NICK ELLIOTT

DARK OCEAN

Seaward Publishing

DARK OCEAN

By Nick Elliott
Published by Seaward Publishing
Amazon Edition
Copyright © Nick Elliott, 2017

ISBN978-0-9929028-4-1

Formatted by Jo Harrison ~ Author Assistant
Ryan Ashcroft ~ BookBrand

To
Liz, Louise and Melanie

"For whosoever commands the sea commands the trade;
whosoever commands the trade of the world commands the
riches of the world, and consequently the world itself."

Sir Walter Raleigh

CHAPTER 1

I'd read through the scanned newspaper report that Claire had emailed the day before. It was headed Special to The New York Times and dated 2 March 1944. The headline read: "Japanese freighter torpedoed off Hong Kong".

The brief dispatch written in the terse, urgent prose of its time, said little more than its headline. But Claire Scott had added her own report explaining that it concerned a cold case we were handling and sketching out the facts. Knowing I was already in the region, she was asking if I'd take it on and if so, get to Hong Kong as soon as possible. I'd called her saying I'd go. That was the previous day. Now I was sitting in front of my old friend Sammy who had other ideas.

Dressed in his colourfully embroidered native costume he sat impassively, cross-legged on the earthen floor of the hut where we were holding the quarterly meeting of our Sarangani Association, a trust we'd set up to help the *B'laan* protect their rights to the ancestral homelands they so cherished. We all feared for the depredations they would suffer in the face of the copper and gold mining project that was rapidly unfolding on their doorstep. The mine at Mount Buwan Bundok was not ten kilometres from where we were sitting.

'Go there, you not come back,' the old man said gently.

'What do you mean, Sammy?'

'Go there, you will die.' He spoke softly but intensely, staring at me with his watery old eyes. The rain hammered onto the thin corrugated iron roof of the hut making it hard to hear what he was saying.

Sammy was the headman of his *barangay*, a village high in the mountains of southern Mindanao. He knew nothing of the case I'd just been assigned. But he was a tribal shaman. Apparently he had entered into a state of altered consciousness in order to reach this conclusion about my impending demise. I'd told him that I had to leave the village as I had business to attend to in Hong Kong. Perhaps his intuition, or something in my own body language, had alerted him and he'd decided to warn me. Now I watched as he came out of a trance-like state. His body convulsed as he muttered strange sounds in this extraordinary ritual that had led him into the spirit world. From there he foretold the future, as well as healing the sick. Sammy claimed to be in touch only with benevolent spirits and not the evil ones that many shamans call upon to bring down misfortune on their clients' enemies. Every village had its own shamans using their unearthly talents to carry out different forms of ritual curing.

'Thanks for that, Sammy. I'll watch out for myself.' Whether or not I believed his premonition, I nevertheless held the old man in high regard. He and his people had come to my rescue once before and I didn't want to sound dismissive of his warning now.

Sammy shrugged but said nothing more. He had spoken.

It was late and we had to get moving. I stood up painfully. Like Sammy I'd been sitting cross-legged for the best part of two hours, only for me it was torture. But the meeting had gone well. Belying their simple lifestyle, Sammy and his lieutenants could teach the corporate world a thing or two when it came to formulating a strategy, and sticking to it.

The idea was to form a stewardship whereby the land would give life to the people and the people give life to the land. It was a three-pronged approach tackling environmental, social and territorial issues, all of which were crucial to the *B'laan*, a peace-loving tribe living in what by western standards would be judged abject poverty, but for them was a natural, healthy lifestyle, though one threatened by the mining companies on the one hand and territorial warfare known as *pangayaw* with their neighbours, on the other.

Carlos stood scrambled up as well. Carlos Torres was a co-trustee of the Association who acted as interpreter when necessary and, as a resident of Mindanao himself, was our principal link with the *B'laan*. Based in Davao, he was also Lloyd's Agent and, like myself, a marine claims investigator.

We said our goodbyes and headed for the door. Sammy had risen too; this small, leathery-skinned old man, bent with age yet dignified. He touched my arm.

'Don't go.'

What could I say? I wasn't superstitious, or was I? 'Don't worry, Sammy. I'll take care.'

***

'Tomorrow's flight leaves at ten,' said Carlos as we drove off heading south to General Santos city. 'Good connection in Manila. You'll be in Hong Kong late afternoon. All booked.'

'Thanks, Carlos.'

It had taken us over an hour just to walk back along the narrow, muddy paths to where Carlos had left his car. To one side were little fields of maize, sugar cane and pineapple, but on the other was the jungle: hot, humid and smelling of putrefying vegetation. The raucous cacophony of the forest's birdlife accompanied us as we went.

Now, as we drove south towards GenSan, the clamour of the jungle was replaced by the chaos of the road. And as we came closer to the city the traffic grew heavier – cars and trucks, jeepnees, tuk-tuks, tricycles, livestock and pedestrians all vying for space on the narrow road, which by now was in darkness. But Carlos was a careful driver – at least by local standards.

'What do you think of what Sammy said?' he asked, 'I mean his warning about Hong Kong?'

I'd been mulling it over. 'Maybe what he saw was my

past, Carlos. My family perished in the landslide there. So did I, very nearly. Then there was my near-miss at Buwan Bundok last year. Maybe it all got muddled up in his dream, his premonition.'

'I hope you're right.'

'Look, it's a cold case' I said. 'The Club want me to review a claim that goes back to the war. The ship sank in 1944, over seventy years ago. Where's the danger in that?'

'Tell me more about the case.' Like all investigators, Carlos had an ingrained sense of curiosity.

I settled back in my seat trying to ignore the growing bedlam in front of me. 'You've heard of Sinclair Buchan, right? Old Scots family business. They've been around the East since the middle of the nineteenth century. Shipping, rubber plantations ...'

'Opium?' Carlos interjected. He knew about the trade between India and China and the opium wars that resulted in the ceding of Hong Kong to the British back in the eighteen forties, around the time Messrs Sinclair and Buchan, a couple of wayward merchant adventurers from the north of Scotland, were seeking their fortunes in the East.

'Sure, that too. Anyway, by the outbreak of the war they were running thirty odd ships. Cargo passenger liners mostly – remember them? And the *Lady Monteith* was the pride of the fleet, delivered from one of the Clydeside yards in 1937, just before the beginning of the Second Sino-Japanese War. So by then things were already hotting up in this region.'

'You're not kidding. So what happened?'

I was reciting what Claire had told me now. 'She was placed on a regular liner service between Bombay and Hong Kong calling at a dozen or more ports in between. But the British government requisitioned the entire Sinclair Buchan fleet at the outbreak of the Pacific War and the *Lady Monteith* became involved in transporting war materials and troops around Southeast Asia.

'In 1941 she was attacked by two Japanese destroyers as she approached Hong Kong. It happened on the eighth of December, the day the Japanese invaded the territory, and the same day they attacked Pearl Harbour. 7th of December in Hawaii, but the 8th in Hong Kong, this side of the date line.'

I stopped talking as Carlos swerved to avoid a pothole that was about to swallow the car.

'Carry on,' he said, unconcerned.

'The destroyers escorted her into Junk Bay out in the New Territories. She became a prize of war. Eventually she was repaired, renamed, repainted, re-flagged and used by the Japanese as a hospital ship. Only she wasn't a hospital ship.'

'She was a POW hell ship, right?"

'Right, that's what they became known as, hell ships. Thousands of POWs were shipped to Japan on them, sealed into the holds. The ships were supposed to be marked with the red cross on a white background to protect them from attack. Presumably the *Lady Monteith* was not, because in 1942 she was used to carry British POWs from the Sham

Shui Po prison camp in Hong Kong, on to Japan. But she was attacked again, shortly after she sailed, this time by an American submarine just south of Hong Kong. She sank and most of the POWs went down with her. Some escaped and were picked up by Chinese fishermen, at great risk to themselves. Others were shot by Japanese guards on the ship as they tried to escape. Most though drowned, trapped in the holds where they'd been kept for days before sailing, awash in their own vomit, urine and faeces. Many were suffering from dysentery, diphtheria, beriberi – all sorts.'

'Jesus! These stories of the war. Even things that happened right here where we're driving now; terrible things.'

We were sharing the road with a variety of livestock and Carlos was having to repeatedly sound his horn to dissuade cows and water buffalo from wandering out in front of us. I thought about closing my eyes but decided against it.

'I know, Carlos. But that's not what this case is all about. Apparently, the ship had performed just one voyage between being commandeered by the Japs and taking on the POWs. She'd been ordered to Rangoon, Bangkok and Beihai in southern China to load cargo for Japan. Just what cargo is a matter of speculation. Whatever it was, Montague Buchan, who's the incumbent *taipan* at Sinclair Buchan nowadays, is laying claim to it as reparation for the loss of not just the *Lady Monteith*, but all the other ships he lost in the war; and for properties lost in Hong Kong and China and a host of other assets too.'

'If he thinks the cargo value will cover all that it must

be something pretty special. Gold is it?'

'I'm sure that's what he thinks it is. Whether he's got the proof, or the means to salvage it is another matter. He's got no cargo documentation of course.'

'There's said to be billions in gold bullion buried here in the Philippines and at the bottom of the South China Sea,' said Carlos warming to the subject. 'Marcos got his hands on a good chunk of it. But there was gold in sunken wrecks too. The *Awa Maru* was one - another so-called hospital ship sunk by a US sub. They say she had, or has, forty tons of gold ingots on board, diamonds too. But China Salvage insist they spent six thousand man hours searching the wreck and found nothing of value.'

'Do you believe them?'

'Who knows? That was back in 1977. Then there was the Japanese cruiser, the *Nachi* in Manila Bay, scuttled by a Japanese sub. She had gold on board too. Both ships were carrying looted treasure back to Japan towards the end of the war.

'But the mother-load was the *Op Ten Noort*. She had 2,000 tons of gold on board - or so the treasure hunters would have us believe. She was a Dutch passenger vessel commandeered by the Japanese, renamed the *Hikawa Maru No. 2* and operated all around the Pacific and Southeast Asia as a hospital ship. Finally ended up being scuttled in Japan. They say when the wreck was found twenty five years ago, they recovered thirty billion dollars' worth of gold, platinum and diamonds from her. Never verified though.'

'I had no idea you were an authority on all this, Carlos.'

'I'm not. It's just what I've read – and what's commonly believed in these parts.'

'So it seems there's more to this than just Monty Buchan replenishing the family coffers,' I said. 'When I talked to the office about it, Claire Scott told me they thought Buchan wasn't the only one in search of whatever was down there.'

What I didn't tell Carlos was that she'd confided her sense of something far more sinister than a disgruntled shipowner trying to hoard a cargo of gold that never belonged to him in the first place. 'Only a hunch,' she'd said.

'Well, good luck to your friend Mr Buchan with his claim, eh?' said Carlos. 'And to you too. Sounds like you'll need it.'

CHAPTER 2

Nowadays Hong Kong's airport is on Chek Lap Kok, a little island off the north western shore of Lantau, the largest of the territory's outlying islands. Once a tranquil retreat for Buddhist monks, fishermen and expats seeking a bit of peace and quiet from the tumult of the city, now they had to share it with the noise of the aircraft and a nearby Disneyland.

I took the Airport Express to Central and grabbed a taxi to my hotel in Western District. The air was warm and humid. Mist covered the Nine Dragons, the hills from which Kowloon takes its name. Victoria Peak on Hong Kong island was the same, shrouded in thick cloud. I couldn't see The Peak but I felt its presence, looming over this town whose only god was Mammon. It was my first time ashore in Hong Kong since I was a child. I remembered very little about the place. Traumatised by the horrors of the landslide that killed my parents, my sister and our *amah*, and buried alive for days, I'd avoided the place ever since, aside from a couple of calls on an old Greek ship I was working on.

As a child, my initial reaction to the death of my family was to shut it out, at the time. The wave of disbelief, the struggle to understand the finality of death, the panic I'd felt, the yawning chasm of abandonment – all these emotions came later, along with unwelcome memories.

But in my line of business, avoiding a place like Hong Kong wasn't always easy. Despite competition from its neighbours in the rest of China, it was still one of the world's busiest ports, and still home to some of the world's biggest shipowners. The grandly named Caledonian Marine Mutual Protection & Indemnity Association, which was the major source of my business, had a dozen or so member shipowners here providing them with third party liability insurance cover under the arcane but effective system of mutuality. And it was one of these shipowners I'd come to see.

Like Carlos Torres down in Mindanao, marine insurance claims investigation was my business. I ran it out of Piraeus where I took care of CMM's Greek clients. The Greek merchant fleet was the biggest in the world, by a mile. The CMM wasn't the biggest P&I insurance 'Club' by any means, but they were my bread and butter and I'd made a reasonable living from them over the years.

But Hong Kong was a city of ghosts for me and despite the lights, the noise and the frenetic energy of the place, I was overcome by a melancholy as impenetrable as the mists cloaking the surrounding hills. By the time I'd checked into the hotel it was too late to call Sinclair Buchan's offices so I ordered room service, downed a couple of beers and watched the news. My mood lightened a bit. Tomorrow would be better. I was glad to get away from Mindanao and back to the work I knew best. The prospect of this case gave me the lift I needed before I turned in for the night.

***

'This way, Mr McKinnon. Mr Buchan is expecting you.' The young woman led the way down a thickly carpeted corridor. On the walls either side were photographs of the many ships that made up the Sinclair Buchan fleet, past and present. I stopped when I noticed the *Lady Monteith*. The old monochrome print had turned sepia with age but showed the ship when she was on her sea trials, fresh out of the yard and cutting through the choppy open waters west of the Clyde.

The woman paused beside me. 'That is why you are here?'

'Yes, I believe so.' She was Asian though not Chinese I sensed.

The door at the end of the corridor was faced with padded red leather dotted with brass studs and surrounded by a rosewood frame. It would have been impossible to knock on such a door and sure enough there was a buzzer. We waited for a green light to come on beneath it and the woman pushed the heavy door open, ushering me in before leaving me to survey the room and its sole occupant.

Montague Buchan got up from behind a large rosewood desk and walked across the vast expanse of deep pile navy blue carpet to greet me, his hand outstretched.

Claire Scott, one of the CMM's syndicate claims directors, had met Buchan and when she'd given me the case briefing, speaking from the CMM's headquarters back in Leith, I'd asked her about him.

'The kind of man a lot of women would find irresistible, actually,' she'd said.

'But not you, right?'

'Not my type, darling. You know the kind of man I find irresistible.' Claire and I had history which we were both pretending to put behind us.

'He's the kind of silver fox I find a bit off-putting. And to be honest, I'm not too sure of his business acumen either. I can understand why he'd want to pursue these claims but to us they look like non-starters. It's more a personal crusade, and of course he's trying to dig the company out of a hole. His fleet's ageing now and he hasn't been very adept at playing the sale and purchase market. He could learn a lot about timing from your Greek friends, Angus. Chartering-wise he picks up time and voyage fixtures as and where he can but it's all a bit ad hoc – no sign of a proper strategy. So I suppose if he could get his hands on a whopping pay-out, it would revive the firm's fortunes.'

'So what's he doing with CMM then?' I'd asked. We were supposed to be highly selective when assessing a shipowner's credentials.

'I'd not have the Sinclair Buchan fleet on our books if it was up to me, but they've been with us from the early days. They were one of the Club's founding members back in the eighteen-eighties. And up till the time Buchan's old man died they were a very well-run outfit.'

'Okay, I'll go through the motions then.'

'Angus, there's something else. This is strictly between us but there's a suspicion that other parties might be involved in the hunt for the *Lady Monteith's* cargo.'

'I'm not surprised. There's no shortage of treasure hunters around the Far East and if everything I hear about the loot that's lying on the seabed from here to Indonesia is true, I'd be surprised if the *Lady Monteith* hadn't come to their attention.'

'Yes, only I'm not talking about your typical treasure hunter. But I can't tell you anymore because I don't know myself, only that there might be dark forces at work. That sounds dreadfully melodramatic but just keep your antennae tuned and I'll let you know more when I can.'

What with Claire's appraisal of Montague Buchan and his plush office on the fifty-seventh floor of one of Central District's most prestigious skyscrapers, not to mention the leather-covered door, I had already formed a picture of the man: a negative stereotype of a none too bright philanderer busy squandering the family fortune on wine, women, lost causes and exorbitant rents. With all this in my mind we shook hands.

'Mr McKinnon. Your Ms Scott told me you were on your way to see us and to render our full cooperation to you in this matter. She spoke highly of you.'

'I was in the region already,' I said as we looked out at what would have been a spectacular view up the harbour if not for the smog carried down from the high-sulphur coal-fired power stations spread along the Pearl River Delta. He sat facing me across the coffee table on which the Sinclair Buchan house flag, company magazine and a couple of shipping journals were artfully scattered.

Buchan matched Claire's description: mid-sixties, tall, tanned, in good shape by the look of it, and wavy silver hair swept back off his forehead. His grey eyes were clear. And he was weighing me up in the same way I was him.

We were discussing the smog when the door opened and the woman who'd shown me in reappeared, carefully backing into the room which enabled her to enter without spilling anything on the tray she was carrying. She placed it on the table bending to unload cups, the cafetiere and a plate of chocolate biscuits; three cups.

'This is Susanna, Mr McKinnon, my daughter and co-director.' Claire hadn't mentioned her.

I stood up and we shook hands. Her hair was almost black with a naturally lustrous sheen. Her high cheekbones, almond-shaped eyes and lightly tanned skin made her effortlessly beautiful. She wore a black skirt and a tight-fitting magenta coloured jacket which accentuated her shapely figure. There was nothing coquettish about her smile. It seemed open and friendly, however fleeting. I guessed her to be in her early to mid-thirties. She walked over to a shelving unit and came back with a hefty green file and a laptop both of which she placed on the coffee table. When she'd served us all coffee she sat down. Every move was performed with a natural, unhurried grace.

'So,' Buchan began. 'You will know something of this strange and harrowing tale but I would like you to hear it from us direct, and then we can discuss the way forward.'

'Sure,' I said, 'but it's only fair to warn you that a provisional assessment by the CMM's claims people doesn't hold out much hope of there being a claim – that is to say against the Club itself.'

'Quite. Claire did warn me of this and I was not at all surprised. But I told her I wanted the best investigator the Club had. She said she had just the man and he was already in the region salving his social conscience in the mountains of Mindanao. She was looking for an opportunity to draw you away from your altruistic exploits and this case she thought would do nicely.'

'She said that did she?'

He smiled. 'She seems to know you only too well.'

'Tell me your side of the story,' I said, 'and I'll see how we can help; even if there's no claim we can maybe render advice. But there'll be a charge for my time and the CMM lawyer's legal opinion in any event. I'm freelance by the way, but in practice I work pretty much exclusively for the CMM.'

'So I was told. She also told me a little of your background here in Hong Kong: a tragedy. Your father was a highly regarded police officer, Mr McKinnon. He might have ended up Commissioner had he lived. I suspect you inherited some of his investigative talents.'

'I hope so,' I said. But I'd spotted the model of a ship on the far side of the office. Monty Buchan noticed my interest. 'Come over and have a look. It's the *Lady Monteith*.'

'I thought it might be.'

The glass case in which the model rested was at least six feet long. The model itself was beautifully crafted from the days when shipyards had their own modelling shops. Such highly detailed replicas were presented to the shipowner by the yard on delivery of the vessel and this was one such example. The *Lady Monteith* was a fine looking ship and the model did her justice: from the tiny windlass and anchor chains laid out on the forepeak to the brass propeller at her stern.

'Beautiful, isn't she,' Monty Buchan said. 'Pride of our fleet.'

'Yes it is.' Buchan seemed visibly moved just by looking at it.

'Shall we get on with this?' suggested Susanna Buchan extracting documents from the green folder and laying them out on the table. And it was she who began by giving a lengthy account of the wreck of the *Lady Monteith*.

CHAPTER 3

I didn't get back to the hotel until well past midnight. We had talked in the office until after dark. The air around the harbour had cleared with a change in wind direction and the extravagant galaxy of lights that was Hong Kong's version of night-time was revealed to its full effect beneath us.

We'd ended up walking to the Hong Kong Club, first for drinks in the Members Bar where Buchan was clearly a habitué, then for dinner in the Red Room, where he was also greeted with deference. And wherever we were heads turned in Susanna Buchan's direction.

By the end of the evening Montague Buchan and I were mildly inebriated, on first-name terms – "call me Monty" - and I thought I had a pretty clear idea of just what their agenda was. Whether the CMM could help or not was another matter but I felt I'd reached that stage in the case where I knew what needed to be done.

When my phone rang at half past three in the morning dragging me out of a deep and dreamless sleep, I cursed myself for not having turned it off before I went to bed.

'Mr Angus?' said an unfamiliar voice.

'*Ne. Legete.*'

'I am Dimitra's nephew,' he said.

'Dimitra?' How many Dimitras did I know?

'Yes, Mr Alastair's housekeeper, on the island.'

I was with him now. 'Yes of course. How are they?'

He hesitated. 'I'm afraid Mr Alastair has passed away.'

Shocked, I was suddenly wide awake. 'God! I'm sorry to hear that. When did this happen?'

'Last night we believe, but his death seems very unusual, sir. And the police here are treating it with much suspicion.'

'Well how did he die?' I asked. Rear Admiral (ret'd) Alastair Marshall was a friend. And though he'd never have admitted it, he was also an intelligence officer, an old spook with his fingers still in many pies, at least until now.

'They don't know for sure but it seems he may have been poisoned. My aunt is very upset. She wanted you to know of this. Mr Alastair had left a note. It gave your name and your telephone number.'

Dimitra had been his housekeeper for years. She lived in, and despite her age, was still sprightly. And she cooked pretty much every meal that Alastair Marshall ate. No wonder she was upset.

'What else did this note say?'

'It makes no sense.'

'Can you read it to me?'

'It says just your name: "McKinnon," then your telephone number, then: "Eastfield 176." That's all.'

It made no sense to me either. My mind was reeling as I tried to gather my thoughts. 'Okay,' I said, 'Where is his body now? And when's the funeral?'

'They have taken him to Thessaloniki for the post mortem already, but they say he will be returned this Thursday for the funeral on Friday.'

That gave me just two days. Despite the interruption to the case I decided there and then to head back to Greece, not just because Alastair had been a friend and something of a mentor to me, but the nature of his work involved maintaining a close relationship with the CMM as well as other P&I Clubs, and that relationship was, more often than not, channelled through myself. If he had been murdered then … My mind began to turn around the obvious questions: who and why?

'I'll be there, Kostas.' I rang off and stood for a long time staring out at the harbour view trying to make sense of what I'd just been told. It wouldn't surprise me if Alastair had enemies. The opaque world of commercial shipping was plagued by crime of one sort or another. Piracy and hijacking were rife off both east and west coasts of Africa and in the waters of the South China Sea as well. Such crimes were usually motivated by simple greed. Demands for astronomical sums of money had to be negotiated and sensitive arrangements made to deliver the ransom pay-offs. Both the CMM and Alastair Marshall were often involved in such negotiations and they were never amicable affairs.

Often there was a terrorism dimension to deal with too.

Then there was commercial fraud: intricate contractual charterparty scams; complex letter of credit crimes and other such rackets. Alastair Marshall was often at the heart of solving these crimes, which was why he kept close counsel with the world of the P&I Clubs who insured the shipowner victims against such losses.

CHAPTER 4

When I arrived on the northern Aegean island where Alastair Marshall had made his home, the church bells were ringing doubles as always on the day of a funeral, calling the mourners together. It was a dismal sound.

Laying the dead to rest involves a certain set of rituals for the Greek Orthodox Church, performed by the local priest. There were hymns and prayers. Then pallbearers carried the casket into the church placing it before the altar. Once the service was finished, mourners filed past the open casket to view the body and pay their final respects. Many left flowers. The priest then anointed Alastair's body with oil and dust reciting verses from the Old Testament.

After all this we boarded the island bus packed with the other mourners and rattled up the hill to the cemetery on the edge of the old village high above the port.

We disembarked into a bitter north easterly wind driving a cold rain directly at us. Although we were now separated, Eleni had travelled to the island with me. She was talking with some of the other mourners and was plainly upset.

Eleni and I had been together for as long as I'd known Alastair. We used to visit him in his sprawling home further up the island and he'd taken to staying with us in Piraeus on his infrequent trips to the capital. Alastair and Eleni had got on well. I think he saw her as a surrogate daughter. He had no children of his own – or not that he ever spoke of. And there was no sign of relatives or any other visitors from off the island on this desolate occasion other than ourselves. And Claire Scott.

Claire, despite her senior position with the CMM, was one of Alastair's people. I had prised this confession from them both following the conclusion to a case just a year earlier. Claire had been enrolled into Alastair's International Maritime Task Force straight from Oxford as far as I could gather. As a talented lawyer, the CMM, which by the nature of its work was down by the head with lawyers, provided an ideal cover for her covert work with the IMTF, a shady offshoot of what was once British Naval Intelligence and was now merged into the Ministry of Defence's Intelligence Department.

It had been set up as a taskforce to investigate the spate of maritime fraud incidents which reached epidemic proportions in the seventies. Its success in getting to the route of these crimes ensured the IMTF's future. Before long they were supplying various EU and NATO naval organisations with intelligence relating to the flood of piracy attacks in and around the Gulf of Aden. It suited the IMTF's masters in the Ministry of Defence to retain its taskforce status, allowing for greater flexibility and less accountability. This much I'd learned. I'd also learned that much of its work was carried out off the books, including Alastair's remit. On the previous occasion I'd become involved with them, he'd made this perfectly clear.

I walked over to Claire. I'd introduced her to Eleni earlier. They both knew about each other. My affair with Claire had started long before I'd met Eleni, only to lie dormant before being rekindled after Eleni and I were together. It was complicated, though less so now that Eleni had a new man in her life. And Claire and her were both mature enough not to show whatever feelings they might have towards each other – or so I hoped.

'He was a fine man and a good friend,' Claire said in a voice filled with emotion. Aside from their professional relationship Claire, like Eleni, had held Alastair in deep affection.

She was shivering. I wanted to put my arm around her but held off.

'We need to talk,' she said, her manner suddenly business-like. She looked at me. 'When are you leaving?'

'Tomorrow night. I want to visit the house, and talk to Dimitra and Kostas, the nephew. Then back to Piraeus. There's an evening ferry.'

'Where are you staying tonight?'

'There's a little guest house here in the village.'

'I'm at the hotel in the port. Can you come down this evening and we can talk there?'

'Sure.'

The priest bestowed the final blessings. We watched as the casket was lowered into the grave. Some of the mourners tossed flowers and soil onto it. After three or four years the grave would be re-opened and the bones removed, washed in wine or olive oil and kept in the *osteofilakio*, the church ossuary. After the burial we went with other mourners for the *makaria*, a meal to celebrate Alastair's life, akin to a wake.

Later I walked down the ancient *kaldirimi* donkey path to the hotel in the port. It was more sheltered down there than on the hill but the storm had still invaded the little harbour and water was washing over the quayside, threatening the tavernas that lined the front.

This was the island where I dreamt that one day I would make my home. Whatever the time of year, it showed nature in all its intensity. Winter snow storms could bring down trees by the force of the wind and the weight of the snow. Sheet and fork lightning accompanied by simultaneous thunderclaps would turn a storm into a drama. In spring the hillsides and meadows were carpeted in wild flowers and in summer the place was alive with the sound of cicadas and the smell of herbs. Off the coast, dolphins played around the local *caiques* as they made their way to and from the outlying islands. Young falcons dived after insects as they honed their hunting skills. It was a magical place and I loved it, but none of this was on my mind as I entered the hotel and spotted Claire in a bar off the lobby. There were no more than half a dozen people in the room but there was a cosy fug about the place. She'd found a table beside a wood-burning stove in the corner, well out of earshot of the Greek islanders drinking at the bar. We'd met in similar places before, usually in Scotland. She loved to find a place by an open fire or a stove if there was one.

'What are you drinking?' she asked.

'Scotch – whichever they've got.' She'd already ordered a Metaxa and a hot chocolate for herself. She signalled the young guy behind the bar and ordered a Black Label for me and another Metaxa for herself. The drinks came. 'I can't get over the measures they pour in this country,' she said.

'It's the only reason I live in Greece.'

She smiled.

'So tell me,' I said to get the conversation on track.

She took a sip of her drink, taking her time before answering. She was like that, always weighing things up judiciously before pronouncing, ever the lawyer. But when I'd first met her she was a reckless young case handler intent on making a name for herself and getting into trouble in the process, from which, many years ago, I'd been sent to extricate her. Marriage to Edward, another lawyer, children and a rapid rise through the ranks at the CMM had followed. But her marriage was faltering and the strain of being called into active field service for the IMTF had taken its toll, in particular the act of killing someone in the course of saving my life not long ago.

I looked at her now. It was some months since we'd last met. Despite her training, I sensed she had never quite recovered from what had happened the previous year on a dark night in the port of Perama when, in defending me she had shot a man. A short time later, on this island, we had been attacked by another, again intent on murder. And again, Claire had helped save us both. I knew at the time these incidents had affected her. Now, despite her natural beauty, I saw the strain in her face and in her body language. Some of that self-confidence that had helped propel her to the heights of a demanding career had slipped away. Perhaps it was just her reaction to Alastair's violent death, but she was normally skilled in compartmentalising her emotions. Now I worried that those violent events had triggered PTSD.

Claire and I had been lovers but parted ways, twice. I'd returned to Eleni and Claire to her husband, for the sake of the children she'd said. I wondered how it was working out, but I didn't ask.

'Monty Buchan has disappeared,' she announced.

'What?'

'Vanished without trace. His daughter called. She's in a state.'

'But why call you?'

'Because she believes it's to do with the *Lady Monteith* case. And she's not calling the police.'

'Let me get something straight, Claire. Given Alastair's murder, is this more than just a CMM cold case. Is it one of his IMTF affairs by any chance?'

The timing of Alastair's death, the note he'd left, had

got me wondering.

She leaned forward. 'Your intuition serves you well. Normally Alastair would have handled this. Now, that's my job. And the IMTF have told me to enrol you – for this case. That's if you're willing.'

I didn't like the way this was going. I wasn't a spook, I was a freelance marine insurance investigator. But I'd got myself involved in the IMTF's murky dealings before and now it seemed I was getting dragged in again.

'Told you to?'

'Well, they asked whether you would be suitable and I said yes, you would.'

'Why, Claire? I need to know what their interest is.'

'This might sound ridiculous but they don't know themselves. Only that Alastair had opened a case file but he hadn't briefed anyone. He died before he had chance, or before he was ready to.'

I told her then what Kostas had told me: that Alastair had left a message.

'I know,' she said. 'I met Kostas at Alastair's house yesterday. He told me about the message. What do you make of it?'

So she was ahead of me. Not surprising, the IMTF was an intelligence agency after all. They'd have wanted Alastair's house, his computers, files, everything locked down. They'd sent Claire to do it.

'I've no idea who or what Eastfield is, never mind 176. I'm meeting Kostas at the house tomorrow.'

'I'll come with you.'

'Sure,' I said, realising I sounded unenthusiastic.

'Angus, are you with me on this?'

'I'll be with you – I'm talking about the IMTF now not the CMM. I'll be with you when I know what the assignment is. And what outcome you're expecting. This works both ways, Claire. You must have a theory at least. I'm not tearing into some dubious escapade blindfold.'

She was trying to supress her laughter.

'What?'

'Sorry,' she said reaching over and putting a hand on my arm.

'What?' I said again irritably.

'It's just the way you sound so indignant when you say that. After the last time, Angus, I'd have said tearing into dubious escapades blindfold was your speciality.'

We both laughed. She was always good at defusing tense situations. I called over for more drinks. This time she ordered just a hot chocolate.

'So what do you reckon? Any theories? And what's the IMTF's daily rate by the way?' I was as mercenary as the next freelance when it came to money.

'Well, to your second question, not too bad: five thousand a day - sterling, plus expenses; as from today.'

That sounded okay. If I'd handled this case for the CMM I'd be lucky to get a third of that rate. The MoD must have been flusher than they made out.

'As to a theory, if I had one I'd tell you. The IMTF

tracks all our cases and most other P&I Clubs' too. You know that. But it would have to be something pretty serious. And that message he left you makes me think he knew his life was in danger. I don't believe his death was from natural causes for one minute. And now Buchan's gone AWOL.'

'So let's assume Alastair discovered something about the *Lady Monteith* case and that knowledge led to his death,' I speculated. 'That's a stretch in itself given all the other cases he'd be tracking that could have caused him trouble, but let's assume for now. It's a cold case. The owner thinks the cargo's something special, possibly gold, and he wants to claim it from the wreck. In the process, he disappears, possibly kidnapped. Alastair's dead, possibly murdered. Someone wants to get to the cargo first.'

'Or cover the whole thing up.'

'Yes, for reasons unknown.'

'Like everything else about this case,' she said sounding exasperated. 'We know bugger all.'

'So what about your theory of something more sinister behind this than just a treasure hunt?'

She took a sip of her drink before deciding, I guessed, what she could and couldn't tell me.

'I meant what I said just now. I'm not going into this blindfold.'

'I can't tell you what I don't know. It's just that we've had an alert from Japan's Public Security Intelligence Agency. A request actually for any information relating to cargo documentation on those British flag ships commandeered by the Japanese and sunk in Asia Pacific waters during World War Two.'

'And Alastair knew of this?'

'Yes, he did. It's an unusual request but we work closely with the PSIA from time to time so we said we'd look into it. The *Lady Monteith* came up of course but there was no trace of any cargo documentation. We asked them what was behind the request and they said it was in response to a query from one of their politicians, and that they'd advise us further when the enquiry had been dealt with.'

'Nebulous then.'

'Yes, I'm afraid so.'

We talked on for a bit. The atmosphere in the bar was cosy but filled with clouds of cigarette smoke. The EU ban was treated as a mere suggestion in these parts.

'I need some fresh air,' I said. 'Then I must get up the hill to the village.'

'I'll come outside with you.'

We walked along the harbour front dodging the waves as they lapped over the quayside.

'I hate this place,' she said.

'It's not at its best at this time of year, and the funeral...'

'It's not that.' Suddenly the mask was gone and there was a look of desperation on her face.

'I know what you're thinking,' I said.

'That Easter night still haunts me, Angus. I relive it when I'm awake and in my dreams. The shooting in Perama was one thing. It was almost like an exercise. I'd been trained for it. But not for what happened here.'

We had been watching the Easter Friday parade from a vantage point on the cliff above where we now walked when we'd been attacked. A man with a stiletto had surprised us. We'd grappled with him and he'd fallen to his death in the crowd of worshippers below almost pulling me over the cliff with him. I had the same flashbacks as Claire.

'Stay with me tonight, Angus.' She was looking directly at me. It wasn't so long since we'd called a halt to our erratic affair but a day hadn't passed that I didn't think about her and our infrequent encounters. And I wanted her now.

'Edward, the family?'

She sighed. 'Please. We tried, believe me. It's so complicated.' She didn't want to go into it any further. We went back to the hotel and to her room.

CHAPTER 5

I stood in Alastair Marshall's living room looking out across the bay. The weather had partially cleared, the late morning sun occasionally shafting through gaps in the ragged clouds to sparkle on the water. The wind was still from the north bringing a chill to the air. Two wood-burning stoves, one at either end of the room, and a log fire on the back wall were throwing out more than enough heat to warm Dimitra's old bones. For me it was too warm for comfort.

The seaward facing wall was mostly glass with sliding doors out onto a terrace. Beyond this the land fell steeply down to the bay where Alastair used to moor his boat in the summer months.

We'd already spent half the day going through his two laptops and his papers. We'd found nothing helpful. Claire had the necessary decryption codes to access his IMTF files and Alastair was a meticulous keeper of his case records but there was no mention of the *Lady Monteith*, of Sinclair Buchan or of its *taipan*, Montague Buchan. Neither was there any reference to Hong Kong. The message he'd left that

Kostas had handed me on our arrival was written on a scrap of paper. It had my name, my mobile phone number and the word, Eastfield and below that, 176. Nothing more.

Dimitra, dressed in black, and her nephew were with us. Dimitra knew both Claire and myself from past visits to the house and we'd talked to her at the funeral. I'd explained what we needed to do. She hadn't objected. Kostas was cooperative too. He seemed more interested in what was going to happen to the house and the land it stood on. There were five hectares of olive groves surrounding the property which Alastair had acquired forty-odd years ago before he'd built the house. I guessed Kostas had his eye on it. Claire and I had both been talking to him already but I liked to get people to repeat their accounts of events in case they differed from the previous version.

'So tell me again, Kostas. Where did you find this note and where did you find the body?' I spoke in English for Claire's benefit, and because my Greek was not as good as Kostas' English.

'I told you. The note was in my aunt's room, in an old jewellery box he had given her many years ago. And *Kyrios* Alastair was lying on the jetty, where he moored his boat.'

'But his boat wasn't there.'

'No. It was taken out of the water months ago. Before the first winter storms, as is usual.'

'So what do you think he was doing down there?'

'If I knew I would tell you.'

'How was he lying?'

He sighed. 'How many times? I have told the police. I have told the *kyria* yesterday.' He nodded towards Claire who was staring out across the bay to the headland beyond, a view that was impossible to ignore. The house had been positioned to show it off to its full effect. Out across the bay was a wedge-shaped isthmus which, at some point millennia ago, had almost broken off from the land of which it had been a part. This rocky outcrop was the site of an ancient city which was believed to have served as a logistical staging post for Agamemnon's forces during the Trojan Wars. Alastair had been an authority on the subject and I guess Claire was remembering his graphically imagined accounts of those times on her previous visits to the house.

I turned back to Kostas. 'And I tell you now,' he said in his assertive Greek manner. 'He was on his front. His face was to one side. There was some, how do you say, liquid from his mouth. It was yellow but with blood too, on the *plakis*, the paving. It was not good to see.'

I thought about that. Arsenic? Wasn't that used in pesticides? Was it available locally? It was too early to jump to conclusions. I thought also of Alastair, a man well into his seventies, dying a hard death so close to his home.

'Was his clothing wet?'

'Yes,' Kostas said as if only just remembering. 'It was, now you ask me.'

'Wet enough for him to have been in the water?'

'Certainly, yes.'

Claire seemed sure she could get hold of the autopsy

report through the IMTF's connections with Europol and through them, the Greek police. By this route she'd already ensured Alastair's possessions, including his laptops and files, should be left untouched for her to inspect further and take what she needed to take, before the police got their hands on them. The report would reveal whether he'd died from poisoning and hopefully where the poison had originated. I was also interested to know whether he'd managed to get to the jetty by himself or whether he'd been dumped there after his death.

'Kostas, can you ask your aunt, as far as she knows, what Alastair ate in the day before you found him?'

'We've been through this with the police too. His routine was the same every day. He ate yoghurt with honey and a *nectarini* or some other fruit every morning, and coffee. Then he worked. For lunch my aunt often made him a *spanakopita* or *tsiropita* served with some salad. He had one glass of wine, always one, and then he slept for one or two hours. It was the same every day. After his rest he went back to work. You understand she was in and out, doing the housework, shopping. She was not watching him all the time.'

'And in the evening?'

'That evening he was out. He went to the port. The police are not saying what he did or where he ate but it was not unusual for him to go there in the evenings.'

'How do you know he went to the port?'

'Well, that's where he went. There's nowhere else to go

apart from the old village on the hill, but there's nowhere open there at this time of year.'

'He could have gone to a friend's house,' I suggested.

'Yes. But he didn't have so many friends that he would have gone to dinner with at this time of year. He was friend-ly with many locals but I don't think he had dinner with them in their homes; in the tavernas, yes. Anyway, my aunt would have known. He would have said.'

He spoke rapidly to Dimitra then said, 'My aunt says he would always tell her but that night he left without saying where he was going; usually though to the port, unless he was leaving the island.

'Any idea where he might have gone? Where were his places?'

'There are not so many open at this time of year. I don't know where he went that night. People in the port are talking about it but no-one saw him. At least no-one is saying they saw him.'

'Did he take his car?' He had owned an old Land Rover.

'Yes, I believe the police found it parked in the port. He'd left it in a side street, not on the harbour front, per-haps because of the weather. The sea was coming over the waterfront that night.'

That was pretty much all we got out of them. Alastair had got up, had his breakfast, worked at his desk, had lunch and a glass of wine, slept, worked, then went into town. The following morning, Dimitra had phoned her nephew Kos-tas who had come to the house and they'd started searching for him.

We walked down to the jetty with Kostas. It was a rough, unpaved path. Steps had been cut into the hillside where the gradient was steep. As we descended I looked around for clues but there'd been high winds and rain since they'd found the body so evidence left of Alastair, in the unlikely event that in his last dying moments he had struggled down to the jetty from the house, might anyway have been swept away.

Although, with the prevailing winter winds from the north we were on the leeward side of the island, the sea was rough enough to be slapping up and over the jetty. I walked onto it and peered down into the water. On a calm day I'd have been able to see to the bottom but now the water was turbid.

'Did the police send a diver down here, Kostas?'

'No. I would have known. I was here all the time that they were.'

'I need a snorkel, mask and flippers, Kostas.' He had a box full of them in his workshop when I was last here. 'Can you get them for me?'

'What, now?'

'Yes.'

'Are you mad?' Claire said. 'It's freezing and you won't be able to see a thing.'

'I'll get them,' Kostas said, and headed back up the path to the house.

The shock of the cold water took my breath away.

Once in I pulled flippers, mask and snorkel on and swam over to my left, to the corner of the search field I'd visualised from the jetty. I peered downwards then dived.

The bottom was no more than fifty feet down. Free divers can reach well over three hundred. I was not up to those depths but reached the bottom without difficulty. I looked around as I swam down but saw nothing other than the murky water and then, as I dived deeper, the sandy bottom strewn with rocks. I came up for air, swam to the next sector of the semicircle I'd mapped out roughly in my mind and dived again. Nothing. I came up for air again and peered up to see Kostas and Claire looking down at me. I gave them the thumbs down for the second time and dived once more.

It was on the fifth dive that I saw it: the blurred outline of a small boat lying on the bottom a little further out from where I'd been looking. I swam towards it. As I came closer I could make out the name on the transom: T/T *Toyama Maru*. I grabbed a rowlock to hold me over the dinghy. It was no more than ten feet long. There was no sign of an outboard motor. Had Alastair rowed this little tender from its mother vessel, the *Toyama Maru*, back to his jetty?

I surfaced again and gave the thumbs down. Then, for the sake of appearances, moved over to the final sector and dived. By the time I climbed out of the water I was shaking with cold.

'You're blue!' Claire said handing me the towel.

'Nothing down there I could see,' I said, my teeth chattering. 'Let's get back to the house. I need a hot shower.'

I had my reasons for not telling Kostas or Claire what I'd seen. I didn't know Kostas well. I couldn't trust him not to tell the local police or his pals in the *cafeneon* what I'd found. As for Claire, I would tell her later. The problem I had was not so much with her but with the IMTF. She would be compelled to report everything back to them, I assumed, and I wasn't sure I wanted that. I preferred to keep as strong a measure of independence as possible. The management of CMM, Claire included, understood this was how I worked. But the IMTF was government, or quasi-government. I knew very little about them and until I did, I'd keep some matters to myself. I was probably in breach of the terms of my enrolment, but since no-one had told me what those terms were, I felt free to make my own rules. Then again, they were paying me handsomely.

I spent a long time in the shower thinking. It was conjecture but it seemed Alastair had rowed the tender ashore from a bigger vessel possibly already knowing he'd been poisoned. Had he eaten poisoned food on the *Toyama Maru*? What had he been doing there anyway? Meeting people he thought he could trust, or was he coerced?

He was a wily old bird and he wouldn't have been deceived easily. Then what? He must have escaped in the tender. Otherwise his captors, having poisoned him, would have simply dumped him over the side with a length of anchor chain round his ankles. But why poison him if they could have disposed of him that way over the side without leaving this trail of evidence? And the tender I'd found was small, suitable for a small yacht perhaps - unless it was used as a workboat by the crew of the mother vessel when they were scraping and painting the hull? Big yachts often carried small dinghies like the one I'd seen for use as work boats.

And he would have written the cryptic note for me before he went out, perhaps knowing his life was in danger? What was that note about? Eastfield must be a place and 176? A quantity, a date, a location? Was it connected to the wreck site of the *Lady Monteith*? It certainly didn't have a nautical sound to it. Claire had told me that Alastiar knew I would be working on that case for the CMM. Perhaps he surmised that I would make sense of these clues he'd left.

My mind was spinning but I had warmed up. I stepped out onto the terrace beside the guest rooms where I'd showered. It had started to rain again but still the sun broke through and a rainbow had appeared arching across the bay. Was it a portent? And if so for good or ill? I wondered what Sammy would make of it. Was I letting his warning get under my skin?

CHAPTER 6

Back in Piraeus I checked on the *Toyama Maru*. She was built in Japan in the early thirties. She displaced eighteen hundred tons fully loaded, was 233 feet long with a beam of 36 feet and a draught of 14 feet. Her two Mitsubishi diesels generated 1,100 horsepower giving her a cruising speed of 13.5 knots. Her flank speed would have been a bit more than that.

She was more a ship than a yacht and had originally been built for a high profile American oil tycoon who had named her *Texas Beauty*. Nowadays her owners were simply listed as Ocean Investments Inc. of George Town, her port of registry in the Caymans.

Furthermore, the skipper didn't believe in the statutory requirement of keeping his Automatic Identification System switched on. There was no trace of her whereabouts which would have been apparent had she been using it. The International Maritime Organisation's Safety of Life at Sea Convention requires AIS to be fitted aboard international voyaging ships with a gross tonnage of 300 or more. The

Toyama Maru was close to 2,500 gross tons. She would have had to be fitted with AIS.

But, confusingly, there was another *Toyama Maru*. She was listed as a Japanese troop transport sailing around the Far East during World War II. On 29th June 1944, this *Toyama Maru* was transporting over 6,000 men of the Japanese 44th Independent Mixed Brigade when she was torpedoed and sunk by a US submarine in the Nansei Shoto, off Taira Jima. 5,400 soldiers and crewmembers were killed during the sinking, although 600 others managed to get off the ship, making this one of the worst maritime disasters in history.

Was there a connection between the two ships, I wondered? I checked on Eastfield too but could see nothing to connect the name to the case. There was an Eastfield College in the States and an Eastfield lighting company in Shenzhen neither of which provided a pointer.

'So what's going on, Angus?' Zoe demanded. Zoe was my assistant, or the office manager in charge of everything during her boss's frequent absences, depending on whose point of view you took. I didn't mind her presumption. She was twenty-five, blond, beautiful and going out with a wealthy Greek twice her age. She was studying law in her spare time and when I was travelling Zoe kept correspondence and our case files as up to date as could be expected. She was indispensable.

'I was hoping you could tell me that, Zoe. Why don't you give me a run-down on the case list.' I'd been away for a couple of weeks. We'd been in daily contact by phone and email but I needed her nuanced version of events now I was back.

'I meant *Kyrios* Alastair. He was your friend. How did he die?'

'We don't know yet, Zoe. It might have been a heart attack.'

'He was healthy I thought. And he wasn't old.'

'He was seventy-two actually, Zoe, so getting on.'

'Yes, but not old, old.'

Greeks perceive ageing differently from many Westerners. Old age is honoured and celebrated, and respect for elders is central to the family, and to your business. The word *Gerondas* means "old man" and is a respectful form of address.

'I know, it's odd,' I conceded. I had to be careful with what I told Zoe. She was a critical part of my business but she knew nothing of my work with the IMTF on the *Lady Monteith* case. And the previous evening Claire had called. She'd received the autopsy report on Alastair's death.

'You were right,' she'd said on an encrypted line. 'Death by arsenicosis. He'd eaten meat and drunk red wine. They found traces of it in his digestive system. Enough to kill him within an hour or two they reckon - circulatory collapse caused by arsenic trioxide poisoning.'

'So what do our wise men at the IMTF make of all this?'

'Give them time. They're working on it but for now they're rather depending on you and I to come up with the answers. They're so preoccupied with counter-terrorism these days and Alastair was a bit of a lone wolf, like you. He pretty much ran their other activities himself – anything maritime that wasn't considered piracy or a terrorism threat was his domain and he'd call on their resources as and when he needed them.'

'Okay. So any thoughts on the choice of poison? Does it give us a clue?'

'Not much. I've done a bit of reading. Arsenic trioxide has long been of biomedical interest to Chinese and Japanese practitioners – it was used in traditional Chinese medicine for over five thousand years, but not surprisingly lost its appeal due to its toxicity. That's as much as I can tell you at the moment.'

'How about the *Lady Monteith* case?' I asked. 'What's the latest on Buchan's vanishing act?'

'Susanna Buchan wants you back there. She seems to think you can help her find him. Of course she doesn't know of the IMTF's interest in the case.'

'Does Buchan have kidnap and ransom cover?'

'No. The CMM has offered it to him through Lloyd's from time to time, but Monty's always said the Sinclair Buchan fleet doesn't trade in pirate-infested waters. Nowadays the high risk areas are off west and east Africa and his tonnage is trading mainly between Australia and north Asia – to China mostly with their bulk carriers. The South China Sea is not free of piracy as you know but he didn't anticipate needing it. It's not cheap and anyway, we're not even sure he's been kidnapped.'

'What are the Hong Kong police saying?'

'She hasn't reported it, for now anyway. She says they don't want the publicity. Her father's a prominent member of Hong Kong society. And she's quite the socialite herself I gather.'

'So she's on her own on this then.'

'So it would seem, except she wants you back there, as does the IMTF – so you better get moving. You can leave Zoe in charge can't you? She's such a bright girl.'

'Yes, she's so bright she'll take over the business before I know it.'

'Well at least you can rely on her.'

'By the way, when I dived off Alastair's jetty the other day I saw something, a little dinghy with the name of the mother vessel on her stern. It was lying on the bottom.'

'So what was the name?'

'*Toyama Maru*. She's an old yacht built in the thirties. Mostly sails around the Far East but suddenly she shows up off Alastair's island it seems. I think Alastair was poisoned aboard the *Toyama Maru*, escaped in the tender and rowed back to his jetty before collapsing. But it's guesswork. I'm feeling my way in the dark. And I get the sense I'm not being shown the full picture, by the IMTF I mean.

'You've made yourself clear, Angus. Stick to the plan – back to Hong Kong, and I'll make sure you're in the loop. The IMTF is very much "need to know" as you can understand, but we don't want you feeling left in the dark to the extent it affects your on the spot judgement.'

'Good.'

She paused. 'How about Eleni? She was very upset at the funeral. Do you miss her?'

'Yes,' I said looking round the flat, my flat. But it didn't look much like a home anymore without Eleni's stuff scattered around. 'I do.'

CHAPTER 7

Susanna Buchan was staring out of her office window. 'Of course he'd tell me,' she said in answer to my question about her father's absence. 'We always know where either one of us is going – for business or otherwise.'

She turned back to me. Despite the concern on her face she still looked very attractive. I found myself wondering what her story was. She wasn't Eurasian and there was something about her which wasn't quite Chinese either, at least not Han Chinese. 'He's been gone a week. No messages. No replies to my texts, voicemails, emails.'

'Where does he live?' I asked. I'd come straight from the airport and was feeling jetlagged after the long flights from Athens.

'The family home is in Mount Cameron Road. I have an apartment there too.'

'But is that where he calls home? I mean does he live there all the time?' I sensed she was being evasive.

She hesitated. 'Let's sit shall we.' We moved over to the L-shaped sofa arrangement where there was a pot of coffee. The office was in noticeable contrast to her father's. Hers was light and airy and the tone, one of muted pastels. Fresh flowers were strategically placed around the room and in one corner stood a huge Nigra bamboo plant.

'He does move around. We both do. But he never goes off the radar like this.'

'What do you mean, he moves around?'

She poured coffee. 'He has his female friends – several. I don't delve into that side of his life.'

'We might have to,' I said.

'Since my step-mother died my father has sought the company of several women but none of them are serious relationships. I mean I don't think they are long-term. But even when he's with them we keep in touch. He doesn't like feeling he's being judged or controlled, by me especially. And I respect that. We're close nevertheless,' she added.

'Okay. But you think his absence, shall we call it, has to do with the *Lady Monteith* case?'

'I don't know. It just seems odd that his disappearance, as I'm calling it, coincides with his resuming the search for the ship. That's all. He was – is - obsessed with the case.'

'Where are the files?'

'There's nothing much on the digital files, just the email exchanges with the CMM. You saw most of the material when you were here before. But there were other documents. He kept them to himself. I can find no trace of them. He often takes work home with him. He likes to work from home. I've searched the house, his study, bedroom. Nothing.'

'So call the police.'

She sighed. 'I can't do that, at least not now.' She saw my questioning look. 'We're a prominent family. We've been here a hundred and fifty years. If his disappearance got out it would create a media frenzy and the whole matter would become impossible to handle. I want you to do some scouting about first. Then I'll call the police if we don't find him.'

'I'm not that kind of investigator and I don't know Hong Kong that well either,' I said. 'You'd be better off with a local private detective. There must be some ex-cops you can call.'

'Same problem as if I call the police. It would get out one way or another.' She paused. 'There is one my father knew and used sometimes. I met him a few times too.'

'Who's that?'

She paused, thinking. 'I'm trying to remember.' Then, 'Eastfield, that's it. His name was Ronnie Eastfield.'

I nearly fell off the sofa. 'Tell me about him.'

'My father said he was a good cop years ago. But he got caught up in the first wave of ICAC arrests – you know, the Independent Commission Against Corruption? Godber was the first to fall, then Hunt. Ronnie Eastfield went down shortly thereafter. My father said they were all at it in those days. That kind of corruption was endemic. Tea money: a brown envelope on your desk every Friday morning. Not just the police, everyone in one way or another was at it. But they targeted the police first to set an example. Eastfield served seven years, but unlike others who went skulking off to Spain or wherever, he toughed it out by staying on here after he'd served his time. He set up as a private detective. He'll be well into his sixties by now so I'm not sure whether he's still active. I only just thought of him, but he did some work for us years ago.'

'He'd be a starting point,' I said. 'Where do I find him?'

'He's up in the New Territories somewhere. Wait.' She picked up the phone. A minute later the Chinese woman who had delivered the coffee came in with a slip of paper.

'Thanks, Esther,' she said then picked up the phone. The call must have gone to voicemail. She left a message asking Eastfield to call her. Then she passed the piece of paper to me. It had an address in Sai Kung and a mobile phone number.

'You know where that is?'

'I can find it.'

'When he returns my call I'll tell him you'll be in touch.'

You bet I will, I thought. Surely this was the break I'd been hoping for: the answer to half of Alastair Marshall's cryptic clue.

CHAPTER 8

The sun was going down by the time I found Ronnie East-field's place. He lived on the top floor of an old four-story apartment block in Sai Kung town in the New Territories, out on the peninsula that bore the same name.

Susanna Buchan had made contact with him so I was expected. Ronnie's home was basic. The floors were tiled and a few cheap rugs were carelessly scattered about. The living room was furnished with a black, faux leather three-piece suite. There was a television in one corner and a cheap dining table and chairs in another. There wasn't room for much else and very little thought had been given to layout. Interior design was clearly not one of Ronnie's interests.

He showed me out onto a small balcony that led off the main room and left me to admire the view, which was probably the reason he chose to live here. It looked out across Hebe Haven, a bay filled with small craft: sampans, junks, motor cruisers and yachts of different shapes and sizes. On the far side of the bay, half a mile away, were waterfront restaurants, their lights glittering in the gathering dusk. Beyond them, looking south, were the hills of Kowloon, the nine dragons forming a barrier between the New Territories and the city's sprawl of Kowloon, the harbour and Hong Kong island.

'I like your view,' I said as he re-joined me carrying two bottles of San Miguel.

'Yeah. Pity about the smell, but this place does me alright.' I hadn't mentioned the stench coming off the water. 'Same smell as comes off Kai Tak Nullah,' he went on. 'When the airport was there the planes' turbo fans would suck that smell into the cabin. Raw sewage and God knows what else. The smell of money people called it.'

He was a dishevelled-looking character. What was left of his grey hair was swept back off his forehead, but wisps of it flew about in all directions. His straggly eyebrows were still black. Beneath them, perched on his nose, was a pair of large steel-framed glasses from some bygone age. He had a grey pallor about him and a sheen of sweat covered his skin. And he hadn't shaved very carefully either. He probably weighed a hundred kilos although he was no more than five-ten. His shirt was tight across his belly to the point that it looked as if his beer gut might burst out unannounced. Ronnie Eastfield had seen better days.

We drank our beer standing there looking out over the bay.

'So Susanna Buchan's filled you in has she?' I asked.

'About her father's vanishing act? Yes. Not much to go on.'

'She thinks it has to do with a Sinclair Buchan ship, the *Lady Monteith*. She sank during the war.'

'Yes, she mentioned that.'

'Know anything about it?'

He took another swig of his beer without answering my question.

'Ronnie, there're a couple of issues here. One is finding Monty Buchan and the other is finding the *Lady Monteith*. The two are connected and they've asked me to look into both.'

'Yes, she told me you insure their ships from some outfit in Scotland. Is that it?'

'That's correct, yes.'

He placed his beer on a small metal table, lit a cigarette and blew smoke out in the general direction of the bay. Then, for the first time he looked me in the eye. 'I knew your father you know. I knew him well. He was a good friend. I met your mother and you and your sister too. You were just kids. You wouldn't remember.'

I just stared at him.

'Even when I went down your dad used to visit me in Stanley. He didn't need to do that. He'd bring me cigarettes, and news of what was going on outside. Stanley Prison wasn't the homeliest of places to spend seven years of your life, I can assure you.

'When he died in that fucking landslide I cried. I cried for him and for you and the rest of your family.'

'I didn't know.' I was taken aback.

'How would you?' He shuffled off leaving me to contemplate what he'd just said. When he came back he was carrying two more beers.

'How would you?' he said again. 'I got out a few months after it happened. I vowed I'd stay on in Hong Kong and the reason for that had a lot to do with what happened to your dad and your family. You were whisked away to Scotland by your uncle, but the memories were left – the ghosts. And I felt guilty, that I'd let him down as well as myself. I was his junior by many years and he treated me a bit like a son. I always felt so anyway. Your dad wasn't just a straight copper amongst bent ones, he was smart too. And now I'm going to tell you something you wouldn't learn from anyone else. Your dad was working on something big. And fucking dangerous too. And it has to do with Monty Buchan's *Lady Monteith*, or so I reckon.'

He looked out across the bay, well into his second large bottle of San Mig now. 'Ever heard of Golden Lily?'

'No,' I said still trying to process what he'd just been saying about his relationship with my father.

'No reason why you would have. But that's what your dad was investigating: Golden Lily.' He sat down heavily on one of the two flimsy metal chairs and gestured me to take the other, our beers on the table between us.

'You know the Japs ran an industrial-scale looting programme both before and during the war,' he continued. 'From Manchuria right across Korea and China down into Southeast Asia. The Emperor Hirohito, appointed his brother, Prince Chichibu, to head a secret organisation called *Kin no yuri* or Golden Lily, for that purpose – to run the operation. The loot – and it was mostly gold we're talking about - was intended to finance Japan's war effort. That was the plan. The Yakuza were involved of course in the pillaging. But there were others too. Secret societies like Black Dragon, and *Genyosha* or Dark Ocean when you translate it.'

'So what's all this got to do with my father?'

'Be patient. Much of that loot was held in the Philippines – buried in sites across the country. There are theories that it was subsequently recovered and formed a massive fund run by the Americans and their western allies to fight the Cold War. But much of it was shipped up to Japan too.'

Still talking, he got up and strolled inside to the kitchen coming back with yet more beer from the fridge. His thirst for the stuff was prodigious.

'By this time though, Japan was facing defeat.' Ronnie slumped back onto the little chair tilting back on its back legs to the point I thought he'd topple over. I was fascinated by what he was telling me.

'Looted gold intended for the war effort was conveniently channelled into the coffers of various organisations, among them Dark Ocean. For years they seemed to have vanished. But then they resurfaced in the early seventies as an ultra-nationalist society harbouring dreams of a resurgent Japan. There were, and still are, many such groups. They'd seem loony to you or me but in Japan they're tolerated, probably because that way the authorities can keep tabs on them. The devil you know and all that.'

A breeze had sprung up and the air was a little cooler.

'So, back to your dad. Dark Ocean sought to launder their ill-gotten gains through banks in Hong Kong and your dad got wind of it. As you know he was attached to the Marine Police and the gold would have come in by sea.'

'Would?'

'Yes, would. Once he'd uncovered their scheme, London got involved. First the Fraud Squad, then it became a matter for the intelligence services – what had been Naval Intelligence but had recently been merged into Defence Intelligence under the MoD. The whole matter was hushed up but the shipment was blocked without a word of it getting out. And your dad was at the heart of it.'

He lit another cigarette. I didn't interrupt him.

'But to uncover all this you might say he had to sup with the Devil. He knew the risks, but life's not always black and white, especially in our business, right? There were those in this town who speculated that your dad was in cahoots with Dark Ocean. That was never proven. I don't believe it for one minute and neither did anyone else who knew him well. After all, he thwarted the whole scheme. But you know how mud sticks.'

The lights glittered as the boats in the bay moved about on their moorings with the easterly breeze.

'Okay,' I said, 'but tell me what all this Golden Lily stuff has to do with the *Lady Monteith*. She was carrying some of this loot back to Japan was she?'

'Yes, she was. One hundred and seventy-five so-called imperial treasure vaults were charted across the Philippines, each with its own map showing the location. There's plenty of conspiracy theories about that, but Buchan's ship didn't go down in the Philippines, did she? She went down not twenty miles from where we're sitting. The *Lady Monteith* became known by the Dark Ocean people as Site 176, the last of the sites, but never properly charted.'

So that was it. I had the second half of Alastair's cryptic message.

'How do you know all this, Ronnie?'

'You may have come across a chap called Alastair Marshall? He's investigating the whole sorry affair. I'm acting for him, in an unofficial capacity of course, as ever with him. I...'

'Alastair's dead, Ronnie - murdered.'

'Christ, no!' He was shaken and stared at me as if not quite believing what I'd just said. 'When the hell did that happen?'

'A week ago. So Alastair knew about my father's involvement in Golden Lily?'

'He ran your dad. He was your dad's case officer and your dad was Marshall's field agent.'

'My father was working for the IMTF then? How did that work?'

'Seconded to them, yes. The IMTF is an offshoot of the Naval desk within Defence Intelligence. Always was.'

This much I knew but other questions were mounting.

Who killed Alastair, and why? Where was Monty Buchan and what was he up to? And where exactly was the wreck of the *Lady Monteith*? I put them to Ronnie Eastfield.

'Sure. Fair questions to which I have no answers,' he said.' But the underlying question is this: what is Dark Ocean's agenda? As I say, on the face of it they're just another one of those ultra-nationalist groups who drive their buses around the streets of Tokyo with loudspeakers blaring out propaganda messages and old war-time songs. There are over a thousand right-wing extremist groups in Japan. Their themes are boringly consistent: anti-leftism, hostility towards China and Korea - North and South; and the justification of Japan's role in the war. But there's a lot more to Dark Ocean than that, only I've no way of telling what they're up to and I wouldn't want to mislead you into thinking I did.'

'Ever heard of the *Toyama Maru*?' I asked him.

'That old tub? Sure, she comes in and out of here from time to time. Why?'

'Because Alastair Marshall was murdered aboard the *Toyama Maru* and it happened on his own doorstep, or just off it.'

'Bloody hell. In Greece you mean? How did he die then?'

'Poisoned.'

'Why'd they kill him? Because he was closing in on them? Are you saying the *Toyama Maru* is connected with Dark Ocean then?'

'It seems possible, don't you think?'

'What was she doing in Greece? There must have been easier ways to kill Marshall than sending a ship all the way from the Far East.'

'I agree it doesn't make sense, Ronnie. There must have been some other reason for the ship being over there.'

CHAPTER 9

It was after midnight when I left. He'd sent out for food and we'd continued drinking his beer, then his whisky. Ronnie was slumped in his chair snoring loudly as I let myself out.

After wandering around Sai Kung for half an hour, I managed to find a taxi and dozed off myself on the journey back into town. Back at my hotel on Hong Kong side I fell into bed and went out like a light.

But I woke in the night, my mouth dry. I'd been dreaming of swimming under water off Alastair's jetty. I reached the little dinghy on the sea floor and as I did, Ronnie's face appeared out of the murk. He moved closer to me, then his face morphed into my father's I recalled from old photographs. I struggled to the surface waking as I did so, my heart hammering in my chest. I got up, drank three glasses of water and sat by the window looking out over the harbour, the air clear and the city lights glittering.

At first it had struck me as a coincidence discovering Ronnie had known my father. But the more I thought about it, the less improbable it seemed. They were both police officers in the same force after all and Hong Kong was a small place. What was more of a coincidence was Ronnie acting for the IMTF with Alastair Marshall as his case officer. But was that so unusual given that they'd both known my father? So the three of them were all connected. And Ronnie was the only one left.

But something else was nagging at my brain. It had been one-thirty by the time I'd got back to the hotel. The lobby had been almost empty. I'd picked up my room key from Reception and headed for the lifts. While I was waiting I'd looked back towards the lobby lounge. The only two people who'd been there when I arrived were now leaving. Two big, hefty Chinese guys, unusually big and hefty in a city of predominantly slender Cantonese. At the time I'd assumed they must be from northern China, or Korea perhaps. I remembered now they'd glanced over at me as they got up to leave; nothing unusual about that since we were the only people around at that time of night so I hadn't given it a second thought. Now I wasn't so sure. Was it hangover-induced paranoia or had they been watching me?

***

My hotel was located in Western District which suited my purpose as well as anywhere and after a largely unsuccessful fried breakfast and coffee hangover cure, I walked out into the hot and humid chaos of Sai Ying Pun. I'd heard it described as the new hotbed of urban cool. I couldn't see it, especially with the headache I was nursing, but I figured I could use this old part of town to my advantage. The brothels and opium dens were long gone now, replaced by hole-in-the-wall restaurants, shops, office and apartment blocks. But the area was run down and the relatively low rents had attracted young expatriates who weren't fortunate enough to be employed on expat terms. I'd seen plenty of these types on the streets around the hotel and figured I wouldn't stand out too much myself with them out and about.

I headed south on Water Street turning left onto Second Street and weaving my way through the crowds of office workers. My plan was to allow my tails, if that's what they were, to follow me, identify them, and at some point turn the tables and observe them in the hope they would lead me to their masters.

My plan failed of course. Before I'd even spotted them they acted. I'd just passed the Memphis Dry Cleaning and Laundry Company, skirting past a group of construction workers removing piles of scaffolding bamboo when I noticed a black Tesla coming towards me down the one-way street. These cars were two-a-penny in Hong Kong and I thought nothing of it. I continued up the hill and as I reached a junction, glanced back over my shoulder. Before I could react the two Chinese from the previous night, my height but twice as wide, came up one either side of me, linked their arms into mine and bundled me into the Tesla. I barely had time to struggle. It would have been futile anyway. Once in the car I was sandwiched between the two of them on the back seat. There was an overpowering smell of sweat. As we drove off the larger of the two extracted a pistol from his jacket and held the barrel to my head.

'You try anything, I shoot you.'

Then the other guy pulled a black hood over my head.

'Where are we going?' I asked in vain.

'Shut up,' said Fat Boy, prodding me hard with his gun again. I followed his advice telling myself this could still work out. After all, I'd wanted to find out who these heavies were and now it looked like I was going to, without the hassle of trying to follow them undetected. That's what I told myself.

We drove through congested streets. After half an hour or so our speed picked up and I could sense we were climbing a winding hill. Magazine Gap Road, I guessed. We must be heading to The Peak. I was wrong about that too for no sooner had I had the thought than we were going downhill, the road twisting. My geography of the place was still limited but if we weren't heading up to The Peak then we must be passing to the south side of the island, to Deep Water Bay, Repulse Bay or Stanley, or anywhere in between. As it turned out I was wrong about that as well. The time the journey took soon told me we'd driven way beyond the south side of the island.

Eventually we stopped and I was hauled out of the car. Despite the hood, I could smell the sea. A strong off-shore breeze was blowing and I could hear waves crashing onto a beach.

I was led across sand then into the sea. Water came up to my knees, then my waist. So was this it? Murder made to look like a drowning accident? The way Alastair had been dealt with, I was ready to believe anything.

The water wasn't cold but there was a swell and an undertow. I struggled then and broke free, tearing the hood off my head, but before I had much chance to look around both the goons had hold of me again. But it was with relief that I saw what was happening. I was being loaded onto a RIB. A third man hauled me aboard and Fat Boy clambered in after me still waving the pistol around. This was the first time I'd had the chance to look at him properly. He was like Oddjob on steroids.

'Hood on,' he shouted, gesturing with the gun to the hood I had in my hand.

'Where are we going?' I asked once in the boat.

'Hood on!' he shouted again, only this time he reinforced his order by kicking me hard in the stomach. For a man of his size he was agile. The boat was pitching. He'd had to raise his foot to the horizontal to get that kick right and it had landed just where he'd intended pushing me, winded, onto the floor of the boat. I stayed there and pulled the hood back over my head.

The outboard engine roared into life and we headed out to sea. For half an hour or more we bounced across the waves. Then the engine was cut as we came up against the hull of a bigger vessel. This time the hood was removed so

I could climb onto and up the gangway, unimpeded. The ship's hull and accommodation were white, her boot-topping dark blue, but beneath the paint I could see that the shell plating was pitted. And the teak decking, onto which I now stepped, was well worn. A slight vibration and the deep thrum of a diesel engine beneath my feet added to the boat's overall feel and I didn't need to see the name on her lifebuoys to confirm what I'd suspected. I'd boarded the *Toyama Maru*.

But what did surprise me was the appearance of Monty Buchan coming out on deck to greet me.

CHAPTER 10

Dressed in cream linen trousers and a dark blue blazer, Monty Buchan looked like he'd stepped straight out of Central Casting. All that was missing was a jaunty Captain's cap.

'Sorry about the subterfuge, Angus. You weren't mistreated were you? Come on in.'

'Never mind the civility. Just tell me what you're doing here. What am I doing here?'

'No need to take offence. Come and have a drink and all will be revealed.'

It was hot and humid and although I was still soaking from boarding the RIB, the ship's air-conditioning was welcome. I was angry with myself for having been so easily abducted; and the hangover from last night still lingered. We entered a saloon, all brass, teak and leather opulence. I looked around as he poured drinks from a bar in the corner. Was this where Alastair Marshall had felt the first twinges which led to an agonising death? I shuddered involuntarily.

'Aircon too cold for you?'

'It's fine,' I said taking the whisky from him.

'Well, here's to our little venture,' said Buchan raising his glass. He took a drink. I stepped over to the bar and added a splash of water to the whisky.

'Okay, so what gives, Monty? Your daughter says you've gone AWOL. She tells me to find you and instead you find me. What's going on?'

'I'm sure you can figure it out, Angus. The Club wasn't much use so I had to strike a deal with the Japs.'

'The Japs? Who do you mean?'

'Dark Ocean. You may not have heard of them, but it's not the criminal organisation it used to be. They're not Yakuza you know.'

'I have heard of them, as it happens.'

'Heard from whom?'

'Your friend Ronnie Eastfield for a start.'

'Oh. So you've met Ronnie have you?'

'It was your daughter who told me about him. And he told me about my father's role in winding up Dark Ocean's money laundering operations back in the seventies. So don't tell me they're some benevolent society, unless the beneficiaries are retired Yakuza of course.'

'Look, let me tell you why we got you here. I know the Club can't help in pursuing a claim but we figured maybe you could, by coming at it from a different angle, on a freelance basis. We'd pay you well.'

'To do what exactly?'

'I'll call Nakamura-san in on this. He's my liaison with Dark Ocean. By the way he calls it by its Japanese name,

Genyosha.'

He picked up the phone, spoke a few sharp bursts of Japanese and put the phone down. 'Handy language to have,' he said.

'I agree. Especially now you're in league with this lot.'

Before he could reply Nakamura came into the room, a short thickset man, grey hair cropped almost to his scalp. Unlike Buchan he was dressed conservatively in a black suit, white shirt and black tie. He looked as if he was due to attend a funeral.

Monty Buchan made the introductions. We shook hands, Nakamura bowing slightly as we did so. Something about his handshake seemed odd to me. I waited for him to speak.

No preliminaries: 'Buchan-san has told me of the work you do in the marine insurance business. You will want to know why we brought you here. How you can help us.' His English was good, if heavily inflected. His face was round and fleshy, his eyes seemed almost buried within it. I sat down in one of the leather wing chairs waiting for him to continue. The *Toyama Maru* rocked gently in the wash of another vessel that had passed. I wondered how close we were to the main shipping lanes. I'd noticed several islands within a few miles of us as I'd come aboard.

Monty Buchan went back to the bar and poured more drinks. Nakamura liked his Scotch too. Monty sat down opposite me while Nakamura stayed standing. As he took a drink I saw what had struck me when we shook hands. Half of the little finger on his right hand was missing. He might as well have been wearing a lapel badge saying Yakuza. I knew that this was *Yubitsume*, a ritualistic act of self-mutilation performed in front of the offended party, usually the boss, as an apology for some misdeed or another. I wondered whether the conservative dress hid a body tattooed with elaborate designs and symbols; and what this man's ranking was in the complex Yakuza hierarchy.

As if reading my mind, he said, 'You are observant. But do not imagine the organisation I represent here today is Yakuza. You might call me,' he paused, 'an emissary.'

'For whom?'

'For Japan!' he exclaimed whether in hope or triumph I couldn't tell. The man exuded volatility bound up with self-control. It was unsettling. I looked at Monty Buchan. He was staring at the carpet.

'Japan?' I asked hoping he would expand on the subject.

He turned and walked over to the saloon window to admire the view of an empty grey sea. Then he turned back to face us.

'Yes, for our future. You will learn more but for now we must turn to business. Do you know where we are now?' he said making a sweeping gesture to encompass the sea around us. 'We are lying off the island of Dangan Liedao, very close to where Buchan-san's ship was sunk by an American submarine many years ago.' He spoke in staccato bursts, his voice almost a harsh whisper. 'But we have been searching for the wreck without success. As you know,

Lady Monteith was carrying valuable cargo which we intend to salvage.'

'So why bring me out here?'

'We could search the seabed with our side-scan sonar and all other technical devices for many months, but never find it if we are looking in the wrong place.'

'And you are beginning to wonder whether you are looking in the right place.'

'Exactly! So you will help us find the exact location, McKinnon-san.'

'And how would I do that?' I asked doubtfully.

Finally it was Monty Buchan's turn to speak. 'We believe your father knew the precise coordinates, Angus. Somewhere, that information still exists.'

'My father died in a landslide. All my family's possessions were lost too. I have nothing left of his. And anyway, how would he know where the wreck lies?'

'Trust me, if anyone knew it would be him. He was involved in the search for gold that the Japanese, let's say "acquired" during the war.'

He glanced at Nakamura almost deferentially. What the hell was Monty playing at? 'He investigated claims, counter-claims, conspiracy theories. He knew more than anyone.'

'Maybe, but I have no records of his.'

'Have you ever looked? Really looked I mean? I have been researching the aftermath of the accident in which your family perished. Possessions were recovered. Some were returned to the survivors or to the next of kin of those who died. You were his next of kin.'

'I was a child. I became a ward of court before they handed me over to my uncle. I received nothing from him relating to my previous life here, or to my father's.'

'That may well be so but your uncle would still have received your father's effects, or what remained of them, perhaps not realising the significance of what was recorded in a notebook, a diary, a coded message somewhere? Did you ever ask about such matters?'

'No,' I lied. I was searching my memory. Years ago my uncle had given me boxes of papers, some photographs, clothing too, but I'd never opened them. It was part of a process of closing off the past. I had no wish to delve into such memories. Now I was trying to recall where those boxes might be. Not at my home in Greece, so in Scotland then? My uncle had died twenty-odd years ago. He'd known that I had no interest in those possessions but would he have retained them anyway? And on his death what would have happened to them? He and my aunt had had no children of their own but what about his will? He'd left everything to my aunt but ... but there was something in her will: a small financial bequest to me; and there was something in it referring to the possessions which again I'd ignored. But I did still have her will, in my apartment in Piraeus.

'Did you hear what I said?'

'What?'

It was Monty again. 'I asked whether you'd ever asked about your father's possessions.'

'No.'

'But they might still exist surely.'

'I don't know. My uncle and aunt are long gone. I would have to make enquiries.'

'We wish you to understand your position in this matter,' interjected Nakamura. 'It will be better for us all if we collaborate.'

'And if I wish not to?' I might as well know where I stood. In my pursuit of Alastair Marshall's killers and what lay behind it, I needed to explore all avenues, including the one into which I was now being drawn.

'To conduct our business by threat is not the way we would choose, McKinnon-san. However,' he walked over to the bar and picked up a remote control. 'your colleague is a very attractive young lady,' he said pointing the device at the bulkhead on the opposite side of the saloon. A screen slid down from overhead and a sense of foreboding swept over me even before the video images appeared.

She was walking down Notara Street in Piraeus, close to our office. Whoever was filming her was on the other side of the street. The next clip had been taken from a greater distance and showed her getting out of her BMW outside a big house. I knew it. It belonged to her parents and was in Ekali, one of Athens' northern and most affluent suburbs. Then it switched to her on the beach. She carefully spread her towel down on the sand and walked purposefully into the water wading out a few feet before diving in. The final shot showed her emerging and returning to where she'd left her towel. Zoe lay down. Then the screen went blank. The sequence had lasted less than two minutes.

There was silence for a moment. Nakamura replaced the remote control on the bar top and turned to me. I glanced at Monty who was inspecting the carpet again.

I breathed in deeply but remained silent not trusting myself to speak and trying to assimilate what I'd just seen.

'She is safe, your Zoe-san, for now,' Nakamura's manner was calm, his voice soft, reassuring.

'Why?' I spoke to Monty but it was Nakamura who replied, his voice strident again.

'You must understand that we are serious in our aims. We would not wish you to think you can play games with us. The girl will be safe but only as long as you cooperate. We do not have the time or the patience to wait while you think up some clever plan to upset our own. So find the location of the wreck for us first. Then we shall see about the girl. We will not put our objectives at risk.'

'And just what are they?'

'Perhaps you will learn in due course. Perhaps you may collaborate further with us in due course. First the wreck's coordinates, then we shall see.'

I cursed myself. So this is what happened when I started playing at secret agents. Now Zoe, who had no knowledge of how dangerous this case was getting, was at risk of becoming a pawn, an innocent victim.

'First I must find them,' I said, 'then we shall see. But do not interfere. You've made your threat clear but if you impede me it will make the job more complicated.'

'We will leave you alone but remember that if you try to double-cross us, we will take the girl. That will not be difficult. And she will be punished for your stupidity. I'm sure I do not need to remind you …'

'Enough!' Monty hissed. 'McKinnon knows what he must do. Let him get on and do it.'

But Nakamura didn't seem to be listening. He made a call from the house phone and in less than a minute Fat Boy appeared. Then Nakamura simply bowed and walked out of the saloon.

I sat down in a wing chair opposite Monty. 'Right! I have a couple of questions.'

He addressed Fat Boy. 'Give us a moment will you, Ah Sun?' Ah Sun just stood there looking vacant.

'First,' I cut in, 'the wreck of the *Lady Monteith* lies in Chinese waters. How do you think the Chinese Coast Guard are going to react if and when you start salvage operations in their back yard?'

'That's taken care of. Stick to what we tell you to do and don't worry about things that don't concern you, Angus. What else?'

'What do I tell your daughter?'

'Tell her nothing. I don't want her involved.'

'Not even that I know you're safe and well?'

'No, nothing! She would interfere and that would endanger her.'

'What? Like you've endangered Zoe? You're a duplicitous bastard aren't you. Is this all about your personal greed? You will put innocents at risk and disregard your own family while playing footsie with a bunch of criminals. And what's their game, Monty? Why is this so important to them?'

'I do what I have to, as do they' he said, agitated by my questioning. 'Now take him ashore, Ah Sun.'

It was dark by this time. They took me back in the RIB to Shek O, the same beach we'd left from. It was a warm humid night, but with an offshore breeze. The lights of a hundred fishing boats twinkled like stars on the dark sea. Under other circumstances it might have been a pleasant end to an enjoyable day out. Instead I felt ill.

CHAPTER 11

'*Beste mou*, tell me,' Eleni demanded.

'Go to the study. The key to the filing cabinet is at the back of the right-hand drawer of my desk. In the bottom drawer of the filing cabinet, right at the back is a file without a name. I think they're there.' It was my uncle's last will and testament and that of my aunt who had died just eight months after him, that I was after.

'You think,' she said caustically. 'Wait while I look.' Eleni was the only person I could trust to root around amongst my private papers. And she still had a key to the flat.

Although Eleni and I were no longer together, we were still on speaking terms and though neither of us found it easy to admit, there was mutual affection. She'd been my anchor for many years but my work, and particularly the travelling, had taken its toll. We'd somehow agreed to part and there was no shortage of suitors ready and eager to offer the kind of stable, long-term relationship she sought.

I was back in the hotel still shaken by what had taken place since I'd left my room that same morning. I could barely think straight. What I knew was that I couldn't do anything to endanger Zoe further. Somehow I had to ensure her safety.

'Got it! Now what am I looking for?'

'Okay. Start with my aunt's will. Look through it carefully until you find the bequests. There's something there about some documents assigned to me. Take your time.'

It didn't take her long. My aunt's will mirrored that of my uncle which she turned to next. They referred to documents to be passed to me upon her death. They were deposited at an Edinburgh bank I'd never heard of.

'Thanks, Eleni. You're a gem.'

'You're welcome, but I'm not your gem, Angus.'

Already there was the making of a senseless argument. 'Just thanks. Everything okay with you?'

'Sure. You?'

We chatted on, trying to smooth things out, not wanting to hurt each other. I asked her about Dimitrios, the new man in her life. She asked me about work – what was I doing in Hong Kong. I thanked her again and we agreed to have dinner at a new restaurant she'd been reading about once I got back. I wasn't sure it was such a good idea.

Next I looked up the Firth Bank. They were in Edinburgh's Dundas Street and according to the website their clients valued their expert investment and wealth management advice. It was still working hours over there. I called them explaining that I wished to take possession of documents left to me and placed in their vaults for safekeeping.

Reassuringly, they advised me to present myself with proof of identity such as valid passport and driving licence as well as recent evidence of my residential status. I hadn't expected anything less.

Calling Claire at this point was out of the question. My assailants had grabbed me off the street when I naïvely thought I could follow them. For all I knew they could have bugged my room. They could track my movements, perhaps even my calls remotely, if I used my mobile phone. If they had been listening in there was no harm in knowing that I was doing all I could to find the wreck coordinates they were so convinced my father's papers would reveal. Claire and the IMTF would have to wait.

The next morning dawned grey and wet. Dawn was hardly the word to describe it. On the assumption that both Ronnie Eastfield and myself were being watched and that my phone was being tapped, or even used as a transmitter to track my movements, I decided to leave it behind in the hotel. If Nakamura and his cronies saw us, so be it. But I reasoned they'd have a job listening into our conversation in such a public place as the Peninsula Hotel which Ronnie had mentioned was a favourite hangout of my father's. I was finding myself drawn into Hong Kong, and my father's ghost no longer seemed something to evade. And anywhere my father hung out I wanted to see for myself.

I called Eastfield from my hotel lobby. 'Leave your phone at home will you, Ronnie? And make sure you're not followed.'

As far as I knew Alastair Marshall had been using East-field as a walk-in agent on the case but I wanted to get this clarified. I wasn't convinced of his reliability either, based not least on his predilection for alcohol. But I'd known plenty of Ronnie Eastfields over the years. Some of them were among the best I'd ever worked with.

I walked up to the Star Ferry terminal in Central. If they were tailing me I didn't notice; neither during the short crossing to Tsim Sha Tsui. But I wasn't about to make the same mistake I'd made the previous day. I ambled up Nathan Road to Grenville Road from where I took a cab north on up into Mongkok. Crowds are good for losing a tail and Mongkok had them in greater numbers than even Tsim Sha Tsui. It also had plenty of narrow lanes and arcades concealed by street stalls and signs as well as the seething throng. I spent an hour and a half at it. At one point I ducked into a clothes shop and bought a baseball cap and lightweight jacket and, since the rain was getting heavier, an umbrella. Eventually I worked my way back to Tsim Sha Tsui on foot and entered through a side entrance of the Peninsula. By the time I spotted Ronnie in the lobby I'd done what I could to shake off any followers and could only hope he'd done the same.

'Don't worry, I was a cop remember? If I was being followed I'd know it.'

'I hope so, Ronnie.' He looked considerably livelier than the last time I'd seen him slumped in his chair drunk and fast asleep. He'd had his hair cut. He'd managed to shave without major incident, and was dressed casually, but smartly enough not to attract attention in the Pen's stylish lobby.

The finest hotel east of Suez was how it was promoted on its opening in 1928. At the time, before land reclamation had altered the geography of Tsim Sha Tsui, the Peninsula was directly opposite the quays where passengers disembarked from the liners that were regular callers from Britain and the ports of empire along the route, notably India, Singapore and Malaya. Kowloon was also last stop on the Trans-Siberian Railway that brought visitors from across Europe, Russia and northern China. The hotel's illustrious past had been carried forward to the present interrupted only by the war. It was on the third floor that Hong Kong's governor had surrendered to the Japanese on Christmas Day in 1941.

We ordered our drinks and I told him of my unplanned excursion to the *Toyama Maru*. 'I have to go back to Scotland if I'm to dig through the papers my father left me. I'll be back here soon. But I need to ask you more about this case.'

He spread his arms. 'Angus, old son, I've told you what I know.'

'I appreciate that, Ronnie. It's not so much what you know as what you think.' Ronnie had been in Hong Kong forever, as a cop, a criminal, a private investigator and until a few days ago, as Alastair Marshall's field agent on the case. I needed someone to talk it through with and Ronnie was my best option.

The problem was that I was used to working in the

comparatively transparent environment of the marine insurance world where rules, regulations and the law governed our business dealings - more or less. There was no shortage of nefarious characters, corruption and criminality, but I was familiar with it, and vigilant. Now I was in another world, one I'd tasted before but now, on the inside, I was no longer a hapless victim of circumstance but an active player. I'd been enrolled into the secretive world of espionage in which I had no training and little experience. Alastair would have been my case officer; now it was Claire. And yet she had admitted that her masters in the IMTF had little knowledge of what this case was about. Was this their method: to let the field agent blunder along in the hope of finding a way forward? Had Alastair enjoyed complete carte blanche?

And as for Dark Ocean, they had found me and shown their ruthless purpose by threatening to take Zoe hostage, and worse. I couldn't risk her life by deceiving them now. Her family were wealthy shipowners who could no doubt afford a ransom. This wasn't about ransom though but hostage taking as security for the fulfilment of a condition: my cooperation.

I voiced some of these concerns to Ronnie as we sat with our beers.

'Listen,' he said. 'Marshall always made it clear that I was on non-official cover. I'm just a NOC in the vernacular with no official ties to the IMTF the MoD or anyone else, and I'm not saying I like it but no-one's going to employ an old soak like me any other way and it pays well so I don't complain.

'You're going to Scotland anyway. Talk to the IMTF people. See what they've got. I'll mind the store here. You can trust me on that. And I'll see what I can dig up.'

'Right. Anything you can find out about the cargo she was carrying, besides the POWs. There might be some records buried away here, no?'

'Monty Buchan never found anything so I doubt I can. But I've got one or two avenues to explore. I'll let you know. By the way, what do you want me to do about Susanna Buchan? Monty doesn't want her to know what he's up to, is that right?'

'Yes, and I think it's best that way. I'll call her before I leave and tell her I've received assurance that her father's safe but I can say no more.'

'And you reckon she'll be content with that explanation?'

'No, but it will have to do.'

CHAPTER 12

The wind buffeted the aircraft as we made our final approach over the Firth of Forth. The flight put me into Edinburgh at seven on a Monday morning. Despite the wind, the sun was shining lifting Edinburgh's gothic mantle and revealing the city's brighter side.

Besides Ronnie Eastfield, Eleni and the bank, I had told no-one of my visit. To go straight to my flat off Leith Walk was out of the question. It was rented by the CMM and although the landlady and her Jack Russell terrier were old friends, I could not be sure that news of my arrival would not get back to the office. So I found a small hotel near the zoo just off Corstorphine Road, checked in, showered, changed and took a taxi to Dundas Street where the Firth Bank had its discreetly located offices. I was there for opening time.

The woman at the reception desk was stern-faced, grey-haired and wearing a grey skirt, white blouse and grey cardigan. She peered at me suspiciously over heavy-rimmed glasses. I was ready for her with the required evidence of my identity, which she inspected carefully as if she was expecting something to be amiss. I waited until she'd finished and she ushered me into a small room with no windows where I was told to wait.

After a few minutes a man entered introducing himself as Mr Johnstone. We shook hands. He was thin, neatly dressed, in his late fifties with a politely condescending air about him.

'I understand you would be seeking your father's papers deposited here by your uncle back in 1992? Am I correct?'

'Yes.'

'Would you mind me asking the reasons for your request, Mr McKinnon? No disrespect of course but ...' He had that manner common to those in his line of work to whom distrust comes naturally.

'No, not at all,' I said. I didn't, so long as he didn't mind me boring him to tears. 'I'm compiling a family history. I know so little and yet it's such a fascinating story. They were out in the Far East for generations. It all goes back to the early part of the last century when my great grandfather went to Hong Kong. He found work as a shipping clerk...' I leaned forward, ready to go on.

'Yes, quite so,' he said interrupting me by standing up. 'It sounds quite fascinating. Shall we pop down to the vaults and see what we can find then?'

I followed him out of the room, along the corridor and through a door which he unlocked. We descended a staircase into another corridor at the end of which was a large steel-fronted door with a wheel at its centre. Johnstone turned it to select the correct combination. Having done so, he swung it open using his body weight as a lever.

'Concrete on the inside,' he explained, tapping the door. The steel's just the casing.' Beyond this was a gate of steel railings which he also unlocked. We stepped inside. I was half expecting to see rows of gold bars. Instead there were just rows of steel drawers.

'Let's see now,' said Johnstone. He found the drawer he was looking for, unlocked it and pulled out a large grey safety deposit box which he presented rather formally to me. 'There,' he said. 'You take that while I lock up here.'

Back outside the vault I was invited to place the box on a table in the corridor. Johnstone gave me a set of two identical keys. 'These are for you, to be kept safe,' he added with a little smile. 'Now, if you'd place one of them in this lock here.' I did as I was told and turned the key. Then he did the same inserting another key into another lock. There was a click and the box was open.

'Now, I'd better lock up here, eh?' he said allowing himself a little laugh for making such a blindingly obvious point, 'and we'll take this back upstairs where you can peruse the contents at your leisure, Mr McKinnon. And Morag will get you a cup of tea.'

Upstairs Johnstone took his leave and I asked the receptionist for a coffee. 'Black with one sugar please, Morag. Biscuits too if you have any.'

Morag appeared with the coffee and a digestive biscuit.

'Only one biscuit, Morag?'

She looked flustered. 'I'll find you another one if you'd like? Have you not just had your breakfast?'

'Another one or two would be most welcome thank you, Morag.' She brought me three.

The box contained a large buff envelope, nothing more. I pulled out the contents. There was a note from my uncle and various papers which I glanced at. The note was scrawled in his handwriting which I remembered so well. It simply said: "Angus old boy, if and when ..."

There were also three notebooks. Each had a blue cardboard cover with the year written neatly in the top right corner. I placed them on the table in date order. The last one was marked 1972. Two of the books had water stains in the bottom corner. On one of these there was a residue of what looked like mud. I ran my finger across the cover's gritty surface. I put them back in the envelope without opening them.

***

'Not coming down for dinner tonight?' the girl at the hotel reception asked when I ordered food to be brought to my room.

'Work,' I said. I'd have preferred some human contact instead of the task that lay ahead. My father's three notebooks lay on the desk defying me to open them. The food arrived: haggis, neeps and tatties and a bottle of Bobbie Burns Shiraz that the receptionist had recommended. 'It goes well with the haggis I'm told,' she'd said, 'even if it is from Australia.'

The 1970 journal contained various case notes none of which followed any standard police crime reports I'd ever seen. There were no personal or domestic references either and at first I wondered why he'd bothered to record cases which surely would have been more formally written up at his office according to official protocols. But I soon realised these were "cases" he chose, for whatever reason, not to record officially. Whether he was in breach of police regulations I wasn't sure. I suspected he was. They covered all sorts of misdemeanours committed by subordinate police officers which it seemed he'd chosen to overlook. Often, they were recorded in a dry, humorous way. He had a fine sense of irony and I warmed to his style. He must have been a tolerant boss considering some of the things his junior colleagues got up to. Women, drugs and, in the case of the expatriate officers, alcohol, all featured prominently.

But it wasn't until I reached March 1971 in the second journal that I found what I was looking for. The entries read:

"24/3 – Jim G called. Tim Younger from South China Bank wants to talk about suspected advance payment con. Off the books. Meet TY Saturday."

I'd already discovered that Jim G was Assistant Commissioner James Graham, several ranks above my father, but from previous references I gathered the two were friends and trusted one another.

"27/3 – Seen similar cases before. Thinking of the charterparty scam on a local shipowner who should have known better. Always depend on greed and gullibility of victim. This one's different. Younger thinks it's a scam but not so sure. Never heard a story like it. Filipino named Santos with Yakuza connections wants to use SCB to monetise gold looted by Japs and promising TY 1pct commission! TY says first consignment is from Sinclair Buchan ship sunk during the war. And more to follow from secret stashes in Japan and the Philippines - Santos was talking billions. TY says Santos will contact him in a week to see if he wants to play. Left no name or contact - naturally. Said I'd look at it. Starting with young Monty Buchan. I know he's looking for the *Lady Monteith* and the gold he thinks is on board – never a thought for the poor bastards who drowned when she was sunk."

So my father had got the bare bones of the story from a banker called Tim Younger. But it was another four months into the journal before I found the next entry relating to the case.

"15/7 – Can't believe it. I get nothing from Buchan on the Jap gold case then Younger calls. Met in Dragon Boat Bar last night. He says *Lady Monteith* is Site 176 – last on a list of Golden Lily sites. He even has wreck location. Says he's playing along with Santos contact telling him the gold can be exchanged for cash, bonds, etc. in Bombay or Cochin. Indian buyers would need to see what they were getting before making an offer. Warned him risk he was taking could land him in trouble. Wants me to play along as the crooked cop who can grease the wheels. No way. Or is there? I'll talk to Jim."

Was this my father succumbing to temptation or what? I poured myself more of Bobby Burns' Shiraz and read on, enthralled. This time there was a gap of just a fortnight.

"1/8 Bloody hot. Aircon not coping. Jim reckons if Younger wants to run with this, let him. It can stay off the books so long as RHKP see no evidence of fraud on bank's part."

I carried on reading. Interesting though it was, I found no further reference to Site 176, Golden Lily, the Yakuza or Tim Younger of the South China Bank. Either my father had dropped the case like a hot potato or he'd decided not to record anything further on it in his notes.

The final entry was made the following year in the 1972 journal. It contained no case notes but was tragically prescient. It was dated 16 June:

"This rain – when will it stop. It's no place to be."

Two days after this we were all swept down the hillside in a torrent of mud and rubble. I drank the rest of the wine and went to bed. But it was hours before I slept.

CHAPTER 13

Had my father known the location of the wreck? Had he noted the coordinates elsewhere? I'd never know. But at some point in the night it occurred to me that, besides Ronnie Eastfield, there were others who might know something more of the history of this bizarre case.

Catriona, the receptionist, asked how I'd enjoyed the wine. I told her it was delicious. 'So it's a full Scottish for you this morning is it?'

I appreciated her cheerful invitation to sample the Scots' proprietary take on the full English breakfast but declined. Instead I went for a walk to collect my thoughts from the previous night.

'Someone called looking for you,' Catriona declared on my return. 'Do you not carry your mobile with you?'

'I left it in my room. Who was it?' In fact I'd ditched my mobile phone for fear that it might be used to track my whereabouts. I was now using burner phones.

She wrote a name and number on a pad and handed it to me. 'She said her name was Morag. Is she your girlfriend like?'

'No she is not, Catriona.' I looked at the note: Morag McRae, Firth Bank, and the number. I went back to my room and called her on the landline.

'Oh, Mr McKinnon, how are you this morning?'

'I'm fine thanks, Morag. I believe you called.'

'Yes, that's right. Mr Johnstone asked me to get in touch. He'd like a word, if you'd hold on.' She put me through.

'Ah, Mr McKinnon. Good morning to you. I'll get straight to the point if I may?' He stopped talking.

'Yes, please go ahead.'

'Right, yes. Well, I owe you an apology, sir. A complete oversight on my part I'm afraid. The items your uncle left: there is something else, a further item which was kept in another drawer in our vault. We have one area for documents you see and another for items of a different nature and value.'

'And?' I asked after he'd paused again.

'Well, would it be possible for you to call by and collect this further item? I'd rather not describe it over the telephone you understand.'

Curious, I took a taxi back to Dundas Street. 'Well now, Mr McKinnon. How nice to see you back again so soon.' Morag was animated this morning, considerably less prim than on our last meeting. 'Mr Johnstone is in a meeting but he has authorised me to take you down to the vault today and young Kirsty will look after Reception while we're down below. We're rather busy today.'

Young Kirsty duly appeared and Morag led me back down to the vault.

What she produced from another box larger than the one my father's notebooks had been in, was a revelation. Folded inside a soft black cloth was a small statue no more than five inches high. I weighed it in my hand. It was heavy. It was either gold or gold plated, I thought, perhaps over brass or some other metal. The statue was a seated Buddha with its right hand raised and facing outwards.

Morag was fidgeting. 'Excuse me for saying so, Mr McKinnon, but this is a very interesting piece. I must say. If you'll forgive me, I am really quite fascinated in the subject of Buddhism.'

This was a different Morag altogether. She was captivated. 'Clearly, this is a Protection Buddha. The raised right hand symbolically represents a shield you see, and its second meaning, overcoming fear, is closely related to that of protection since one who is receiving protection would be less fearful, do you see? This statue signifies courage and offers protection from fear, delusion and anger. It looks Chinese to me, from Yunnan maybe – certainly southern China.'

'I'm impressed, Morag. Do you know how old it is by any chance, or what it's made from?'

'Ah now.' She held out her hand and I passed the statue to her. Holding it close to her face she peered over her glasses at it. 'I couldn't tell you for sure but it looks to me like it's solid gold. It's old and there are scratches. If it was gold plated the base metal would show through so I don't think it's gold plate. Many were cast in silver or brass and gold plated. Not this one though.'

'How old would you guess?'

'Well now, don't hold me to this. There are others better qualified, but certainly over a hundred years. I'd get it assessed if I were you: a proper acid test done. As to its value, I really couldn't say. I rather think it's worth is more sentimental for you is it not?'

'Yes, you're right. Thanks, Morag. I'll take it with me for now.'

'Aye, well if you want it kept safe, you know where to come.'

And with that I signed for it, we parted and I returned to the hotel.

***

The two men my father had mentioned in his notes were Jim Graham and Tim Younger. Graham's name appeared online but only in a brief obituary in the South China Morning Post from four years earlier. He'd died in New Zealand to where he'd retired. I was luckier with Younger. He had retired from the bank years before but his name appeared in a story from six months ago in The Scotsman. Younger, it seemed, was alive and well and living in Perthshire.

The story covered the opening of a new cattle mart and Sir Timothy Younger of Canmore had performed the honours. Canmore was his 2,000 acre estate in the hills north of Pitlochry. Unable to find a phone number or email address I decided to pay him a visit.

I asked the car hire firm for something fast and was given a Jaguar. My reasoning was that if I was being followed I could shake off the tail. After my encounter with Oddjob and the video of Zoe they'd shown me, I wasn't taking chances. If I was followed to Younger's place they could, after I'd left, and if he had them, force the coordinates out of him. This seemed unlikely since with Zoe held to ransom they knew I would willingly surrender the wreck's location in return for her liberty. Indeed, to force this case to a conclusion, it was crucial that they did learn the wreck's whereabouts, the sooner the better.

I took a circuitous route via Loch Tay stopping along the way, but at no point in the journey did I sense I had company, except for the little Buddha statue on the seat beside me. Younger's Canmore estate was up a B road some miles north of Pitlochry. The sign at the old stone gates said West Port. There was a lodge inside to the left of the entrance. Despite a light rain that had begun to fall, washing was hanging out in the garden. I pulled up and got out of the car as an elderly man appeared in the porch of the cottage.

'Aye?' His manner was neither friendly nor hostile.

'I've come to visit Sir Timothy.'

He eyed me and the car at some length. 'Are you expected?'

'I'd like you to tell him I'm here. He was a friend of my

father - Kenneth McKinnon.'

'Aye, I'll call the house for you.' He went back inside. It was fifteen minutes before he reappeared. 'Just go on up to the house then.'

I drove for half a mile or so through rolling parkland scattered with huge oaks and sycamores that must have been there for a hundred years or more. Herdwick sheep grazed alongside shaggy Highland cattle. The house appeared, framed artfully between the trees, a white, turreted baronial pile somewhere between Medieval castle and French Renaissance chateau, a style much favoured in Scotland.

A woman was waiting, dwarfed by the huge wooden door. I guessed she was the man's wife from the lodge. They were of an age. I wondered what she'd say if she knew he hadn't brought the washing in. I parked and she ushered me indoors.

Younger was standing in front of a large stone fireplace occupied by a log fire which blazed and crackled. He was lighting his pipe. His glasses reflected the light from the fire making it difficult at first to see his eyes. He must have been well into his eighties. His corduroy trousers were worn at the knees and his cardigan looked moth-eaten.

He extinguished the match by waving it around in the air then used the match box to pack down the tobacco as he sucked on the stem of the pipe to ensure its successful combustion. Sparks flew out onto the rug. He stamped on them aggressively but I could see small black holes where the same thing had happened. I waited while he completed this ritual then stepped forward to introduce myself.

'I apologise for arriving unannounced. I couldn't find your phone number.'

We shook hands. 'You look like your father. I suppose people have told you that?'

'My uncle said I did.' Ronnie Eastfield had too but I wasn't going to bring his name into the conversation.

'Same shaped head. Same build.' He spoke in a distracted way as if disoriented. I sensed he was a little senile.

He gestured to an armchair beside the fire and settled himself down opposite me.

'So, what can I do for you? You'll not have come all this way to discuss old times.'

'Actually, I have,' I said, taking a direct approach. I feared if I didn't his mind would wander. 'Did you ever learn the exact location of the wreck? The *Lady Monteith*?'

'Bad business,' he mumbled. 'So many dead. Your whole family.' He was talking about the landslide now, not the victims of the *Lady Monteith* sinking. I tried again.

'Yes, but the *Lady Monteith*: do you remember that case? Golden Lily's site 176, do you know where the wreck lies?'

The woman had brought in tea and a fruit cake.

'What? Oh, yes of course. Another bad business. These things trouble you more as you get older you know. They don't fade with time. Not for me anyway. Yes, I know exactly where the damn thing lies.' He looked at me, a sideways look and I wondered if he was really as dotty as he seemed.

'You'd better tell me what this is all about, eh?'

So I told him a version of the facts leaving out the IMTF and Alastair Marshall's death. I described the cold case I'd been assigned by the CMM, of Buchan's determination to claim the cargo, of my encounter with Nakamura on the *Toyama Maru*, their threat against Zoe and of my father's notebooks which led me to where I was now sitting.

'Yes, a rum business if ever there was. So young Monty Buchan wants to claim the treasure he thinks is on board and replenish his bank account, but where the devil does Dark Ocean fit in? You say they're helping Buchan salvage the cargo but not just to see him rescue his ailing business surely. They were never noted for their altruism. If they were just a bunch of Yakuza hoodlums I wouldn't be so worried but as you say, they have an ultra-nationalist agenda. Did you know that they harbour the ambition of a Greater East Asia Co-Prosperity Sphere? As you no doubt will know, that was an imperial propaganda concept formed at the outset of the war but behind it lay a far more sinister ideal. And the Dark Ocean I encountered forty-something years ago had some very disturbing ideas as to how the region could still be shaped by the will of a resurgent militaristic Japan. So I wonder what they're about now, umm?'

The man's earlier vagueness had gone. He was sharply focused now, leaning forward in his chair and looking intently at me as he spoke.

'Tell me,' I said, 'back then how did they think they could realise their ambitions? My father's notes say you were contacted by a Filipino who was acting for them.'

'Yes, Santos his name was. He offered me a commission if I'd help them monetise the gold from their wartime lootings. He wanted me to be his laundryman.' Younger laughed to show his disdain. Then he got up and started poking at the fire. 'A hundred and seventy-six of them but most of those had already been recovered I was told. The *Lady Monteith* was the last known site: number 176. But I don't have the answer to your question. They didn't share their strategic plan with me if that's what you're asking. I don't think they shared it with Santos either. He was just acting as a broker.'

'What did my father think of all this?' I asked 'He says he met you and he didn't like the idea of playing the crooked cop. But he said he'd talk to Jim Graham. After that there were no further references to the case in his notes.'

'Yes, Jim Graham and your father were close. In case you're worried, your dad was a straight arrow. I wouldn't have talked to him if I'd thought he was corrupt. Anyway, I told Santos to find someone else to wash his dirty linen.'

'But Santos gave you the wreck coordinates.'

'Not exactly gave. I led him on at first you see. I was curious. I said if he wanted the Bank to consider his request I'd need to show the Board some evidence. He couldn't expect us to just take his word for it. It was a highly irregular transaction he was proposing.'

'And he gave them to you?'

'Yes, reluctantly. He scribbled them on a piece of paper. I later plotted them on the Admiralty chart. It showed a position a few miles south west of the Jiapeng Liedao islands.'

'The *Toyama Maru* was anchored off Dangan Liedao when I was on board. They believed they were close to the wreck there.'

'You'd need to check that but as I recall, Dangan Liedao and Jiapeng Liedao are two separate island groups; in the same chain but separate.'

'So how did Santos take it when, having given you the location, you told him there was no deal?'

'Ha! He did what I guessed he'd do. Nothing. He was a flunky. He couldn't risk telling his masters in Tokyo that he'd disclosed such priceless information. God knows what they'd have done to him.'

'I'd like to see them.'

'I have them somewhere. I'd need to rummage through some drawers. But even if you get this Zoe of yours off the hook this time, who's to say they won't come after her or you or someone else close to you if you don't do their bidding. Seems to me you must either barter the information for a safe passage as it were, or join with them.'

'Yes. That's pretty much the way I see it,' I said. That wasn't the way the IMTF planned it, but the IMTF and those who worked for them were subject to the Official Secrets Act. Whether they expected me to break the law in pursuit of this case had not been made clear. I hadn't even asked. In the meantime I'd stick with my cover of investigating a possible insurance claim on the *Lady Monteith's* cargo. But I wasn't finished with the old boy yet.

'What can you tell me about the ambitions of Dark Ocean back then?' I asked him, returning to my earlier question.

'They believed wholeheartedly in the principles behind the Co-Prosperity Sphere: the subordination of other nations, the superiority of the Japanese over other Asian races. It was part of an explicit policy before and during the war, and afterwards Dark Ocean adopted it. Fanciful to put it mildly. They were full of hot air I thought. Initially it was talk of controlling the trade routes of the region, then the world. Nonsense!'

'And this all came to you via Santos?'

'Yes. Of course he wasn't privy to the whole plan. And being a Filipino, I don't think he believed half of what they told him. But he was an opportunist, an unscrupulous one. He wanted me to meet with his masters. I declined but by this time I was more nervous than curious. Talked to your dad and he arranged police protection for me.'

'Where do you think they went after you turned them down?'

'I told him to head for Cochin if he wanted to cash in the gold. At that time, Cochin or Bombay were the centres for easy gold transactions, monetising it I mean. Never heard another word. To be honest I was very glad to see the back of Santos and the whole shady business.'

I drank the tea and ate a piece of cake while he tried to get his pipe going again. Then I pulled the Buddha statue out of my bag.

'What do you make of this?' I asked him.

He finished re-igniting the pipe and took it from me. 'Was this with your dad's stuff too then?'

'Yes. He didn't get it from you I presume?'

'Never seen it before.' He handed it back. 'Looks old. You think it's to do with this case of yours do you? Things like this were not uncommon out there. Might have just been some artefact he kept on his desk with his papers, a paperweight to stop stuff flying around, pre-aircon you know when we all had fans on our desks.'

'You're probably right,' I said taking it back from him. 'What about the rest of the loot? I've heard much of it was shipped to the States after the war.'

'Well now. That's never been proven of course. But yes, that's always been rumoured: that the Yanks got their hands on billions which went towards financing the Cold War. Bankrolled dictators on every continent, bribed officials from the UN to KGB agents, even influenced the outcomes of American elections. But that's another story altogether. Prove it if you can!'

'It might help support Buchan's claim if I had some documentation. Cargo manifests would be useful as a start.'

'Funny you should mention manifests. I remember Santos going on about manifests. He said they existed but he never showed them to me. I wasn't interested you see.'

We talked on but I learned little more from him. He was reliving the past, his memory of those days vivid still. I think he was reluctant to let me go. I promised I'd keep in touch and let him know how the case panned out.

'My apologies again for appearing unannounced,' I said standing up. 'And I need those coordinates, Sir Timothy.'

'I know you do. Just wait here, my boy.' He struggled to his feet and tottered out of the room.

CHAPTER 14

I returned to Edinburgh by another route and once back in the hotel, keyed the *Lady Monteith* wreck coordinates Younger had given me into a reverse geocoding tool. It showed a point two or three miles south of the Jiapeng Liedao islands, which themselves were several miles to the southwest of Dangan Liedao. As I'd suspected, they'd been looking in the wrong place.

Nakamura had told me to bring the coordinates to him personally. But before I did so I had to be sure Zoe's life would no longer be at risk. Dark Ocean had shown itself to be a dangerous bunch of criminals, their modus operandi one of ruthless violence in pursuance of their megalomaniacal aims. But they had offered to bring me into their scheme, whatever that was, and if I was to get to the bottom of the case, to understand what their real aims were, I needed to join with them on the inside, or at least appear to.

But my first priority was how to protect Zoe. She was better off not knowing the danger she was in, for now. I would need to arrange for her to simply disappear – melt away before her watchers' eyes. For that to happen I needed to speak with my case officer.

After following an elaborate contact protocol Claire and I arranged to meet outside the Royal Botanic Garden Glasshouses the following morning. It was close to where she lived and when I arrived she was already waiting. She had a dog with her – a black mongrel puppy.

'Who's this?'

'Asbo. The kids found him and begged me to take him in. He's a nightmare.'

Asbo was wrapping his lead round Claire's ankles and barking at the same time.

'More training needed.'

'Yours you mean or the dog's?'

'You're cheerful today,' I said, but I wondered how much was an act. It couldn't be easy managing the CMM while doing her undercover work and running a household of two young children with a husband who was rarely home and with a marriage that was disintegrating. And I still wasn't sure whether she'd recovered or would ever fully recover from those violent events of a year earlier in Greece.

'It's seeing you, darling,' she said squeezing my arm. 'Here, you take him.'

She passed me the dog's lead. I tightened it and pulled him to heel. "Heel!" I said sharply in a commanding tone of voice. The dog took no notice and Claire laughed.

'He's Iona's dog but of course she expects Nanny to walk him. And Nanny's back in Oslo on holiday. Anyway, I don't mind. We all love him really.'

As we walked I brought her up to date ending with my father's notes, my meeting with Tim Younger and my concern for Zoe's safety.

'I have a plan for Zoe,' Claire said. 'We'll get her over here for a month's training and familiarisation at the CMM. She's never even visited us because you always kept her to yourself. She can stay with me, come into the office every day, and that way we can keep a close eye on her.'

I was sceptical. 'I'm not sure how safe she'll be. For a start you'll have to smuggle her out of Greece without these bastards noticing. When they do see she's gone, they'll start looking.'

'Angus, I know I downplay the reach and resources of the IMTF but believe me, they're highly competent in these matters. They'll keep her well shielded wherever she is, don't worry.'

'If you say so.'

'I do. But listen, it's time you heard what they've got to say - the IMTF. I've arranged a meeting up here the day after tomorrow. Can you be at South Queensferry, Hawes Pier 0800? And don't forget the coordinates.'

'I won't. But tell them to have a BA chart of the Outer Approaches to Hong Kong: Number 3026; the paper version.' I needed an Admiralty chart to see exactly where the location was in relation to Hong Kong and its other outlying islands but I'd learned there was no chart agent in either Edinburgh or Leith these days.

We walked through the Gardens enjoying the spring sunshine. She held my arm and once we were on the move, Asbo more or less behaved himself.

'How are you, Claire? Personally I mean.'

'Absolutely fine, darling,' she said airily, avoiding a proper answer. 'Anyway, it's me who should be asking you. I'm your case officer, remember? You're such a lone wolf, Angus. We trust you. Or rather I tell my masters at IMTF they can trust you. But we need to talk more often. They need to know what's going on and I look foolish if I don't know what my own field agent is up to. My Joe,' she added leaning her head against my shoulder.'

'I understand, but it's not always easy.' I didn't want to make things difficult for her but neither did I want people telling me how to handle the case.

'I have something to show you,' I said changing the subject.

'Ooh! I love surprises. I noticed that fancy man bag on your shoulder. What's in it? I hope you're not carrying anything classified in there.'

I ignored her mockery, so easily accepted when it comes from someone you love, and fished out the Buddha statue. 'Take a look at this.'

She took it from me and inspected it. 'Where did this come from then?'

I told her, and of what Morag and Tim Younger had said about it.

'But you think it might be linked to the case? I suppose it could be symbolic in some way of what the ship was carrying.'

'That's a fair assumption. The Japanese plundered everything of value they set their eyes upon. The Buddhist monasteries and temples were not exempt.'

'You'll find out when you find the wreck, darling.'

'You make it sound like Pokemon.'

'She laughed. You've no idea what Pokemon is, have you.'

'No. And you do?'

'Of course. The children are into it. Get a life, Angus!'

CHAPTER 15

I arrived at Hawes Pier ten minutes late. Claire was already there standing, arms folded, beside her black Porsche. There was no sign of Asbo.

'Traffic?' she asked, 'or a protest in support of your anti-establishment tendencies?'

I had overslept but she'd guessed right too. Her intuition was unfailing. I was sensing a certain officiousness that had crept into my limited dealings with the IMTF, even into Claire's own behaviour. I wasn't one of their flunkies.

'Their RIB's out there,' she said waving to the little craft, its White Ensign fluttering manically in the wind. As we watched, it started moving towards the pier.

It was a choppy ten minute ride across to the anchorage off Rosyth. The Navy coxswain drew the boat alongside in a well-practised manoeuvre and we clambered up the gangway to be greeted by an officer in naval uniform. He introduced himself as the chief officer.

If I'd expected to be piped aboard a state-of-the-art warship of Her Majesty's Royal Navy, I was to be disappointed. The RFA *Sir Gareth*, a thirty year old converted ro-ro vessel, was anchored off the naval dockyard at Rosyth undergoing routine maintenance and repairs.

'We're not part of the Naval Service as you may or may not know,' the chief mate explained when I asked him how the Royal Fleet Auxiliary fitted into the Royal Navy hierarchy. 'Us officers wear Merchant Navy rank insignia and naval uniforms. We're only under naval discipline when the vessel is engaged on "warlike operations". So you can relax.'

He led us into the sparsely furnished wardroom. A cheap blue carpet covered the deck and the utilitarian furniture and fittings were typical of what you'd find on any merchant vessel.

A man and a woman dressed in civilian clothing, and a naval officer stood up as we entered. The woman introduced herself as Commodore Amber Dove, the man as Benedict Wood, seconded, he explained, from Britain's Secret Intelligence Service, MI6. The naval officer, who said his name was Randolph Carvill, was wearing a dark blue sweater with epaulettes signifying he was a Vice Admiral. He must have been close to retirement by the look of him.

We sat down and Amber Dove poured coffee. Claire obviously knew her and Benedict Wood. There was an easy familiarity to their exchanges.

'Well, at last,' said Amber Dove. 'Welcome to the IMTF, Angus. Please forgive the spartan surroundings but I'm sure you're used to worse.

'Let me explain. Admiral Carvill here has kindly agreed

to sit in. It's quite possible, given the nautical dimension to this case, that the advice, and possibly the intervention of the Royal Navy may be necessary, so we agreed it was best that a senior officer was present from the beginning. Admiral Carvill is fully conversant with the case. Not only that but he has broad experience of the Far East having completed several extended tours of duty in the Pacific theatre.' She smiled across at Carvill who nodded and smiled back condescendingly, in the way senior officers do when they're having to defer to those they consider their subordinates.

'Now, Benedict here,' she continued, 'is on secondment from Six; across the river,' she added in case I didn't know what she was talking about. 'We do work closely with our colleagues in the other intelligence agencies and Benedict has been with us for almost a year now. He also has Far East experience having been assigned to the SIS station in Hong Kong for eighteen months up until last year.

'Finally of course, Claire here who you know well already.' She gave me what I interpreted as a knowing smile but maybe I was imagining it. 'As you know, Claire is your case officer, Angus, and we're very confident that arrangement will work well.'

Amber Dove was in her mid-fifties I guessed, short silvery grey hair, earrings but no other jewellery. She wore a simple black woollen dress. Her manner was relaxed, and I detected a sense humour in her manner.

Wood was considerably younger, in his mid-thirties and sporting a beard which seemed incongruous with his tight-fitting suit. He deferred to Amber Dove and said little, watchful.

Claire sat, elegant as ever, an expression of mild amusement on her face. She knew how frustrated I was at having been shielded from the inner workings of this secretive organisation, and now I was face to face with them. Did she already know what the agenda was and was awaiting my reaction?

As if reading my thoughts, Amber said, 'I know how impatient you are to know more of our plans, Angus. And we are equally interested in sharing your own thoughts. Let me say first though that Alastair Marshall was not just a valued colleague, he was a dear friend. I was and still am devastated by his death. In our line of work, we are so often close to such calamities, whether our adversaries or among our own people, but Alastair had been with us from the start, when the IMTF was first formed following the disbanding of Naval Intelligence back in the sixties. We grew out of what the old timers like him knew as Room 39. And although we became part of Defence Intelligence at the MoD, the IMTF's task force status gave us a measure of independence; and much of the old culture which had been such a force within Naval Intelligence was retained, cherished even. And Alastair, although latterly he chose a reclusive life, was very much part of that whole transition.' She paused to drink her coffee. 'In recent years the IMTF, as you can imagine, has become somewhat preoccupied with the issues of the day. Piracy and the maritime dimension of terrorism have kept us fully stretched despite, as I say, the alliance we enjoy with our colleagues at the SIS and other agencies.

'But Alastair was always more concerned with maritime fraud, the commercial aspects of crime on the high seas, which is why he took such an interest in the P&I world, including Claire here and yourself through your work at the CMM.'

'Which leads us to the present,' Claire interjected. Amber Dove laughed. Her face lit up taking on an attractiveness which was hidden before.

'I know. I've been going on a bit.' The two women had a friendly rapport. There weren't the underlying tensions so often present when men converse in a competitive environment.

'So, you now have the coordinates revealing the whereabouts of the *Lady Monteith*. You will pass these on to Mr Nakamura and his Dark Ocean or *Genyosha* cronies. They will attempt to salvage cargo from the wreck believed to be gold in one form or another, for the purpose of what exactly? And what about Buchan? Do we know his agenda?'

'I thought I knew why Buchan wanted to get his hands on the cargo: to replenish the family coffers,' I said. 'But from my enforced meeting with them on the *Toyama Maru*, Buchan's role in all this isn't clear: whether he's really collaborating with Dark Ocean as he claims, whether he thinks he can double cross them and seize the cargo for himself, or whether he's being blackmailed or otherwise coerced.'

'Surely he despises Dark Ocean. They were part of the

imperial Japanese war machine that commandeered his fleet and wrought havoc on his family business,' Wood contributed for the first time.

'Yes, but Buchan is an opportunist,' I said. 'He might think it better to make a pact with the Devil if he can see something in it for himself.'

Amber Dove spoke. 'So let's just reiterate what we believe to be Dark Ocean's aims: the revival of Japanese imperialism; turning the concept of a Greater East Asia Co-Prosperity Sphere into a present-day reality; an ultra-nationalist agenda; what else?'

'Are we sure they're serious?' said Benedict Wood. 'I mean could they pull it off?'

'They're deadly serious,' I said. 'They're a lot better organised and resourced than the other ultra-nationalist groups blaring out their fanatical rhetoric and martial music on the streets of Tokyo. Whether they can pull it off, I couldn't say until we know more of their plans, the specifics I mean. By the way, did you get the Admiralty chart I asked for?'

'I have it here,' said Wood bringing it across to the table along with a set of parallel rules and a pencil. He unrolled it keeping the corners down with four brass paperweights.

I found the coordinates that Tim Younger had given me and marked the location where they intersected with a cross. We could now all see clearly where the wreck apparently lay and its proximity to the Jiapeng Liedao islands, and to Hong Kong itself.

'So, with these coordinates which I'll give them, they'll be able to locate the wreck,' I said. 'They'll need a sonar fish for that. Then ROV-mounted cameras can probably identify what cargo she had on board allowing them to decide how to salvage it. From what my father knew and what Younger told me, Dark Ocean know the wreck is Golden Lily's Site 176, and that there's something of great value there, probably gold, which they wish to claim, as they have so many of the other one hundred and seventy five other treasure troves.'

'And,' added Ben Wood, 'we can assume they intend to use the proceeds of all this loot to fund their imperialistic dreams in the region, for which they will need very deep pockets indeed.'

'Quite,' said Amber. 'So, Angus, after we've got Zoe out of Athens, you get back to Hong Kong and do everything you can to help them find the wreck.'

'And then what?'

'Don't worry. We have something in mind which we'll share with you when the time is right. But there's something more I need to tell you, and I'm taking this opportunity of briefing Claire and Ben here too. Admiral Carvill is already aware of it.

'You know that after Alastair's death we removed all his records: laptops, back-ups on external drives, everything. He didn't use the Cloud of course. It was all encrypted and much of it we already had, but when we got all his equipment back to London we did find some notes that caused us concern. They were notes that he'd obviously felt he could not trust to be shared even with us. And they were highly speculative too; he was making some pretty huge assumptions so perhaps he simply wasn't ready to share them until he'd gathered more evidence.

'They amounted to a dossier. They concerned this case, the *Lady Monteith*, Site 176 and Dark Ocean. They made reference to your father's own investigations too, Angus.'

I looked at Claire. She raised her eyebrows indicating that she was hearing this for the first time.

'The gist of the Marshall Dossier as we're calling it, was that there was a direct link between Dark Ocean and its aims on the one hand and those of another organisation, the Foundation for Oriental and Asian Studies, on the other. He described it as a symbiotic alliance.'

'And just who are they?' asked Claire.

'A right-wing think-tank based in Switzerland. On the face of it they just publish learned papers on the state of Asia's economies.'

'But?'

'But, one of their members and contributors is a right-wing economist by the name of Ikuo Takahashi. Alastair had spotted one particular treatise he'd written on how he surmised that the Greater East Asia Co-Prosperity Sphere might yet be achieved. I'll let you see it but believe me it's inflammatory to put it mildly. It was never published by the Foundation so we're not sure how Alastair came by it.'

'So what's your conclusion?' I asked.

'We haven't concluded anything but you'll agree it seems quite possible that Ikuo Takahashi is associated with your Dark Ocean. And here's what concerns us. His paper outlines a proposed economic model for wresting control of all ocean transport and trade as well as port redevelopment programmes throughout the Far East. In effect it would form the basis of a modern co-prosperity sphere.'

At this point Admiral Carvill lifted his heavy frame out of his chair. 'Look at this,' he said looking out of one of the portside windows. We all got up and moved over to watch as the Royal Navy's new carrier, all 3.5 billion pounds worth, move past on her way out for sea trials.

'Big Lizzie we call her,' said the admiral proudly. 'Pride of the fleet. Mind you, it'll be a while before she's ready for active service.' I counted seven tugs fussing around her as HMS *Queen Elizabeth* was manoeuvred under the Forth's three iconic bridges.

'I read they're still using Windows XP software on her,' chipped in Ben Wood. 'A bit risky I'd have thought.'

'Well I wouldn't know about that,' blustered Carvill.

'Nothing wrong with Windows XP, in its day,' said Amber Dove defensively, 'and anyway, there'll be a team of cyber specialists on board.'

Besides the 65,000 ton aircraft carrier, a small product tanker was making her way westward to load at the Grangemouth refinery. To the east of the bridges a supertanker was loading North Sea crude at BP's Hound Point terminal. Even a small nation like Scotland had the benefit of North Sea oil to sustain its modest economy, for now at least. But Japan had no such resource.

As we returned to our seats I asked, 'How practical is it, this economic model?'

'We've had a couple of tame UCL transport economists go over it. They tell us it's well postulated and feasible, but only if all the pieces fall into place for them. There's a lot of theory ...' Amber Dove tailed off not needing to add that it hadn't been tested in practice.

'And the end game?' I asked. 'As I recall, the term co-prosperity sphere was one of the greatest euphemisms of the twentieth century. Surely they don't think such a concept can be justification for Japan's wholesale invasion and hegemony of Asia.'

'No, of course not,' she said. 'That was put to the test and look what happened. No, this is more subtle, more sleight of hand, but nonetheless devastating, potentially. And whether bonkers or not, we cannot afford to ignore the threat it presents.'

'So where from here?' Claire asked. If she had her own ideas on how to handle this she wasn't revealing them, instead deferring to Amber Dove.

'Securing Zoe is our first priority,' I interrupted deliberately including everyone in the task.

'I've thought of that,' said Claire reiterating what she'd voiced to me in the Botanic Gardens. 'We'll bring her over here for a month or so. She can get experience in the CMM office. I'll assign her to one of the syndicate claims managers. She can continue her legal studies while she's here and be safe too without knowing anything of what's behind it.'

'We'll need to extract her covertly,' said Benedict Wood. 'We can use the SIS Athens station to handle that.'

'I'll handle it,' I said. 'I know her, the whole scenario.'

They looked at one another before Amber Dove replied. 'No disrespect, Angus, but extraction is a job for professionals. It needs planning. It's a process.'

'And it needs to look natural,' I said. 'I don't want a posse of spooks trailing around after her. I'll go to the office, tell her what the plan is and we'll catch the EasyJet flight to Edinburgh.'

'What about the watchers? Once they see you both on the move they'll act. They'll snatch her,' said Ben Wood.

'Not the way I'm planning it they won't. I know how to do this, trust me.'

'You'll need backup.'

'I don't need backup. It's a distraction.' I said trying not to sound obstructive for the sake of it.

After umming and ahhing over this for a while they eventually agreed on the condition that I liaised closely with Claire, as my case officer, who would be in Leith ready to receive Zoe.

We returned then to the subject of FOAS as we were now calling the Foundation for Oriental and Asian Studies. 'You leave them to us,' said Amber. 'We've got people working on it.'

'Who else is in FOAS besides this Takahashi?' I asked.

'At present we have very little to go on. And I'm afraid what we do know we can't share with you just yet, Angus. It's need-to-know but Claire will brief you as and when it becomes relevant to your side of the case. For now, you get Zoe over here safe and sound then take your lead from Claire.' She began to tidy the papers in front of her signalling the end of the meeting. Then she stopped and looked up as if she'd just remembered something. 'Oh, by the way, we're treating this as an off-the-books case, Angus.'

'You sound just like Alastair,' I said. 'Are they ever on the books?'

She smiled. 'Worst case, we need to have deniability in place, you understand.'

***

I had dinner that night with Claire. We went to a Spanish place in George Street and sat in a discreet booth where we could speak privately. Claire said she had something important to talk to me about.

'Angus, I'm sorry if I sound a bit bossy at times. It can be difficult to separate the professional from the personal.'

'Forget it,' I said. 'I'll be sure to let you know if it's getting to me. Let's just deal with the business at hand.'

'It would be tragic if this arrangement, me as your case officer, ended up fracturing our, she hesitated, our love for each other.'

I moved closer to her. 'It won't do that, Claire.'

'Promise you'll tell me. You're not the best communicator, especially when it's personal stuff, are you?'

'I promise.'

'Good.' We kissed, both of us aware that our relationship was complicated by circumstance, and far from secure. How could it be otherwise?

'I wanted to give you some pointers about this business. You could say it comes under tradecraft. I can't tell you everything I've learned about how to stay safe and how to get results, but I'll tell you a few things that might help.' She took a sip of her wine. I could tell she'd been preparing this speech and I gave her my full attention.

'When you are trying to get information, say anything to get the answer you want. Just for example, it helps to share your own doubts with someone to build rapport and trust. Empathise with them as if you're on their side even though you're not. Exude confidence too, play the role of certainty in an uncertain world, reliability in the midst of madness. Build trust by sharing your own vulnerabilities and then show how you deal with them. I know some of this sounds contradictory but you need to learn to act a part.

'Also, when you need to, develop a story, a legend that you're comfortable with in a difficult situation. If you believe it you can get away with it. With the right cover story anything is possible. Again, it's about acting.

'Don't be surprised what these Dark Ocean people uncover about you. They'll already know about your past, the landslide, maybe your affairs. But they'll dig into your psyche too, your character. You can think on your feet. You learn quickly, but think about your appearance too, your body language. Look normal and you can stay hidden in plain sight. And control your emotions. Learn to switch off your anxiety.'

She talked on, downloading what she'd learned from her photographic memory, speaking intently, determined that I should absorb what she was saying.

'Thanks, Claire. I'll bear it all in mind.'

'It will take its toll, this case,' she said. 'Believe me.'

CHAPTER 16

'I've been watched by these people for the past weeks and you never thought to tell me? What is going on, Angus?'

Zoe was reacting to my news that she was under surveillance. It was taking time as at every indignant outburst on her part I had to start explaining again. Yet I could only tell her a small part of what was going on.

'As long as you didn't know they were there, you were safe,' I said. 'I couldn't risk you knowing and reacting impulsively. You must see that. Imagine if you'd decided to run off, or worse, to rashly challenge them. They would have seized you there and then, Zoe.'

'What does "rashly" mean? I don't know this word.'

'It means foolishly.'

'Ah! So I'm foolish now.'

There was no placating her. She just had to blow off steam. After a while I told her that the CMM wanted her to attend a six-week training course at their headquarters in Leith.

'You'll love Edinburgh,' I said, 'especially at this time

of year. It's one of the most beautiful cities in the world and they'll look after you well. You'll be wined and dined. You might even meet a handsome young Scotsman.'

'What, in a skirt? What's wrong with handsome Greek men? Anyway, if I said yes, when would this be?'

I'd known she'd jump at the chance despite her protestations. She'd been nagging me for a trip like this ever since she'd joined.

'Wednesday.'

'Wednesday? That's two days from now. How can I be ready? And what about the work here? Will you be in the office or swanning around as usual?'

"Swanning around" was a phrase she'd learned from me, and which she used frequently to describe my business trips, or any other absence from the office.

'Anyway Angus, there are things I need to speak to you about. Urgent things.'

'Go ahead,' I said, but at that moment the phone rang. It was Eleni and she was in tears.

'I need to see you, Angus-*mou*. Can you come now? I want you, *agape-mou*.'

'What's wrong, Eleni, tell me.'

'It's Dimitrios. He's gone. He's left me, Angus. I can't explain over the phone. I'm at the flat. Please come.'

'Okay,' I said. 'I'll be with you in half an hour.'

'Now, please *agape-mou*.' She rang off, distraught.

'Zoe, I have to go. That was Eleni. Dimitrios has left her apparently. She's upset.'

'Go! She needs you, poor girl. You should still be together anyway.' Zoe never missed an opportunity to proffer her advice on the state of my domestic affairs.

'We'll talk tomorrow,' I said.

'Tomorrow? I can't come in tomorrow. If I'm to go to Scotland I need to buy clothes and other things. I need the day off.'

'Alright. That's fine. I'll tidy up the case files and collect you from your parents' house at five on Wednesday morning.'

'Five! Why so early?'

'Because the flight's at seven-fifteen, Zoe.'

'Oh God! Do I have to take such an early one?'

'Yes, I want you on that flight, it's all arranged,' I said. 'No arguments. And we'll talk on the way to the airport.'

'If you insist.'

***

Thinking back to that early morning journey to the airport, what I remembered was Zoe's excitement. She was a bright young law student and I'd given her the chance to get good practical experience, both in my Piraeus office and now, in the CMM's headquarters back in Scotland. She'd been reading up about Edinburgh and how many Greek students attended the universities there. She'd asked whether Brexit would prevent Greeks studying in Scotland. I began to worry that she might want to stay and I wouldn't get her back.

They came as we were sitting having a coffee in a restaurant up on the mezzanine floor above the main departures hall. They would have tracked us all the way from when I'd collected her from the family home in Ekali. It was almost casual. Two of them, tall men in their early thirties I guessed, one I recalled wore a black leather jacket. It was him who came up behind her and jabbed the needle deep into her neck. The next sensation I remembered was a white light bursting behind my eyes.

When I came round my head was thumping with a pain that was off the scale. I was being lifted from the floor onto a stretcher. I opened my eyes. It hurt. I tried turning my head, and felt sick. I had to get up. Instead I let them lift me but I remembered straight away what had happened, what I'd seen. They'd taken Zoe, and it was my fault. Why hadn't I followed the IMTF's advice and had them extract her – the experts? Because I'd been too bloody obstinate.

They took me to a small clinic on an upper floor of the terminal building. A doctor came and shone a light into my eyes, felt my pulse and took my temperature. He asked me my name, what day it was and whether I felt nauseous. Then he cleaned the blood from the back of my head, dressed the wound and gave me two paracetamol for the headache.

'The police want to see you,' he said. He went out of the room and I was left alone to reflect on what had happened, and what an idiot I was.

CHAPTER 17

'I am Captain Stathakis,' he introduced himself. 'I understand you were present when the young woman was abducted.

'Yes, I was.'

'I would like you to come to my office now and I will take a statement, if you feel well enough. It is very close and the doctor has agreed.'

I stood up and the room began to tilt. I sat down again.

'Wait,' I said. I stood again, more slowly this time. I knew I had to work with this guy. He wasn't taking an aggressive line. In fact he held me by the elbow as we walked slowly down the corridor to his office.

It was a functional room looking out onto the airport's apron where a number of aircraft were parked loading and unloading passengers and baggage - a useful viewpoint for a police officer.

'I am the senior officer of the airport police. I am calling in a colleague to assist me with this interview. First give me your name please.' I told him.

'*Perimenete.*' He dialled a number and spoke rapidly telling a colleague to come to his office.

My mind was still reeling. I tried to process it rationally but couldn't. More than anything I was racked with guilt. Shouldn't I have seen them approaching? My reactions had been slow. We'd been talking and laughing together. I *had* seen them approaching, but there was nothing unusual about them, except they looked like a couple of toughs. But then half the male population of Athens dressed and looked like them; big burly guys, swarthy, unshaven, long hair.

I must have groaned for Stathakis looked up suddenly. 'You are disturbed. Do you want something? Water, coffee?'

I took a deep breath. 'Both please.'

He added this to the orders he was giving over the phone.

Despite the nature of my work in Piraeus, I'd had little contact with the Hellenic Police in the years I'd lived here. I sat back and concentrated on the man opposite me. Captain was a senior rank, but then Athens Airport was a high-risk beat for any cop to have under his control. Stathakis was maybe late forties, a wiry man with thinning hair plastered to his skull and a neatly trimmed moustache. Despite his unprepossessing appearance there was something authoritative and oddly reassuring about him. I was thinking how much I should tell him about the background to what had just happened.

Another officer came in, a young woman bearing coffee and a jug of water. Having gone through some introductory formalities, and with a video camera running on a tripod in the corner, they took my statement.

I hadn't had chance to fabricate a cover story so I told them the truth, or the partial truth, that Zoe worked for me and I was taking her to the airport for her flight to Edinburgh where she was due to attend a six week familiarisation and training course at the offices of our principal, CMM, the Caledonian Marine Mutual Insurance Association. I gave them full details of my business and of Zoe's parents' address in Ekali. Then I gave a description of the two men I'd seen approaching our table. More than that I did not know I said, other than that there must have been a third man who had come up behind me.

'The other customers in the restaurant must have a better idea of what happened,' I added.

After a few more cursory questions the interview was terminated, the video camera switched off and the young assisting officer dismissed.

'Now, Mr McKinnon,' said Stathakis, settling back into his chair, 'suppose you tell me the full story. Why do you think your young colleague was taken, snatched violently in a busy restaurant when she was about to leave the country? Before you start, let me tell you that I am already well aware of your activities in Greece serving our shipowners. Your reputation is, how would you say, impeccable. But I have a job to do and I believe our interests in this matter are mutual. We would both like to find the people who did this and who is behind them, who ordered it. I suggest we collaborate. Do you agree?'

'I agree. But I don't know the answer,' I lied. I knew damn well. Whoever had been watching Zoe on behalf of the Dark Ocean gang had either received instructions to snatch her, or in the absence of such instructions, had taken matters into their own hands when they saw she was about to leave the country.

'Let me help you,' Stathakis announced staring at me intently. 'Do you believe the kidnappers were Greek or foreigners?

'They looked Greek to me. I can't be sure. Dark, swarthy looking. Sorry, I'm stereotyping. No, I remember now, one was wearing a ski-cap. Not the one with the syringe, the other guy.'

'Did you recognise either of them? From Piraeus perhaps?'

'No, I'm afraid not.'

He stood up and looked out of the window. An Emirates plane was disgorging weary-looking passengers. Stathakis turned away.

'Well, we are fortunate perhaps,' he said, returning to his desk. 'While you were unconscious we spoke with other customers in the restaurant. We have reasonable descriptions of all three men but one witness had the foresight to follow the men, one of whom was carrying Miss Papado-poulos in his arms, as they ran down the escalator and out of the terminal building. This witness has told us that she was still conscious and struggling as she was bundled into the back of a silver-coloured van without number plates.

As you'll know Mr McKinnon, it is an unfortunate legacy from earlier times in this country that the police feel free to remove the number plates from vehicles they believe are illegally parked or have committed some other offence.' I knew only too well. It had happened to me and I'd had to fight my way through acres of red tape to get them back.

'Of course, the kidnappers might have removed the plates themselves. This also is not uncommon amongst criminals.' He had the habit of methodically speaking his thoughts as if preparing his report. 'What our star witness also noted though was that one of the three rode off on what he believes was a Ducati motorcycle which was parked behind the van right outside the terminal building. I believe this offers us our best lead.'

'How did he know it was a Ducati?'

'Its distinctive red and white bodywork and frame made him certain. And it had a pillion, which helps narrow the field further.' He tapped into his laptop and swivelled it round so I could see a picture of the bike.

'Like this he thought, the Multistrada. So, we shall see. But for now you may go, Mr McKinnon and we will keep in touch.' He passed his card to me. 'I shall be leading the investigation. You may reach me at any time.'

'Thank you. My priority is to find her and bring her to safety.'

'Yes, I understand, but I caution you not to take the law into your own hands. This is a police matter. Oh, and please do nott leave the country until I authorise you to do so.'

CHAPTER 18

Without Zoe in the office a backlog was accumulating. I realised just how much I missed her – not just for her productivity but her cheerful, feisty presence too. In the days that followed I tried, without much success, to focus on work. I called her father's office but he didn't want to see me. I'd give it time. Eleni called. I told her what had happened. She was distraught, again. What kind of business was I mixed up in? How could I let a young woman like Zoe be exposed to such dangers? It was time I grew up. I had listened to this viewpoint before. She was probably right.

Claire was more business-like. She didn't need to remind me I'd screwed up. Instead she wanted to know what Stathakis was up to.

By the Friday I was getting on top of the caseload but had barely slept. When I did it was only to be awoken by a recurring nightmare of Zoe's head jerking violently to one side as the syringe was plunged into her neck. It haunted me when I was awake too.

To my relief Stathakis called late that Friday afternoon.

He wanted to meet away from both his office and mine. I walked to a café bar near Zea Marina, close to where I lived up on Profitis Ilias, the hill that rises above the noisy bustle of Piraeus. The spring orange blossom had just come out, filling the streets with its heady scent. I barely noticed it.

There had been very little I could do to follow up on Zoe's disappearance until this point, and now I was glad to be out seeing the man who could. I found him in the bar tucked away down a side street. After the bright sunshine the dark interior was almost impenetrable. Stathakis was sitting at a table in the back smoking a cigarette and nursing a cup of coffee. I ordered a beer and sat down opposite him.

'Your colleague, it seems, was taken for reasons we had not guessed at,' he began.

'What do you mean?'

'We found our Dukati man in the leather jacket, and his associates too. There aren't many bikes fitting the description we were given. All three of these individuals are ex-military. They work for a private security firm now – or did until we arrested them.'

'And they talked?'

'Yes, they talked. Do you know the most effective way to extract a confession from a Greek?' he asked.

'Tell me.'

'Not by means of physical coercion. No, you don't need that. Place a Greek in solitary confinement for a few days and he will talk. The very thought of being isolated from his fellow man is enough to send a Greek into a state of such anxiety he will do or say anything you ask.' He spoke without irony. 'And believe me, it worked. We kept all three in solitary confinement after their initial interrogation. I told each of them they would remain there until they were ready to talk. The first broke his silence after thirty-six hours. Once the others realised he'd talked, their resistance soon cracked too.'

Stathakis stared down into his coffee for a moment before looking at me and continuing.

'Zoe Papadopoulos is a brave young woman, but a foolish one. It seems that once she saw she was being watched she thought she could turn the tables on her watchers.' I winced. She hadn't told me. And it was what I'd thought I could do in Hong Kong a couple of weeks earlier. 'At first she succeeded, which of course emboldened her further. She tracked one of them to the offices of a local shipping agent, a small family-owned outfit on Akti Miaouli. It happened that she knew the owner's daughter. They are studying maritime law together at Piraeus University. What this girl, Fotini, told her was that they had acted as agents for a large private yacht and our Dukati man, his name is Mardas by the way, had been to their office to settle the disbursement account covering the vessel's stay in Greek waters. He had paid an amount of several thousand dollars in cash.

'Fotini was only too happy to tell her friend about this vessel, the *Toyama Maru*.' He said it slowly, struggling with the pronunciation, 'including the fact that a further group of five passengers had joined the ship in the port of Iraklion. This group consisted of four Europeans and one Japanese national. Ms Papadopoulos obtained from her friend the passenger list naming all these nine men: the original four Japanese who were on board when the vessel arrived in our waters and this latest party. I have that list.'

Stathakis took it from his pocket and passed it across the table. Two of the Japanese names jumped out from the page: Hachiro Nakamura and Ikuo Takahashi.

Takahashi. This was the economist who had written the paper on a reborn Asian Co-Prosperity Sphere. Nakamura I'd already met. The others on the list, the Europeans, were names I didn't recognise.

'That copy is for you,' Stathakis said, pre-empting my next question.

'So far so good,' he continued, 'but this is where she made an error. Mardas is not stupid and Zoe was careless. When we interrogated him he admitted that the decision to abduct her was taken when they learned she was spying on their activities. Taking her from you at the airport was convenient for them, you see.'

'Why? They could have taken her earlier.'

'Oh no. They were watching you too and they wanted to see what you were up to. When they saw you heading for the airport with her they knew they had to act. And it turned out perfectly for them for another reason.' He paused.

'Which was?' Stathakis liked to string a story out.

'They had a private jet waiting. We have learned that this aircraft had arrived the night before from Zurich. It seems when he had reported to his masters, Mardas had been instructed to seize Zoe and deliver her to the hangar where the plane was parked.'

'So how did they manage to get their unconscious passenger airside without going through Security and Immigration?'

'I'm afraid they bribed certain individuals. Such arrangements are not uncommon, as you will know.'

'And the plane departed for where?'

'The pilot filed a flight plan for Dubai. Whether that is the final destination or not, we don't know - yet. But we will find out, be sure of that. We are talking about the abduction of a Greek citizen, and one from a rich and influential family. I have already spoken with Interpol and they will ascertain the aircraft's final destination. The plane left here on Wednesday. It is in Dubai now.'

'Thank you,' I said. He was not obliged to keep me so closely informed and I appreciated it.

'And in case you were wondering about Mardas and his associates, we have already charged them with kidnapping. They face a lengthy stay in Koridallos. And I'm sure you know something of the conditions there.'

Koridallos was Greece's main prison located just outside of Piraeus. Amnesty International and others, including the Committee for the Prevention of Torture, often expressed concern about the place for its overcrowding and inhumane treatment of prisoners.

***

Stathakis was true to his word. He phoned early on Saturday morning and told me the plane had just taken off from Dubai bound for Hong Kong.

Zoe had blundered into the case not realising the danger she was placing herself in. She was headstrong even by Greek standards. She was brave, she was loyal and had the inquisitiveness of a good investigator. Sure, she had been foolish but I could not deny my own inadvertent role in her abduction.

I couldn't deny either that she had uncovered vital evidence. She had discovered the names of the key players in what was turning out to be a global conspiracy, and had proved beyond doubt a clear connection between Dark Ocean and the Foundation for Oriental and Asian Studies by placing Nakamura and Takahashi on the *Toyama Maru* together. It was up to me now to find her – before the bastards decided she was superfluous to their needs. I shuddered when I thought of what they'd done to Alastair. Was arsenic their murder weapon of choice?

'You will be returning to Hong Kong I presume?' Stathakis said.

'Yes, of course.'

'Normally, I would be obliged to inform Interpol of this latest development, you know that. However, I have received instructions from my superiors to the effect that no further action is necessary on my part. It seems you have friends in high places, otherwise I would not be extending such independence of action to you. And yes, I am aware of the death of Admiral Marshall. I have spoken to my counterpart handling the case.'

I thanked him and promised to call him on my return to Greece. He was a good friend to have. Then I called Claire to discuss my return to Hong Kong. Having seen how efficiently they had spirited Zoe out of Greece, and how susceptible public authorities can be to a well-timed bribe, she insisted that I should return to Hong Kong covertly.

'Nakamura and his gang may well have access to Hong Kong Immigration's air passenger arrival data,' she said. 'It's safer this way.'

'And how do I accomplish this magical deception?' I asked her.

'Just leave that to me.'

CHAPTER 19

The IMTF had routed me via Bangkok and on from there to Guangzhou. I came through Guangzhou Baiyun Airport armed with a passport and a six month multi-entry visa. My name was Jeremy Watson and I was representing a firm of Edinburgh solicitors seeking a partner firm in China.

A thin, middle-aged man came up to me as I entered the greetings area.

'Taxi to Shenzhen?'

'Is it far? I've come a long way.'

'You must be tired,' he said. 'What was the movie on the plane?'

'Didn't watch it,' I replied.

With the IMTF's code phrases out of the way he took my bag, introduced himself as Mr Au and led me out to a green taxi waiting at the curbside.

I'd been told it was a two hour drive to Zau Zai Tau near the town of Xia Sha in Shenzhen. I settled back to relax and maybe catch up on some sleep after the flight but Mr Au was nervous. He'd struck me as nervous from the moment we'd met but as we drove his anxiety seemed to increase.

'Is there something I should know, Mr Au? You seem worried.'

'No, no. It's okay.'

'Then what?'

'No. We have very fast boat for you. Get you to Tung Ping Chau Island double quick.'

'It needs to be fast does it?'

'Yes. In case, you know. But Coast Guard never come near Tung Ping Chau.'

'So nothing to worry about then.'

'No, nothing to worry about. Don't worry.'

The journey turned out to be nearer three hours and by the time we reached the beach it was midnight.

Mr Au insisted on carrying my bag down to the dilapidated wooden jetty where a speedboat was tied up. A man was bending over one of its three big V8 outboards. He stood up as we approached. He was young and skinny and was wearing an Iron Maiden t-shirt. He seemed as stressed out as Mr Au.

'Okay! Let's go,' he called, firing up the engines.

'Quick,' yelled Mr Au handing me my bag. 'You go now!' I jumped aboard.

The night was starless and moonless. The continuous urban sprawl that was Shenzhen lit up the coast like a fairground but where we were on the Dapeng Peninsula was a remote spot, its mountainous terrain home to bandits, smugglers and pirates for centuries, Mr Au had told me. Isolated as this place was, I found no comfort in his assurances regarding the China Coast Guard and their prying eyes, although I'd been told that their attention lay elsewhere these days.

I'd learned that the island of Tung Ping Chau where we were headed had a chequered history. Guns and opium had been smuggled from here since way back. Then in the war it had been used as a staging post to smuggle a one-legged Nationalist Chinese admiral out of Hong Kong along with a dozen or so British soldiers and sailors. Later, in the seventies and eighties, the route across the channel to the island was one that illegal immigrants used in their bid for freedom and a better life in Hong Kong. As they swam, many died from shark attacks or drowned from exhaustion. Others paid snakeheads to take them across by speedboat only to be picked up by the Hong Kong Marine Police and returned to the mainland. My father would certainly have been involved in the early days of those operations.

The route was still used for smuggling but tonight the waters seemed quiet between Zau Zai Tau and Tung Ping Chau island, which I could make out as a black silhouette a mile away across the channel.

Mr Au cast us off from the jetty and we accelerated away with an ear-splitting roar, leaving a bright opalescent wake behind us. I found a seat and clung on. After a few moments I looked back to the shore. Mr Au was waving. I couldn't tell whether it was a farewell or a warning. I waved back. Then I saw what he was waving at. Coming round the headland to our north was another craft, bigger than ours, much bigger: a sleek, modern-looking cutter, white-hulled with the distinctive blue-red-blue diagonal hull stripes of the China Coast Guard.

The cutter wasn't making anything like the speed we were, but despite that she had an advantage. The distance from the headland, round which she had appeared, to Tung Ping Chau was only half our own distance to the island. They could intercept us before we were halfway across the channel unless we outmanoeuvred them.

Iron Maiden opened the throttle further and the boat surged forward. The Coast Guard cutter was no more than half a mile from us now and, so long as we held our present course, would close on us. We altered course towards the south, still heading for the island, and as we did so a cacophony of high-pitched Cantonese reached us above the noise of our engines. Ignoring what I assumed was a warning to stop, Iron Maiden turned and gestured for me to get down. The gap between our two vessels was still narrowing and unless we overshot the island altogether, we would continue closing on them. And I guessed we were already well within range of their guns.

Then Iron Maiden did what I'd been hoping he'd do. He turned away from the island altogether and headed south into the open waters of Mirs Bay. We were tearing along now on a straight course for the Sai Kung Peninsula and Hong Kong territorial waters.

The threat of interception was gone and we were gaining ground away from the cutter, but as it seemed we were getting clear they started firing. At first their machine gun was well off target but as they found the range rounds began spitting into the water all around us. I lay in the bottom of the boat but it afforded little protection. It was only a matter of time before they scored a hit, and no sooner than I'd had the thought, they did. It took out one of the outboards which stopped with an ominous grinding sound.

Iron Maiden was not deterred. He was weaving the boat, zig-zagging through the darkness but still keeping an even distance from the cutter.

I risked a look ahead and could make out lights on Sai Kung Peninsula. We were heading for more islands now but still taking fire. Once past these little islands they would provide us with cover. Our boat was quick and manoeuvrable and Iron Maiden handled it with confident skill. We dodged behind the first of the islands in what I knew to be the entrance to Tolo Harbour. The cutter's gunfire stopped and as I looked I saw her turning back.

Despite the one country-two systems relationship with China, Hong Kong's territorial waters still prevailed and extended for three nautical miles from its coastline. The Chinese Coast Guard cutter had almost certainly violated the law, technically at least, and the skipper wouldn't have wanted to create any more of an incident. He'd probably guessed one of Hong Kong's marine police launches would intercept us.

Iron Maiden put me ashore at some steps alongside a busy road under a row of high-rise tower blocks. I handed him a thousand Hong Kong dollars as a bonus. He seemed happy with that. Whoever employed him would take care of the ruined outboard I hoped.

So much for the nice quiet entry I'd been promised I thought as I watched him pull away. I couldn't have made more of a commotion if I'd landed in Statue Square under a Union Jack parachute trailing red smoke flares behind me.

At least I was back in Hong Kong, but Ronnie Eastfield had arranged for me to be picked up on Tung Ping Chau. Now I was in Sai Kung. I found a small park with trees and a children's playground. It was one o'clock in the morning and the place was deserted. I sat down on a bench and opened the bag to get at my phone. Inside Mr Au had placed a Glock pistol and a box containing a hundred nine millimetre rounds. No wonder it had seemed heavy. I wondered where he'd got this little arsenal from and whether he thought I was planning to start a war. Had this been Claire's doing?

I called Ronnie and explained what had happened. He had already heard from his gofer who'd witnessed the incident from where he'd been waiting for me on the island we'd just overshot.

'No problem,' he said, his voice slurred either by sleep or alcohol. 'I'll come and get you.'

He collected me an hour later in his dilapidated army Land Rover that he'd picked up cheap when the British garrison had left town twenty years before. It was open to the elements with a fold-down windscreen and a spare wheel screwed onto the bonnet. It belched black exhaust fumes and sounded like a bronchial Spitfire taking off. That was Ronnie: this old jeep reflected his whole persona and would allay the doubts of even the most suspicious adversary. It wasn't a contrived façade, just the way he was.

We drove back to his place and sat on his balcony with our beers looking across Hebe Haven as we had a few weeks earlier. Ronnie had been told of Zoe's abduction from the IMTF with whom he was now in direct contact, and I filled in the detail before moving on to my father's notebooks, and my meetings with the Firth Bank and Tim Younger.

I placed the little Buddha statue on the table between the San Miguel bottles. He picked it up. 'I remember this,' he said, turning it in his hand. 'Your dad kept it on his desk in his office.'

'Where did he get it from?'

'Buggered if I know, but there's someone you'll be meeting tomorrow, or today rather, who might.'

'Right, Ronnie, our first task is to find Zoe. What's the latest position of the *Toyama Maru*?' I thought that would be the most likely place they'd hold her after she'd arrived by air. The vessel had departed Greek waters three weeks earlier so could be due in Hong Kong any time.

'Vanished,' he said. 'And before you ask, her AIS is switched off so there's no easy way of tracing her unless the IMTF can spot her via satellite.'

'I'll ask Claire about that. So who are we seeing that's so important?'

'A man with a very distressing story to tell. Oh, and we're meeting Susanna Buchan there too.'

CHAPTER 20

Leaning forward he pointed a crooked finger at me. His hand shook. In fact his whole body trembled.

'James Brodie, 2nd Battalion, Royal Scots,' he announced. The Royal Scots had been the oldest regiment in the British Army raised over four hundred years ago. They'd been merged with the other Scottish infantry regiments a few years earlier, but didn't tell him this.

We were sitting in Brodie's private room at a nursing home in the New Territories. Seated beside me was a middle-aged Catholic nurse called Sister Alice, and on the other side of Brodie's bed were Ronnie Eastfield and Susanna Buchan. Brodie himself was slumped in a wheelchair beside his bed. He wore striped pyjamas and a red dressing gown. Perched on his head was his regiment's black woollen Glengarry cap with badge and a red and white band round it.

Ronnie had tracked down the only survivor of the Japanese prison camp at Sham Shui Po still living in Hong Kong. Not only that, Brodie had survived the sinking of the *Lady Monteith*. He was ninety-four years old and his memory, at least his long-term memory, seemed to be intact.

We spent an hour and a half with him. At times I worried I was pressing him too hard but he didn't seem to mind, despite the appalling memories he was dredging up. I was reluctant to dwell on the brutality of his time in the camp, the atrocious conditions or the horrors of those final hours trapped under deck with hundreds of other POWs who had been herded onto the ship and down into the hold. But Brodie didn't shy away from any of it. It was almost as if he had to relive it.

'Sham Shui Po was bad enough. Conditions were dreadful there. The rice we were fed was sweepings off the warehouse floor - had all sorts of rubbish in with it including weevils and worms. And there was diphtheria. I can still hear the poor buggers coughing. They sounded like dogs barking. Then it would paralyse them. We lost a lot from that.'

He started coughing himself, as if in sympathy with his fellow prisoners.

'The reprisals were wicked, if anyone escaped or tried to. Don't want to talk about that. Savage, it was. I signed the no-escape chit, you ken. Was like a promise not to try and escape. I knew what would happen if I didn't sign. I saw what the Japs did to some of the poor bastards. Beatings, and much worse.' He pulled off his Glengarry and put it on his lap. 'Quite a few of our lot refused to sign the no-escape. Hard men. And they were the first to be shipped off to Japan to work in the mines. We thought they might get better fed because they'd be working so they'd need to be kept fit. Turned out to be wrong. They were worked to death.'

'How long were you in Sham Shui Po?' I asked.

'We surrendered on Christmas Day '41. I was there until end of '43. Best part of two years. But they weren't all bad bastards. I remember we'd go foraging in the brush around the camp, mainly grasshoppers we'd find to boil with the rice. I was out there one day when I see this Jap officer on the other side of the fence. "What do you want?" he says. I thought he was challenging me, then he asked again and I just said, "Bread." First thing I thought of. I'm out there the next day and there he is. It was winter and he's wearing his long coat. He looks about then pulls a couple of loaves out and tosses them over the wire. I'd keep an eye out for him after that. He used to give us bread once or twice a week. Then he stopped. Never knew what happened to him.

'But if we thought the camp was bad that ship was worse. Herded like cattle. Some of us were almost dead on our feet. Not me, ken,' he said looking at me, proud that he'd retained his spirit if not his health.

'The *Lady Monteith*, that wasn't her name then of course. They'd renamed her. Gives me the shivers to think about it. She looked alright as ships go. But we were put into the hold. Crammed in like sardines; herded like cattle.' He cackled at his mixed metaphors then began coughing again. Sister Agnes bent over him wiping his mouth with a tissue. He brushed aside her fussing. I used the interruption to steer him onto the question of the ship's cargo.

'When you were being herded aboard, Jim, did you notice anything about the cargo? Or hear anything about it?'

'Aye, we did.' His old eyes lit up for a moment. 'See, the ship's crew were Japs but they weren't like the soldiers. It was the soldiers were the worst, brutal bastards. But the ship's crew were more reasonable. A few of our boys had picked up some Japanese lingo in the camp, believe it or not. I was with some of my pals. One of them, Archie, asks this Jap crewman for a cigarette. Secretly, ken? He gives us a packet of ciggies. Archie gets talking with him. Asks what the crates are on the hatches. We'd seen them when we boarded. We're in a hold just for us POWs but she was a big ship, ken? And on one of the hatches they'd lashed a big crate, really big. So Archie had seen this and he asks what's in it. And the Jap goes all cagey like. Then he says there's all sorts loaded in the hold. And on deck is a gold statue. At least, that's what the crew reckoned it was. Said it'd been made to look like stone, but why ship stone statues back to Japan?'

'What was the statue then?'

'Didnae ken at the time but later we heard it were a Buddha from some temple. It'd been loaded before the ship came to pick us lot up.'

Brodie was tiring now, I could see. His breath was rasping and Sister Alice was casting warning looks in my direction. But he hadn't finished.

'The whole lot went down with the ship, and us lot trapped in that hold. We were only an hour out of Hong Kong. Sailed straight into that American sub's line of fire. They had no way of knowing POWs were on board. They were supposed to paint the ship white with a red cross on the side but the Japs weren't interested in the Geneva Convention were they. But that same Jap sailor who'd given us the ciggies pulls back the canvas in one corner of the hatch, then he opens up the hatch cover. There's a ladder and we all start scrambling for it. Then one of our officers gets us organised. The ship's listing heavily by this time but lucky for us, once we get up on deck we could just jump for it over the ship's rail.

'We just swim for it to get away from the ship before she comes down on us. I cannae remember how long we were in the water but eventually I was picked up by a Chinese fishing boat and taken to one of the islands. I found out later that only sixty-one out of over three hundred of us POWs survived the sinking. The Jap sailors and soldiers? And that statue? I dinnae ken.' His head sagged. He was done in and I didn't push him any further.

Brodie had ended up back where he'd started – in Sham Shi Po POW camp. It had all happened late in 1943. Within a few weeks he was shipped off to Japan ending the war half-starved in a POW camp there. He and the other prisoners were rescued by the Americans and began their long journey home. Eventually, after the war, he'd returned to Hong Kong, joined the Royal Hong Kong Police and married a Chinese girl. I wondered if my father had known of his story.

Before we left I crouched down beside him and held his frail, bony old hands. 'Thanks, Jim,' I said. 'You're some man right enough.'

CHAPTER 21

Susanna Buchan hadn't spoken much while we were with Jim Brodie. 'Can we talk?' she asked now as we left the nursing home.

'Sure. What about Ronnie here?'

'No just you and me, if that's okay?' she added turning to Ronnie.

Ronnie didn't look too concerned and I told him I'd be in touch.

'You know you can kip down at my place, any time,' he said and with that he rattled off down the road in his Land Rover as we climbed into the back of a large black Mercedes and glided off, cocooned in leather and soft Oriental music.

'Do you recognise this music?' she asked. 'It's from Vietnam, where I come from.'

'Oh.'

'I'll tell you over dinner, if you're free?'

'I'm free.'

We went to the Beas River Country Club, set amongst rolling hills in the northern part of the New Territories. Susanna was greeted at the door in much the same way I'd seen her and her stepfather welcomed at the Hong Kong Club.

'Drinks first?' she asked leading the way to the bar. She ordered a Margarita for herself and a Scotch for me. The barman was over eager. Not obsequious, he was just entranced by her. It wasn't just her beauty as much as her easy-going manner: cool but friendly. There were a dozen or so others in there, a mix of Chinese, Europeans and Americans and she greeted those she knew without stopping to talk.

'I thought I'd better tell you a little bit about myself,' she began. 'It will help explain things, to do with the *Lady Monteith* I mean.' We'd sat in a quiet corner waiting for our drinks to be brought over. She took a sip of her Margarita before starting.

'I was rescued from the South China Sea when I was two. Of course I only know what I've been told. I was on a boat full of people fleeing Vietnam for a better life. The boat was overcrowded – over eighty of us on board. The food and water had run out. Conditions were dreadful, there was no sanitation. And that night when the ship found us, it was stormy and the boat was taking in water.

'I was passed to one of the ship's crew who was standing at the bottom of the gangway. Our boat was slamming against the ship's side. It sank within minutes before anyone else could be taken off. I lost my family that night, my parents and two brothers.' She spoke without emotion.

'The ship that rescued me, and a few others who'd

managed to get off, was the *Lady Maree*, one of Sinclair Buchan's. When we arrived in Hong Kong, Monty came aboard. I was the only child who had been rescued. The others were adults and were taken to a resettlement camp, at Sham Shi Po, on the site of the Japanese POW camp ironically. They were resettled in England eventually.'

'And you?'

'You can guess. I was adopted by Monty and his wife. She was Chinese, my stepmother. She couldn't have children of her own so I was special to her. And I loved her so much.' Her voice trembled for a moment. 'I was lucky. I grew up in a privileged environment. I received the best education here, then in England and the States.'

'And after that?'

'I worked for a New York sale and purchase broker for a couple of years after I graduated. Then Monty brought me into the company here. So you could say the sea really does flow in my veins.'

'Quite a story,' I said thinking too of the one we'd heard earlier from Jim Brodie. 'Have you ever been back to Vietnam?

'I've visited. The people suffered so much. Really, for twenty-five years there was war. Indo-China became a buttress against Communism. The French and the Americans were trying to keep the Soviets out of the region. The Americans backed the south against the north and lost. The Communists took over the whole country and killed so many or sent them to re-education camps where thousands more died. It was illegal to leave the country so many fled by boat thinking they could start a new life somewhere else. The fishing boats were not built for the open sea. Escaping in this way was very dangerous. They think a million and a half people took this route and hundreds of thousands are believed to have died, mostly by drowning, though many were attacked by pirates and murdered or sold into slavery and prostitution. Some countries in the region turned the boat people away even if they did manage to land. And some shipowners instructed their captains to follow a more easterly route up the South China Sea to avoid the boat people. Sinclair Buchan was not one of them.'

She looked directly at me. 'So I was lucky, but we're both orphans aren't we. You were lucky too.' That connection hadn't crossed my mind until she said it. We were on our second drink and she was looking lovelier than ever. We were both silent for a while.

Finally, smiling, she said, 'Don't worry, Angus, I wasn't trying to draw anything out of you, just saying we have that in common.'

'I can sense that.' And I could. 'And I didn't think you were - trying to draw something out of me. Have you heard anything from Monty?' I asked, feeling clumsy by switching subjects and altering the mood.

'He's not in Hong Kong, but I got a message a few days ago. Just a text saying not to worry, he was alright.'

'No idea where it was sent from?'

'No. I thought you could trace a text back to a location

but I couldn't see how. Anyway, let's go into dinner shall we? I'm hungry.'

The Grill Room was quiet. We ordered and she asked me to choose the wine, though I sensed out of politeness rather than confidence in my decision.

I had to make a judgement. Susanna Buchan was a big part of this case. I was holding much back from her but if I revealed part of what I'd learned then she'd want to know the rest. And the rest involved matters of international security. She had a right to know. It concerned her father's wellbeing, the family business and possibly her own safety. It came down to whether I could trust her to keep it to herself. I told her pretty much everything without disclosing the IMTF by name, only that the CMM routinely shared its case files with Whitehall - which was true - and that they'd been asked to pursue this one to its conclusion. I told her of my meeting with her father and Nakamura on the *Toyama Maru*, of Dark Ocean's ambitions, of the Foundation for Oriental and Asian Studies' involvement and of Zoe's abduction. Finally, I told her of my father's golden Buddha that the Firth Bank had been keeping.

She didn't question my vague reference to the British Government's interest or how they could expect a marine insurer to play such an unlikely role. Perhaps she guessed there was more to it than I'd revealed. Whether she liked it or not, through Monty's obsession, she was involved and I sensed she was just glad to have someone she could rely on.

'Will you come with me tomorrow?' she asked. 'I want

you to meet people who can help.'

'Who?'

'Let them tell you. I'll arrange a meeting. They contacted me and said they have news but they wanted to
see you too.'

'Have you met them yourself?'

'Briefly, yes, or at least one of them. They are very secretive but he told me when and where to go. All I know is
that they have an interest in the *Lady Monteith.*'

She dropped me off at Ronnie's place before heading
back to Hong Kong side. I was about to get out of the
car when she held my arm and leaned across, separated by
the armrest.

'I will help you, Angus. Everything I can. We will help
each other. I have many contacts. But don't worry, I will be
discreet.'

We kissed, lightly at first then more eagerly. Her per-
fume was intoxicating. I pulled her to me. After a while she
drew away.

'I'll pick you up here at midday,' she said breathlessly.
'Oh, and bring your father's golden Buddha with you.'

CHAPTER 22

Kowloon Tong is Kowloon's version of the leafy suburb. Its villas, built in the nineteen thirties and fifties, came with their own gardens, garages and, since the area was on the flight path into the old Kai Tak Airport, no high-rise blocks for the neighbours to peer down from.

We drew up at a two-story villa in the local art deco style, surrounded by a two-metre high wall topped with razor wire and CCTV cameras at either end. At the back of the house was a garden that stretched for fifty yards or so back from the house. It too was surrounded by a wall and more razor wire. It was also populated with Banyan trees providing both shade and privacy.

Susanna pressed a buzzer beside an outer stainless steel door. After a while there was the sound of bolts sliding and the door opened. I froze. The man standing there occupying the whole door frame was Oddjob, aka Fat Boy, only this time he was beaming from ear to ear. I turned to Susanna. 'What the hell?'

'This is Ah Sun,' she said to me, then greeted him in

what I recognised as Putonghua, the modern version of Mandarin based on the Beijing dialect.

'Come in, come in. Welcome!' He extended his podgy hand. I took it cautiously. 'What are you doing here?'

'We explain. Come in. Welcome,' he repeated.

He led the way across the front garden and into the house. Inside the hall it was cool, a wooden ceiling fan disturbing the air, wood panelled walls and a parquet floor partly covered by a large rug with a dragon motif. Two stone Buddhas stood sentry on either side.

'This way please,' said Ah Sun leading us into another room. More parquet flooring and another huge rug, this one in pale gold silk patterned with deep blue motifs. Heavy rosewood and lacquered chests stood against the walls which were painted in a deep vermilion red. Where there was space, elaborately framed paintings depicting Chinese mountain landscapes of lakes and forests hung from the walls.

Ah Sun gestured towards a rosewood sofa adorned with silk cushions, more ornamental than comfortable. I remained standing.

'What's going on?' I asked Susanna. 'What's this guy doing here?' I gestured to Ah Sun who was now standing in the corner of the room with his arms folded across his chest, still beaming.

'Ah Sun? There is much to be explained, Angus. Ah Sun is a good boy, really. But you weren't to know that when you last met him.'

A man entered the room, so quietly out of the shadows that I barely noticed him.

'Nya Wang will answer your questions,' Susanna said gesturing to the new arrival.

He was tall for a Chinese, five-ten maybe, and slim. I guessed his age at sixty but he could have been ten years either side of that. He was dressed in a simple black robe and wore sandals. His head was shaven. There was something about his movements, spare and calm lending an aura of serenity to the man. He made no attempt to sit down. When he spoke his voice was soft and hesitant as he chose his words with care.

'Susanna has told me much about you; and Ah Sun here also. I will explain why we are meeting now, but first, please, we shall drink tea together. He clapped his hands rather theatrically and a small woman emerged from nowhere carrying an ornate silver tray.

'This is Dianhong tea from Yunnan province, Mr Angus. It is where our Order was founded. Our monastery became a cradle of Chinese Buddhism. It is still there today, in the far south of the province at Ganlanba near Xishuangbanna, a beautiful place.' The woman poured the tea from an ornate porcelain teapot then left the room.

'Mr Angus ...'

'Call me Angus.'

'Angus, very well.' We sat now, Nya Wang at the end of the rosewood table. 'Let me first tell you something of the background to why we have found each other, you and me.

'You may know that Bodhidharma was an Indian Buddhist monk. He lived fifteen hundred years ago, and he brought our *Chan* Buddhism to China. He also began training the monks of that Order and this led to the creation of our own Kung Fu martial art, which so fascinates people in the West. Our traditions and practices have been preserved and revered for many centuries. Chan Buddhism emphasizes attaining Buddhahood, the supreme Buddhist religious goal, through enlightenment of one's own mind. It spread to Japan where it was named as Zen. One day I hope to explain more of our beliefs and our philosophy to you.

'But for now we move forward. We know that the ship, the *Lady Monteith*, belonging to the family of Susanna here, was carrying a much cherished item belonging to our monastery. It was taken by Japanese troops during the war. They transported it from Ganlanba to Beihai, a port in the south of China, and there it was loaded onto the ship. It was on its way to Japan when the ship sank close to where we are now. The item was a statue of the Buddha.

'The Japanese wanted it for its gold, to melt it down and add it to the other gold they had taken from our country and from our neighbours. But to us, this Buddha means much more than the value of its gold. Our Buddha gave protection and helped us conquer fear and anger. It gave us courage too.'

He paused and I placed my father's Buddha on the table. 'Like this?'

'Yes,' he said. 'Where did you get this?' He picked it up

and examined it closely.

'My father kept it on his desk, here in Hong Kong.'

'It is old, and yes, it is our Buddha. I mean it is a model but exactly like our Buddha, a replica, and gold too. You know, the Buddha has thirty-two major characteristics and another eighty minor features. Believe me, this matches our Buddha statue in every way. We can only guess how your father came upon such a rare object. Our own golden Buddha is over three hundred years old.'

'I understand, but what is your own role in all this?'

He hesitated giving a little cough. 'I am an emissary sent by the head of our monastery to retrieve the Buddha and return it to our temple. This is not an easy task. It is lying at the bottom of the sea and now some Japanese want it, again it seems for their old imperialist plans. We also must plan. We have many obstacles to overcome, but with your help and Susanna's, we will return our Buddha to its home.'

He had sketched out his case concisely. 'How big is the Buddha? Do you know what it weighs?'

'It is one of the largest such statues, perhaps even the largest. It is over five metres high. It weighs nearly six tons.

'Now, Ah Sun here is a member of our Order. He is already close to the *Genyosha*, the Dark Ocean as you know them. But his position is dangerous, extremely dangerous. If they learn of his true allegiance they will surely make things very hard for him. Yet his presence in their camp is essential. For example, he knows that they wait now for you to give them the exact location of the shipwreck, and that they are holding your young friend from Greece.'

These revelations were a game changer. The fact that this mild-mannered monk and his cohorts had infiltrated Dark Ocean moved everything forward. What I'd feared was becoming a tortuous process of pursuing dubious leads up blind or murky alleys suddenly seemed a lot less daunting.

'Where are they holding her?'

'On their ship. The *Toyama Maru*. Ah Sun can help you rescue her.'

'I would greatly appreciate that. And of course I will help you,' I said. 'But it will not be so easy to snatch something the size of your statue from under their noses.'

'I have a proposal to make,' Nya Wang said. 'You must provide them with the information they seek so they can start their salvage operation. Ah Sun says they have all the equipment available to do this: a tug and a special crane mounted on a barge, an underwater vehicle, and a team of divers.'

'What about the China Coast Guard? Don't tell me they are not curious about such activities taking place in their waters, or do they want a piece of the action?'

'Do not worry about that. We have an arrangement with the China Coast Guard to, let us say, turn a blind eye to the salvage operations. They were very appreciative of our generous payment. Furthermore, much of the equipment to be hired by Dark Ocean is Chinese as are some of the crews and divers. They have all been vetted by and are acceptable to Dark Ocean and will arouse less suspicion than if only non-Chinese personnel are engaged. It was the only way to arrange matters, and it depended on Ah Sun and his team gaining their trust. There is no need for you to suffer anxiety about this.'

'You must have good contacts here to pull all this off.'

Nya Wang laughed. 'Of course. There are many disciples of our Order here in Hong Kong. They come to Ganlanba to train in our martial arts. And they are well connected to the Chinese authorities.'

'We are talking about Triads?'

He laughed again. 'If you wish to call them so.'

'Alright, supposing the Buddha is salvaged, I can't see Nakamura and his people standing around while you tow it off to China.'

'It will then be the time for us to seize it from them.'

'I agree this would be the most desirable outcome but it is not without its difficulties, you will admit.' I was unconsciously adopting his elaborate manner of speech.

'Of course, but understand please, this is extremely important to us. We will give our lives if necessary to bring the Buddha home. And even this simple plan is better than no plan. You agree? We must begin somewhere.'

I had visions of a gun battle at sea and wondered how well Nya Wang had thought it all through.

'I understand you also seek to destroy these people,' he continued. 'They have killed your friend and seized the girl.' He spoke vehemently now, his earlier serenity replaced by fervour. 'With your help we can find our statue and bring it home. Will you help us?'

I remembered something Claire had said that evening back in Edinburgh when she was schooling me in the dark art of tradecraft. "Remember, Angus, failure in the art of intelligence comes to those who cannot or will not distinguish between what they know to be facts and what they wish were true. It's a matter of keeping an objective viewpoint even when tempted otherwise."

Was I facing a comparable situation now? Here there was the danger that two parties might seek to convince each other of an unrealistic objective through a mutual need to secure a preferred outcome. Nya Wang was as passionate about his Buddha as I was about finding Zoe. And Alastair Marshall's killers. Over-arching these aims was the threat Dark Ocean posed to the security of the region with its outlandish ambitions. The danger was that neither of us were viewing the situation objectively. But we talked on and by the time we left we had a plan of sorts. It remained to be seen whether we could make it work.

I picked up the little Buddha statue which he'd placed back on the table. Did my father know of its protective properties? 'I'll leave this with you, Nya Wang,' I said handing it to him. 'I'm sure it belongs to you.'

He weighed it in his hand. 'It will protect us all.'

CHAPTER 23

Susanna offered me a lift back to Ronnie Eastfield's place in Sai Kung but I said I'd take a taxi. I needed to think. How did Nya Wang's quest for the golden Buddha fit in with what I was trying to achieve for the IMTF? Was the involvement of Nya Wang and Susanna an added complication or a welcome opportunity? And I had a message from Claire to call her.

I remember checking the time after I'd paid off the taxi. It was ten past three and I was hungry but first I found a quiet spot by the waterfront and called Claire on another of the burner phones I was using. I brought her up to date on my meetings with Jim Brodie, and now Susanna Buchan and Nya Wang.

'So what is this magical plan?'

I gave her the bare bones of it.

'Will it work?'

'Yes,' I said cautiously. 'If the stars are aligned and the Lord Buddha so decrees it.'

'Very funny. Now then, can you be in Tokyo on Thursday? We're meeting some guys from Japan's Public Security Intelligence Agency. They're handling the Dark Ocean end of things.'

'What do you mean handling?'

'Things have moved on, Angus. They're our counterparts, on this job at least. They're sharing intel on Dark Ocean's activities and on its collaboration with the FOAS. It's the only way to nail this whole crazy scheme before it becomes a reality.'

'So who is we? Who's attending this meeting?

'Amber Dove, Ben Wood, you, me and two senior guys from the PSIA: Takeo Ishikawa and Saburo Akimoto.'

We talked on for another five minutes or so and she told me where and when to meet them in Tokyo. Then I walked the hundred yards back to Ronnie's. I've replayed that walk in my mind a hundred times, just as I had the minutes before they snatched Zoe back in Athens. Was there anything I'd missed? I'd become more alert to danger recently, keeping an eye out for anything unusual, anything or anyone out of place. I tell myself there was nothing.

I reached the entrance to the four-story block and with my mind on one of Ronnie's ice-cold beers, pressed the buzzer for his apartment on the top floor. The flash came an instant before the sound of the explosion. I was thrown backwards onto the ground. Dazed, I looked up. I could see the top floor was ablaze. I could hear nothing other than a high-pitched ringing in my ears. I stood up as slowly my hearing returned. Car alarms were going off and people were beginning to gather around the building. The main entrance door opened and three or four Chinese stumbled out. The lobby was full of smoke and dust but I went in keeping low, looking for the stairs. More people were coming into the hall as they descended from other floors. I pushed my way past and went up the stairs two at a time. The smoke cleared a bit as I ascended. I reached the third floor surprised that the fire wasn't more intense. Then I saw what had happened. The blast had blown the top floor off the building. I was looking up from the third floor through a tangled mess of broken concrete and twisted rebars, up to where the top floor had been and was now open to the sky.

'Ronnie!' I yelled. Had he been in? I recognised mangled bits of his furniture, smouldering rugs, the fridge door hanging off its hinges, the contents blackened. I moved across the third floor still looking upwards. Then I saw Ronnie, or what was left of him. The blast had blown him apart. What I was looking at was part of the upper part of his body including his head, charred, blackened and still smouldering. I knew it was him from the steel frames of his glasses. The glass had melted across his blackened face but the frames, unfashionably large and round, were intact.

I stumbled back down the stairs worrying that the 9mm ammunition I'd left in the flat would start going off. The Glock was in there too. Outside on the street I could hear sirens wailing. The crowd had grown but the emergency services hadn't arrived. No-one took any notice of me as I walked away.

Poor old Ronnie. Pressing that buzzer had killed him, I was sure. What else could it have been, a gas explosion? I doubted that. Given what we were involved in I'd put my money on Dark Ocean. Had they hoped I'd be in there too with him? No, they weren't after me. They needed me. I had the location of the wreck. Ronnie was dispensable, but then so would I be after I'd revealed the coordinates.

CHAPTER 24

Tokyo's New Otani was built by an ex-Sumo wrestler on a site he had owned. It had once been the residence of a samurai lord and the hotel's traditional Japanese décor expressed timeless ambience, or so its public relations people said, and it seemed to have worked. But it was the four-hundred year old, ten-acre gardens that made it special and it was through them that I now walked with Claire.

We'd stopped by a waterfall. 'You know what these gardens remind me of?' she said.

'The Botanic Gardens in Edinburgh; me too. This is all a bit grander though.'

We walked on stopping again on a red ornamental bridge over a small lake with koi carp swimming beneath us.

'I never met Ronnie but I could tell you liked him.'

'Yes, I grew to like him. He had this connection with my father too which gave us a kind of bond I guess.'

'You can't let it get to you, Angus. These things can happen in our business. You know that.'

'Sure.'

'You think it was Dark Ocean who did it?'

'It seems likely. I wasn't aware he had any other enemies. He was pretty much retired.

'You know, Clinton and Putin have both walked
through these gardens when they stayed here,' I added to
change the subject. She was right, I had liked Ronnie.

'Not together hand-in-hand I imagine,' she said grabbing my hand.

'Probably not. But I presume the management
can accommodate a small meeting of spies without too
much trouble.'

'That's all been taken care of,' she said. 'We're starting
at eight tomorrow morning.'

We met in a large conference room overlooking the
gardens. Japan's Public Security Intelligence Agency had
fielded four of their own officers to match ours. After introductions and an appropriate, if awkward for the *gaijins*,
bowing session, we all sat down.

I sensed awkwardness among the Japanese too. Japan
was still close to bottom in the gender equality rankings and
I could tell these guys were not used to dealing with women
at this level. Amber Dove and Claire Scott both outranked
Ben Wood and myself and once this became obvious I
could sense not hostility, but an unease, and there was un-
disguised curiosity too.

Green tea was served by a hotel employee. After the
woman's departure Amber asked if the room was clean. After some confusion as to what she meant she was reassured

it was and the meeting began; and by prior agreement she then presented the IMTF's findings ahead of the PSIA's.

'As already reported,' she began, 'a clear link has now been established between the Geneva-based organisation known as the Foundation for Oriental and Asian Studies, which henceforth I shall refer to as FOAS, and *Genyosha*, which, if I may, I shall refer to as Dark Ocean. Our evidence for this connection is based firstly on the findings of the IMTF's late Rear Admiral Alastair Marshall who we believe was murdered by one or other of these organisations to prevent him investigating their activities further; and secondly, corroborated by Ms Zoe Papadopoulos, our Mr McKinnon's assistant in Greece, who obtained a passenger list from the vessel, *Toyama Maru*, listing Messrs Hachiro Takahashi, Hachiro Nakamura, both I now understand proven members of Dark Ocean, and four Europeans, all members of FOAS according to Marshall's own investigations. We are calling this body of evidence the Marshall Dossier and it forms one of the principal cornerstones of the case. I should add that Ms Papadopoulos has been abducted and is held by Dark Ocean and it must be a top priority for all of us around this table to secure her earliest possible release.' She looked around, eyeballing each of us in turn and drawing earnest murmurs of agreement.

'Alastair Marshall had, prior to his death, also discovered a confidential, unpublished economic feasibility study on how a Greater East Asia Co-Prosperity Sphere, albeit considerably modified from the original concept, might yet be achieved. This also forms part of the Dossier.'

At this point there was some fidgeting from the Japanese side of the table.

'We appreciate, gentlemen,' Amber continued showing commendable diplomacy, 'that this makes for uncomfortable listening, but have no doubt that the presence of an organisation such as FOAS in the midst of democratic Europe is no easier for our own intelligence community to digest either. Whilst we might ask why you, as your nation's principal intelligence service, have let such activities go unnoticed, we would also have to ask the very same question of ourselves with regard to FOAS.

'This cabal's strategy, based upon Takahashi's study, is to gain control of the major shipping and trade routes of the Asia Pacific region, which is taken to comprise China including Hong Kong and Taiwan, both Koreas, the countries of Southeast Asia including Singapore, and eventually both Australasia and the Indian subcontinent.

'You might well ask how such a daring, not to say outrageous plan could ever be executed. The answer is by sleight of hand.' Ishikawa muttered a translation of the term and was rewarded by nods and whispered *So desu ka?* from his colleagues.

'The feasibility study asserts that the shipowners, the charterers (by which I mean those exporters and traders of goods and raw materials who charter tonnage to carry their produce to market), and the privately owned ports and terminals throughout the region responsible for handling its imports and exports, are vulnerable to hostile takeover. Given sufficient financial resources, by which they mean a war chest worth many billions of dollars, controlling shares and voting rights in these commercial maritime entities can be acquired, seats on boards taken and domination of their strategic and operational activities thereby accomplished, all in relative secrecy by the use of multiple offshore entities serving as their acquisition vehicles.

'Any remaining shipowners, charterers and ports, particularly state-owned entities, would in time be progressively weakened by the cabal's stranglehold over this huge region's trade. I don't need to remind you that some five trillion dollars' worth of maritime trade passes through the South China Sea every year.

'Furthermore, it is our fear that the cabal is already well on its way to acquiring the billions it would need. The attempt to seize whatever valuables might be salvaged from the wreck of the British cargo vessel, the *Lady Monteith*, which Mr McKinnon here is attempting to thwart, is only the tip of the iceberg. Other such recoveries of World War Two loot have already been made over a period of years, in the Philippines and from shipwrecks in and around the South China Sea.

'Now Mr McKinnon here has uncovered further evidence of Dark Ocean's past activities, and of another dimension to the case which will have a strong bearing on how we handle things going forward. Angus, would you elaborate please?'

I gave them an account of my father's investigations into the attempted money laundering of gold looted by the Japanese in the war, of my meeting with Tim Younger, and an account of Nya Wang's quest to reclaim the golden Buddha and return it to his monastery.

'I would add,' continued Amber returning to the cabal's strategic aims, 'what must be obvious to us all, and that is the immense geopolitical destabilisation such events would most certainly cause, should they succeed. Particularly, given China's own ambitions to secure hegemony in the South China Sea and the tensions such behaviour is already creating across the region, the escalation of such tensions would represent a profound threat to regional, not to say global peace and security.

'As we all know, in addition to building artificial islands, China has also constructed military outposts in the region to assert its dominance, even though their claims to the region were discredited in a ruling by the Permanent Court of Arbitration, and despite the deployment of US and other nations' naval assets aimed at deterring China's illegitimate territorial claims.

'And may I quote from a speech given by a prominent US Navy admiral. He said: "We will not allow a shared domain to be closed down unilaterally no matter how many bases are built on artificial features in the South China Sea. We will cooperate when we can but we will be ready to confront when we must." That statement was made prior to the Trump presidency I might add. Furthermore, I see the Pentagon has just sent a destroyer on another "freedom of navigation" operation within twelve nautical miles of Triton in the Paracels, just a few weeks after the last one. The Chinese are calling it a serious political and military provocation.'

'And you are aware from our earlier briefing on this matter,' Ben Wood interjected, 'that none of the intelligence we are sharing with you today has been communicated to our American cousins for reasons we are all well aware of.' He was referring to a recent loss of confidence that had emerged, within the SIS particularly, towards its American counterparts.

'He's right,' said Amber Dove, 'It's a situation we very much hope is of a temporary nature. But you can see, we already have a cold war on our hands in this region with the Chinese escalating their expansionist plans, and this Dark Ocean/FOAS conspiracy can only serve to exacerbate matters ten-fold.'

'So, at this point do you have any questions?'

'At this point, no,' replied Ishikawa.

'Very well. Now, returning to Takahashi's paper, this has been analysed by our own economists. They assure us that it is well postulated and, in theory at least, feasible.'

She pulled bound copies of the paper from her briefcase and passed them around the table. 'Here is the paper in both Japanese and English. You will see in Addendum 7 a list of those entities which we understand have already been targeted for hostile takeover.

'So that, in a nutshell, is what we are facing and I invite

you to present your own, the PSIA's that is, ideas as to how to deal with the situation.'

The Japanese were anxiously leafing through their version of the Takahashi report. I went straight to Addendum 7. It ran to over twenty pages and listed what I could see were all the major shipowners, operators, traders, charterers and privately-owned port and terminal operators across the region. Banks active in ship finance and a number of leading brokers were in there too.

Something else caught my eye. 'I see they've got a couple of big FPSO operators in their sights,' I said.

'Yes, I noticed that,' Claire added.

Floating Production Storage and Offloading vessels are converted supertankers positioned near an offshore oil platform. They process crude oil and store it until it can be transferred to another tanker for onward shipment to a refinery ashore. You wouldn't acquire a fleet of such sophisticated vessels unless you had access to an oilfield in the first place.

'The Chinese reckon there's two-hundred billion barrels of oil and up to seven-hundred and fifty trillion cubic feet of natural gas in the South China Sea,' I said. 'I'm sure Dark Ocean and FOAS have their eyes on that as well as the annual five trillion bucks' worth of trade.'

That took a little time to sink in. After some whispered conferring with his colleagues, Ishikawa-san spoke: 'Thank you. This is a very serious matter. Please allow us one hour to discuss. We will meet again after lunch. We have arranged for sandwiches.' And with that they got up, bowed hastily and left the room.

***

Exactly one hour later Ishikawa returned, alone. This time, gone was the formality, the hesitancy and the polite mannerisms. Instead this was the westernised Ishikawa who, as one of Japan's leading spooks, had spent years in Washington, Berlin and London and must now have been in the final years of a successful career. Claire had told me he'd been a field agent in his earlier days too, working out of Burma and Thailand during the CIA's secret war in Laos. He took off his jacket and sat down, his manner brusque.

'I have reached a consensus with my colleagues. They have agreed for me to discuss this matter with you directly, for the sake of expediency.'

'That sounds sensible,' said Amber Dove.

I smiled. I suspected the consensus was a case of Ishikawa telling his colleagues how he was going to handle things rather than discussing it with them at any great length.

'We follow the activities of Dark Ocean of course,' he said. 'But at first our understanding was that they were just one of our many nationalist groups who take to the streets of Tokyo from time to time. Since we heard of their recent emergence we have been building our own dossier on their activities. However, the picture you have painted shows that you have made considerable progress. I confess we find it embarrassing to be told that such things are happening so rapidly under our noses, and on my watch.

'First though, I will tell you about Hachiro Nakamura.' Ishikawa looked around the table before continuing. 'Today, this man is indeed the head of *Genyosha*. And he has a very disturbing background. His father was murdered by an opposing Yakuza faction when his son was an infant so father had little or no influence over son. But Nakamura's grandfather was a notorious gangster during the war. He was what we call *kuromaku*. It means black curtain and refers to someone who directs the actions of others from behind the scenes.'

'We would say *eminence gris* or grey eminence,' said Claire.

'A power broker,' Ben Wood added.'

'Yes, exactly. During the war Nakamura's grandfather made deals with many gangsters around Asia using coercion, trading opium for gold, and often arranging the elimination of those who crossed him. He did the dirty work for the politicians and the princes back in Tokyo. He was a fanatical ultra-nationalist and after the war he was imprisoned for several years. Shortly after he was released he went to the Yasukuni Shrine in Tokyo and in front of many of his followers sympathetic to his beliefs, committed *seppuku,* or you may know it as *hara-kiri,* suicide by disembowelment. His grandson was there watching. It must have had a profound effect on the boy. He grew up a gangster and through his grandfather's connections, joined *Genyosha*, as it became resurgent. This is what we know.

'We will now of course work closely with you to put an end to these organisations and their activities. If what you say is true, then I fear their wealth has been accumulated through collaboration with banks, government agencies, politicians and others in high places here in Japan. We have indeed had our suspicions for some time that such allegiances exist.'

Amber spoke. 'We are pleased to hear this, Ishikawa-san. We are both seeking the same outcome: the complete dismantling, preferably the total removal of both these organisations to put an end to their outlandish plans.

'Our aim is also, of course, to secure the safe release of Ms Papadopoulos, and indeed the safe return to its home of the Buddha statue. However, our absolute priority must be the destruction of this cabal that threatens the security of the region's nations and their peoples.'

'I agree.' Ishikawa said. 'I have already scheduled an appointment with my colleagues in our defence ministry's intelligence department. When the time is right, I believe military action may be necessary. We will of course liaise closely with yourselves should the need arise.'

'Yes, of course. Mr Wood will be our liaison with MI6 and other agencies back in Europe. But Ms Scott will be your point of contact in all matters out here, and we in turn will channel any relevant intelligence through her to yourselves. She will base herself in Hong Kong until this matter is resolved, but she will make herself available for meetings with you when and where necessary.'

'We are agreed then,' Ishikawa concluded and with that we said our goodbyes. I was impressed by the man. He was a pragmatist and I was glad he was in charge of the case here at the heart of the matter.

CHAPTER 25

Claire and I returned to Hong Kong the following day. She felt as responsible for Zoe as I did but the IMTF wanted her on hand as liaison officer for what could be the final phase. And, if it came down to it, I knew Zoe's safety would be sacrificed in the blink of an eye if the greater good was to be served. I wasn't happy about this but as Claire reminded me, she was my case officer and not the other way round. But what I didn't want was her dragging around Hong Kong challenging my decisions. For me, Zoe came first.

Claire was going to be ensconced in the British Consulate located in Admiralty district between Central and Wanchai. So they had booked her into the nearby Conrad Hotel.

'Do IMTF staff usually slum it like you?' I asked as I saw her into her hotel limousine. My hotel was a quarter of the price she was paying.

She gave me an arch look. 'You can always come for a sleepover, darling.'

Tempting though it was, I had no intention of becoming further involved in Claire's romantic plans at this stage. I'd decided to visit Nya Wang and went straight from the airport to Kowloon Tong. The wind was getting up. 'Number three now. Number eight tomorrow morning,' said the taxi driver referring to Hong Kong's system of typhoon signals. 'Maybe number nine,' he added for dramatic effect. 'Very early this year.'

'Must be climate change,' I said.

'Yeah, must be. Climate change everywhere now,' he said cheerfully. I suppose it gave everyone another excuse to talk about the weather. I stared out of the car window at the profusion of street debris being chased round in circles by the sudden gusts of warm, rain-laden wind. The worsening weather seemed like a bad omen and I had to force myself into a positive frame of mind. It wasn't easy.

Nya Wang had told me he'd be at the house at all times. I rang the bell. This time the steel door was answered by a man I hadn't seen on my last visit. He was dressed in a monk's robes and moved with the quiet grace I'd seen in Nya Wang. I was ushered into the same room that we'd been in before and Nya Wang appeared as tea was being served.

'I have news from Ah Sun,' he announced without preamble. 'The *Toyama Maru* is here at the Pun Shan Shek anchorage. And there is a foreign woman on board, possibly your colleague from Greece. He does not know for sure.'

'When will Ah Sun come ashore?' I asked. 'I need him to help me get aboard.'

'Do not be hasty. I have asked for more information.

He will contact me again. You must understand he is in a dangerous position. He cannot risk being uncovered.'

There was nothing more I could do but wait. At least it seemed Zoe, if it was her, was alive. He promised to call me when he had news so I left to return to my hotel.

The taxi was coming out of the cross-harbour tunnel onto Hong Kong side when Claire called. She had news too and wanted to see me. She sounded agitated. I redirected the driver to the Conrad and met her in the lobby. We went to her room, which was in fact a suite with a separate lounge-cum-office.

'What's happening?'

'Amber's been in touch,' she said. 'Ishikawa has fresh intel on Dark Ocean and FOAS. Their plans are much further advanced than we'd guessed. The PSIA have been digging and it seems the hostile takeover strategy is already being implemented.'

She handed me a printout. 'This was delivered by the Consulate an hour ago. It's been decrypted. It's the same list of targets we had in Tokyo but look at the names in red. They're already under their control. They're using proxies to acquire them but the PSIA have linked the proxies to Dark Ocean and FOAS members. Amber says she has had all these acquisitions checked out.'

I looked more closely. There were eighteen companies in red, all in the Asia Pacific region including three in Australia. I recognised most of them: small to medium-sized shipowners and charterers; nothing that was going to grab headlines in the international business press.

'They're moving fast,' I said. 'These deals have all been concluded within the past six weeks. In relative terms this is an avalanche. And no-one's standing in their way.'

I walked over to the mini-bar and poured us both a Scotch adding a splash of water to each. Claire took a cautious sip of hers and set the glass down gently on the coffee table. 'There's worse, Angus.'

'Go on.'

She hesitated, uncertain of where to begin. 'Have you ever heard of VX?'

'I presume you're not referring to Vauxhall Cross.'

'VX is an incredibly toxic organophosphate nerve agent. It makes sarin look like cough mixture. It's ten times more toxic and it's classified as a weapon of mass destruction by the UN. Ishikawa believes Dark Ocean has access to old stockpiles of the stuff. It's reckoned to be by far the most lethal of all chemical weapons. It works by inhibiting the production of an enzyme in the nerves; creates a storm of constant activity in the nervous system that overwhelms the body and kills within minutes. Death is caused by paralysis of the diaphragm muscle – so by asphyxiation. And it can be dispersed as a vapour over large populated areas.'

'How the hell did they get hold of the stuff?'

'That's what I asked. Back in 1969 there was a leak of chemical weapons from a secret depot on Okinawa. The Americans were storing stockpiles there. A big row erupted between the Americans and the Japanese government. The

Americans were forced to remove the stuff and dispose of it off some Pacific atoll. The removal operation was known as Red Hat. What Ishikawa's discovered from his Defence Intelligence people is that some stocks of VX were diverted to another island in the Yaeyama group down towards Taiwan. Dark Ocean has some kind of logistics base there, all under cover of a legitimate freight forwarding company.'

'You're not telling me they're planning to use this stuff are you?'

'The PSIA believe it's a threat, the ultimate sanction if you like. The worry is that these people are fanatics. They are committed to their cause. They've already shown they'll kill with impunity haven't they.'

She paused taking another sip of her drink. 'Not only all of this,' she went on, 'but Ishikawa says he has reason to believe there are those in the Japanese government who are acquiescent, or at least turning a blind eye to Dark Ocean's activities, because they see them as a means to foil China's hegemony in the South China Sea. You remember he referred to this yesterday but he seems to be verifying it now.'

'So where is the VX now?'

'Ishikawa is working on that. But I'm afraid, Angus. You're planning to get aboard the *Toyama Maru*. I know you have to find Zoe but for God's sake watch out for yourself too. They're killers: Alastair, then Ronnie…'

Ignoring my previous resolution, I stayed with her that night. At five-fifteen next morning Nya Wang called. 'Go to the old Sham Tseng ferry pier in Tsuen Wan now. Ah

Sun is on his way and will wait for you. You will go aboard with him.'

Claire held onto me, no longer case officer but anxious lover. 'Don't go. We can get others to do this. There are assets in the region – special forces. It's not part of your remit.'

'You know I have to do this,' I said, gently untangling myself from her.

After my shower I went over to the bed. 'I know,' she said. 'Go.'

CHAPTER 26

The weather had worsened overnight. Signal 8 was up and the streets were more or less empty as rain squalls swept across the city's landscape.

Ah Sun and Nya Wang were waiting at the pier. Ah Sun had been sent ashore to buy provisions from the chandler and engine parts from a local repair shop. A scruffy-looking sampan was bobbing up and down a few metres offshore in water littered with oil-stained polystyrene and stinking of raw sewage. As we spoke a white van arrived, the sides painted with the name Ah Fai Ship Chandlers. The sampan came alongside the jetty and they began man-handling boxes of fruit, vegetables and canned goods aboard. The last item was a wooden crate containing parts for one of the ship's generators.

Ah Sun was supervising the operation. I called him aside. 'Ah Sun, tell me about the girl. Have you seen her?'

'They keep her in the hospital, locked up. They give her drugs.'

'What drugs?'

'To keep her sleeping. Then give her food once a day.'

'Do you have a key to the hospital?'

'Yes, have key.'

'What does she look like?'

'Very beautiful. Gold hair. But sick - not well.'

That was as much as I could glean from him but I was sure it was Zoe.

'Okay, Ah Sun. Between us we must get her off and to safety.'

He looked at Nya Wang for confirmation.

'This man is helping us, remember?' Nya Wang said. 'And with his help we can return our great Buddha to Gan-lanba. He deserves our help too. Do as he says.'

That was enough for Ah Sun. I asked him about the ship chandler. Would he have another crate like the one they'd just loaded? He spoke to Ah Fai who said he did and would be back with it in half an hour.

Then Ah Sun spoke rapidly to the sampan's coxswain pointing at me as he did so. He took out a wad of hundred Hong Kong dollar notes, peeled off a few and handed them over. 'He will help us,' he said.

The chandler returned after twenty minutes with an empty crate the same size as the one containing the generator parts. We loaded it onto the sampan's deck and I squeezed inside, knees against my chest as the top was nailed down.

The sampan was rolling heavily in the swell from the approaching storm and it took us the best part of an hour to reach the *Toyama Maru*. Peering through a narrow slat in the crate's side I could see she had now been renamed and painted grey above the waterline. Her port of registry was still shown as George Town. It was a thin disguise.

I didn't like this ship. I thought of Alastair suffering the first agonies of the arsenic poisoning; now of Zoe's incarceration, locked up, drugged and fed once a day like an animal in a zoo. I thought of Nakamura and his missing finger. And I asked myself, not for the first time, what the hell I was doing caught up in this business. What was I trying to prove? It wasn't just about the money. Neither could I argue that I was simply a hapless victim of circumstance. I didn't have a ready answer, but I knew one day I would have to come up with one. In the meantime I fought to prevent a sense of fear from creeping over me.

The sampan came up against the ship's side with a thud and Ah Sun called up to attract the attention of crewmen on deck to help transfer the stores. The ship's gangway was lowered and two men came down to help. The hook of a small deck crane was lowered to lift the heavy crates including the one I was cooped up in. The crate swung wildly as it rose up and over the ship's rail before landing hard on the hatch cover. Ah Sun was speaking with the Filipino crewmen in his broken English. 'Get stores to pantry and tell second engineer his parts arrive. I open crates.'

'Okay, okay,' came the reply.

After a moment I heard him prising open the top of my crate. 'Out, quick,' he whispered. I climbed out and ducked down beside the hatch coaming before the engineer with two of his ratings came to collect their engine parts. They didn't bother to ask about the empty crate I'd been in.

Once they'd gone we made our way to the accommodation. Now that the crew had brought the stores and spares in there was no sign of life. It was mid-morning but almost dark. Great gusts of wind swept sheets of rain across the deck. Lights were on in the accommodation but the weathertight doors were shut against the storm. Ah Sun opened the portside door and we entered cautiously, closing it behind us. The hospital was one deck up. Still there was no-one around and we reached it without being seen. Ah Sun unlocked the door.

I had had little time to think what condition I would find Zoe in although Ah Sun's account had given me some warning. The hospital was a cabin-sized room with medical equipment lining the bulkheads and an operating table in the centre, from which Zoe now arose. But she was not the same ebullient young woman I knew. Her time in captivity, and for all I knew her mistreatment at their hands, had changed her dramatically and I could see she was vague and confused from the effects of the drugs they'd given her.

As she lowered herself from the operating table she stumbled. I reached forward to grab her and she collapsed in my arms. I pulled her to me to hold her upright. She was sobbing, softly at first but as I held her the sobbing intensified until her whole body was shaking uncontrollably.

'Zoe, it's okay,' I said. 'We'll get you out of here. Go

with Ah Sun. He'll take care of you.' She just clung onto me.

'Oh, Angus,' she moaned.

'You're safe now, don't worry. We'll have you home soon. It's over now.' I carried on comforting her, holding her and stroking her dishevelled hair until Ah Sun tapped my shoulder.

'Time to go.'

I tried gently to pull Zoe away from me but she only clung tighter, her sobs reaching a hysterical pitch. Ah Sun read my mind. He went over to a metal cabinet and started searching. Within a few moments he came back with a syringe and jabbed it straight through the fabric of Zoe's top and into her arm. I was becoming seriously impressed by Ah Sun's resourcefulness.

It took a while but eventually Zoe just slumped against me. I lifted her into my arms like a sick child. We went along the passageway, back down and out onto the deck to signal the sampan. I knew this was where things could get difficult and they did. The *Toyama Maru's* regular Filipino crew were one thing but the two guys who came out from the other side of the accommodation were something else: tough looking security guards, Koreans I guessed. I knew that if we didn't deal with them quickly and quietly we'd have others joining them. Ah Sun obviously had the same idea.

I laid Zoe gently onto the deck in the shelter of the hatch coaming and crouched down beside her. Ah Sun knew these guys. He was part of their team. I watched guardedly as he walked over to them nice and relaxed. They weren't sure what to do but it seemed they hadn't seen Zoe and me. He spoke easily gesturing to the wind and rain whipping around us. One of the thugs laughed at something Ah Sun said.

Zoe was collapsed against the hatch coaming but then without warning she sat up and started shouting in Greek, her words slurred but clearly audible. I pulled her down holding my hand over her mouth but it was too late. One of the heavies came loping across the deck towards us. He'd heard Zoe but hadn't seen us. I waited until he was virtually upon us, stood up and grabbed at him awkwardly. He was my height but heavier, and a trained fighter I quickly discovered. Almost straightaway he had me in a choke hold, his right arm round my throat, his left hand pulling on his right to further tighten his grip. I leaned forward lifting him off his feet. We struggled but he still wasn't loosening his hold. The deck was slippery with rain on the oily steel surface. I pushed back to throw him off balance. We crashed into the corner of the hatch coaming and fell to the deck. He was underneath me now but still his grip didn't relax. I was having difficulty drawing breath and could feel myself weakening. But my arms were still free. With what strength was left in me I reached forward and grabbed the boot of his right foot in both hands. Then pushing backwards into his body I wrenched hard twisting his knee upwards towards my chest. With a scream he released his grip on my neck. I kept twisting his knee upwards while still lying back across his body to prevent him getting free.

We were at an impasse and not knowing what my next

move should be but having the advantage, I released his foot, turned and grabbed at his head with the idea of smashing it onto the steel deck. The bastard was quick and had the same idea. Now he was straddled on top of me, his hands at my throat trying again to choke me. But he'd made his mistake. I brought my left knee up into his groin with all the force I had left. He shrieked in pain and released his grip long enough for me to push him off me. This time I took my opportunity and leaning over him, slammed his head against the deck. He lay still.

Zoe had stood up, still looking vacant. I pulled her back down telling her to stay where she was. Ah Sun was grappling with the other thug now. How long did I have? I grabbed Zoe and rushed her to the ship's side where the gangway was still down. Lifting her in my arms again I struggled awkwardly down towards the sampan where I could see the coxswain was watchful and prepared. As he saw us he brought his craft neatly alongside the gangway and despite the swell slamming the sampan's gunwale up and under the foot of the gangway, we managed to get Zoe aboard.

'Go!' I yelled. He needed no further encouragement. The little boat disappeared into the rain squall, Zoe standing in the cockpit staring back at me.

I climbed back up the gangway to be confronted by Ah Sun and behind him, the thug holding a pistol to his head.

'Hands up!' he shouted. I didn't argue. He hustled the two of us back into the accommodation. His mate was still lying on the deck where I'd left him.

CHAPTER 27

We were back in the same saloon I'd been taken to on my previous visit, only this time I wasn't offered a drink. The ship was rolling in the swell which had reached into the sheltered anchorage of the harbour. The lighting was low and there was the smell of alcohol and cigarettes in the air. As the minutes passed the Korean who was minding us began prodding Ah Sun in the chest with his gun, goading him. Ah Sun didn't react. There was just the three of us in there. Was there an opportunity for the two of us to take him on, if I could divert his attention? I was sure Ah Sun was thinking the same, but then the door opened and in walked Nakamura.

He was dressed not in a suit and tie this time but tan-coloured chinos and a black cashmere sweater with the sleeves pushed up to reveal a solid array of coloured tattoos on both arms. And he too was holding a gun.

'Such a disappointment you - both of you.' He spoke softly, with a note of regret. The man was an enigma. His squat muscular physique, the tattoos, the missing finger -

none of these matched with the soft-spoken eloquence of his manner.

'Ah Sun, can you explain yourself?' he asked.

Ah Sun's cover was blown. He had betrayed those who thought him a loyal servant. He didn't reply, so I did.

'You and I are going to make a deal,' I said to Nakamura. 'You're going to release him and you can keep me. I have the information you need, and a whole lot more besides. I can help you. Now you decide.'

He smiled. 'I expected better from you, Mr McKinnon. You promised to deliver the wreck's coordinates and we hear nothing from you.'

'You kidnapped the girl. Did you think I'd ignore that?'

'She was foolish. She interfered in our business.' He was referring to the passenger list Zoe had obtained from her friend, Fotini. It had been the breakthrough we'd needed in making the connection between Black Ocean and FOAS, but it had sealed Zoe's fate.

'We had to keep her silent. Now it seems she is gone. But if you think you can trade the coordinates for this man's freedom you are wrong. We already have them.'

This threw me. Was he bluffing for some reason? If he wasn't how could he have obtained them, and from whom? The only people who knew the coordinates besides myself were Claire, Amber Dove, Ben Wood, Admiral Randolph Carvill and Tim Younger. Had one of them revealed them and if so, deliberately or in error? Had Nakamura got hold of the Admiralty chart on which I'd marked them? Or had he found them from some other source? I was about to challenge him to show them to me, if only to buy time, when Ah Sun made his move.

Having the gun had made his minder complacent and Ah Sun saw his chance. His arm shot out, the flat of his hand chopping down onto the man's arm. He didn't release the gun but he'd been caught off guard and Ah Sun had planned the outcome. In one fluid movement he turned to face his opponent and, using his bulk, drove him back hard against the wooden panelling of the bulkhead. Holding the man's gun hand high above his body he slammed his arm against the panelling splintering the wood. The gun went flying across the carpeted deck and Ah Sun felled the man with a chop to the side of his neck.

I went for Nakamura but he fired twice before I could stop him. I felt a searing pain at the top of my right arm. I managed to grab him round the neck with my left arm but his gun hand was still free and he fired again. This time he hit Ah Sun who fell heavily to the floor. He lay there doubled over in a foetal position, moaning as he clutched his stomach. It had all happened in seconds: three shots, the sound still ringing in my ears.

I let go of Nakamura and moved towards Ah Sun.

'Leave him!' shouted Nakamura. Blood was already seeping through Ah Sun's fingers and onto the carpet. The minder had staggered across and retrieved his own gun and was covering me with it.

Nakamura spoke. 'He is dying. You cannot help him.'

I knelt down beside Ah Sun. He was alive, breathing in shallow gasps, his face contorted in pain.

'He needs morphine' I said. 'You must have some in the dispensary. Please.'

'He has betrayed us. Let him die in pain.' He was standing with his back against the panelled bulkhead, the gun pointing down at us.

I stood up and faced him. 'Until I have verified the coordinates you cannot be sure of finding the wreck. Do you want to take that risk? I don't know who gave them to you but can they be trusted? There's been plenty of false information put about over the years. Are you really sure of your source?'

He hesitated, staring at me angrily. 'Very well!' Then he spoke rapidly to the Korean minder who left the saloon.

I grabbed a waiter's cloth from the bar and knelt beside Ah Sun. Rolling up his shirt sleeve I tied the cloth as a tourniquet round his arm. Gently I pressed on the skin above the vein in his arm to help draw it closer to the surface. He was groaning loudly now but I could see the vein I was looking for and placed a finger over it pressing up and down. Gradually the vein began to protrude. After a couple of minutes the minder lumbered back in with a tray and a box of syringes.

People with abdominal gunshot wounds bleed internally and die slowly. Chest wounds, even low ones which can get the liver, are what kill you fast. The kind of wound Ah Sun had suffered might not kill him for two or three hours. If that was how Ah Sun was going to go I didn't want to see him suffer – and he was suffering. He'd also begun to shake, his great body convulsing as he lay there. There was no one here who could operate on him. I felt his pulse. It was erratic. All I could do now was ease his pain.

I knew that I had to give him the morphine intravenously. Given intramuscularly to a patient in shock it would take too long to work. A normal dose would be five to a maximum of ten milligrams. Although I knew ten would be a huge dose, that's what I gave Ah Sun. I fixed the needle to the syringe, drew the liquid up from the ampoule and jabbed it into what I hoped was the right vein: the median cubital.

I stayed kneeling beside him. He gripped my hand but as the drug took effect his grip weakened until finally he let go. I stayed there as he bled out onto the carpet. At least he was out of pain now. And all I felt was a slow burning anger.

'Right. Give me the coordinates and we will see,' said Nakamura. 'Now.'

I stood up slowly. 'Give me paper and pen and you can have them,' I said, 'but tell me, Nakamura, what do you hope to get out of this? Are you hoping to find some vast treasure trove down there to fulfil your crazy dreams? I don't think there's enough gold on that wreck to satisfy them if that's what you're thinking.'

My words sparked an angry response. 'You think we don't have plans. Our nation has been humiliated. We, *Genyosha*, are the means by which Japan will regain its pride and its dignity. We are our nation's destiny. I will not share our dreams as you call them. They are not dreams. They are clear objectives which will soon become reality. No, of course the financing needed cannot be met from what we find down there. The wreck and its cargo are only a small part. But it is the symbolism that counts. How would you know the influence Buddhism has had on the development of our society and our culture to this day. The Buddha beneath the sea here is the biggest such statue in the world. It will be taken to Japan and become the symbol of our cause.'

He'd regained his composure but still spoke with passion. 'Our followers expect us to bring to Japan the fruits of Golden Lily, denied us in our war against the Western imperialists. This wreck is the final site that was identified. Number 176. There are many more sites to be searched, but the cargo salvaged from this site will truly be proof of our commitment, of our achievement, our triumph!

'Here,' he said walking over to a desk in the corner of the saloon and handing me pen and paper. 'Write them down. Where does it lie?'

I wrote them down for him, then knelt beside Ah Sun again. He lay still now and I could feel no pulse. If I was to avenge Ah Sun's murder, then I must help retrieve his temple's lost Buddha. Seizing it from Dark Ocean's grasp was something else but right now I had traded the coordinates for a peaceful death for Ah Sun. Now I had to fulfil my side of the bargain.

Nakamura took the paper I'd written on and made a call on the ship's sound-powered phone. We stared at each other until the ship's captain arrived with the Approaches to Hong Kong chart and his parallel rules. They pored over it together. Finally, Nakamura turned to me. 'The coordinates match, but until the wreck is located you will remain aboard, as our guest.'

'And after that?' I asked unnecessarily. He didn't bother answering.

CHAPTER 28

Out on deck there was no sign of the man I'd left unconscious by the hatch coaming earlier. I was taken to the bosun's store in the ship's forepeak, a familiar place from my
seagoing days. It was where everything from ropes and
chains to paints, grease, luboils and all manner of tools were
kept. As a ship's bosun, the store had once been part of my
domain. Now it was to be my prison.

There was little light in there to explore my surroundings but I could see it was well kept with ropes coiled neatly
on the deck and shelving with drums of oil, tins of grease,
tools and assorted weather-proof clothing and footwear.
But what I saw next sent a shock through my nerves. Lined
up on the starboard side shelving were eight crates. In the
dim light I could make out a series of letters and numbers
stencilled onto their sides. There were only two letters that
made any sense to me: VX.

They kept the stuff on board! The implications crowd-
ed my mind. If these were the canisters taken all that time
ago from Okinawa during Operation Red Hat, what condi-

tion were they in after nearly fifty years? Was it stable? Was it still potent? I backed away involuntarily.

Then, as I stood next to the door I felt the throb of the ship's engines and shortly after, the nearby racket of her anchors being hauled up through the hawse pipes. We were on the move. But were we heading for the wreck site in the teeth of a typhoon or shifting to another in-port anchorage? It didn't take long to find out: we were entering open waters. The ship began to pitch and roll, gently at first but then with greater strength as her speed picked up and the seas became angrier.

The storm had passed over Luzon and headed northwest. The Philippines gets the brunt of the tropical cyclones that develop out in the Pacific, but they have a bad habit of barrelling straight across the Philippine archipelago and on into the South China Sea. And that's what this one had done. A mature tropical cyclone becomes a typhoon when wind speeds reach between seventy and ninety miles an hour; a severe typhoon has winds of at least ninety-two and to qualify as a super typhoon winds must reach a hundred and twenty, at least. This one was brewing into a severe typhoon but before I'd left the hotel the weathermen had been predicting it would reach landfall south of Hong Kong down towards Hainan. But they'd added that this one was a straight track storm with a particularly wide radius of maximum wind, meaning Hong Kong and its surrounding waters could expect winds in excess of eighty miles an hour with accompanying storm surges and likely damage to fixed structures and floating craft.

I began groping around searching for something I might be able to force open the weathertight door with. It had hatch dogs on both sides but a locking device had been fitted on the outside preventing it being opened from within. I gave up after a while and sat there nursing my arm which was aching and seeping blood. I tried to think the situation through but all I could think of was those eight crates marked VX. Eventually I started searching again and this time got lucky in the form of a two-foot long Stillson pipe wrench which must have weighed close to twenty pounds. I moved across to the door with the idea of using the wrench to force the lock on the other side by levering the dog hatch handle of the door open. I was getting it into position when I heard a noise. The door was being opened from the outside. Standing back I waited, holding the wrench with both hands. A man entered carrying a torch in one hand and a gun in the other. It was the Korean I'd fought with earlier. I guessed he'd been sent to check on me, but considering our previous encounter he might have had other ideas. He certainly wasn't carrying a drinks tray. He shone the torch around the store, then, when he didn't see me, moved further in, searching. I came up from behind and caught him on his left ear with the wrench. He went down without a sound. I dragged him inside and bent down to feel his pulse. It was faint but his breathing was even. I took his gun, his waterproof jacket and a bunch of keys from one pocket and loose ammunition from the other.

I looked at the VX crates again to memorise the lettering on the first crate. Then I left locking the door behind me, well armed with gun, ammo and the pipe wrench.

The weather had worsened. Waves were washing over the forecastle. Rain and spray blended into a white vortex coming from all directions at once. I stood for a moment in the shelter of the forepeak gripping the door and getting my bearings. I was pretty sure we were heading southeast away from Hong Kong's Pun Shan Shek anchorage. Typhoons spin anti-clockwise and the wind was now on our port beam. We were in open waters but looking aft through the spray I caught glimpses of the dark silhouette of an island with a cluster of lights along its shoreline. From its position I guessed it was Lamma island.

The *Toyama Maru* had begun to slam as her bow heaved out of one trough and ploughed into the next mountainous wave, vibrating with the impact. Under normal circumstances in these conditions the ship would have been slowed or her heading changed to reduce the risk of damage to her bottom plates and her cargo. I'd seen forty-foot steel containers virtually flattened by the effect of slamming. What worried me most now were the crates of the lethal nerve agent stowed just a few feet away and vulnerable to the pounding the ship was taking.

My choices were limited. I couldn't take over the ship by strolling into the wheelhouse and telling them to head back to Hong Kong. I needed to get off the ship. Zoe, I hoped, was safely ashore. Ah Sun was dead, and I wasn't keen to be anywhere nearby if the VX started leaking – or worse, was detonated. I had no idea whether those crates contained canisters, or whether the VX had been weaponised in the form of missiles or mines.

But to jump for it hoping to swim ashore in this weather wasn't an option either. I presumed we were heading for the wreck site. That was just off the coast of Wenwei Zhou, the southwestern-most island of the Jiapeng Liedao group. If the wind continued to blow from the east then the wreck site would be in the lee of Wenwei Zhou, possibly providing a safe haven for her to wait out the storm.

I was banking on something else too: that the ship had a functioning radio room, and that I could get into it undetected. I worked my way back along the main deck towards the accommodation block, clinging onto the starboard side ship's rail. Twice I was knocked off my feet by the force of the waves sweeping across the length of the ship. The second time the wrench slipped from my grasp and slid across the deck before I could retrieve it.

Eventually I made it to the weathertight door and into the relative calm of the ship's accommodation. I stood still, dripping water and listening. The sound of the storm was muffled in here although the ship was still heaving about violently in an awkward corkscrewing motion.

I made my way up to the bridge deck. I knew the officer of the watch and the helmsman would be in the wheelhouse, others too possibly. When I got up there, the door to the wheelhouse was closed. The door to the radio room, adjacent to the wheelhouse, was closed too but not locked. I went in, closing it behind me.

The ship was old and so was most of the radio equipment arrayed around the operator's table. This was from the days of Morse, when ships carried a dedicated radio officer. Until satellite communication, the ship was a remote out-station, but to my relief, a laptop and satellite router sat on the table in front of me. I clicked the mouse and a password request came up. On a shelf above me were piles of books, mainly manuals of one kind or another, and beside them a stack of discs. I sifted through them and found what I was looking for: the installation disc for the computer's operating system. I inserted it, rebooted the computer and entered the BOOT menu selecting the installation disc.

It was all coming back to me from one day a couple of years ago when we'd had a computer meltdown in the office. It was Zoe who'd figured out how to repair it and I could see and hear her now as she tapped away, cursing softly as I stood watching over her shoulder. Now, expecting someone to burst into the radio room at any moment, I forced myself to think back. Suddenly it all seemed intuitive and I could see how to reset the computer's password.

This led me into Inmarsat's Fleet service, and another password request. I tried the ship's call sign: 3LXY2. It worked. My message to Claire's encrypted email address was short: "Eight containers of VX in Bosun's store, forecastle. Unsure whether weaponised. Believe on course for wreck site. ETA imminent. Advise."

I sat and waited, and watched the door. She'd promised she'd be manning her station 24/7. I had her reply within two tense minutes: "Get off when you can. Believe Buchan on board. We have eyes on you. Standby pick-up from portside. Try signal to rescue team as you leave."

Did she mean the Special Boat Squadron she'd alluded to back in the hotel? Despite its lineage the IMTF rarely mentioned the resources at its disposal but I knew from my past encounter with them, that they could literally bring down shock and awe from the skies when necessary. It would make sense for them to call upon the Royal Navy's resources to help me out. I deleted our messages which removed them permanently; no deleted items folder here.

I was sitting there considering her reply when the door burst open. One of the ship's officers stood there, frozen in surprise.

He was wearing tropical whites with two-bar epaulettes on his shoulders. I turned and raised one hand in greeting. 'Hello there, Second Mate. Just finishing off,' I said, standing up and pulling the gun from my pocket. 'I'm going to kill you now unless you do what I tell you. All clear?'

'Okay, okay,' he stammered, instinctively raising his arms.

'Good. There's a man on board called Buchan. Do you know him?

'I know him. He's locked in cabin.'

'Right, we'll go and see him.' I prodded the gun into his chest and he backed out of the door. 'One sound and you're dead,' I whispered in case he hadn't got the message. The wheelhouse door was still closed. I guessed the second mate had been coming into the radio room to check for traffic.

CHAPTER 29

We headed down the stairway to the deck below and along the portside passageway.

'Here. He's in here,' the officer said, stopping at the last cabin door. He turned to me nervously. 'Don't shoot, okay?'

'Who's in the next cabin?'

'Nobody.'

'Do you have a key for Buchan's cabin?'

'No key.'

Here, try these,' I said, handing him the keys I'd taken earlier. He gave me an enquiring look.

'Just do it.'

He found one that fitted and opened the cabin door. And there, lying on the bunk, was Monty Buchan looking dishevelled and forlorn, though when he saw me his expression brightened and he struggled to his feet. Monty Buchan was not cut out for this kind of thing.

'Ye gods, Angus! Am I glad to see you,' he said dabbing the sweat from his forehead with a paisley handkerchief. 'And Watanabe too.' He grabbed our hands in turn. Second officer Watanabe was grinning.

'You two know each other then,' I said.

'Of course,' said Monty.' He used to sail for us when he was still a cadet. Imagine my surprise when I saw him here.'

'Can he be trusted?'

'You can trust me,' Watanabe interrupted. 'I didn't know about these bad things when I joined this ship. I just want to leave.'

'Are you off watch now?'

'Yes. I came into the radio room to check for comms but off watch now.'

'Okay, just sit down there,' I said pointing with the gun to an office chair beside the desk. It was cramped in the cabin for the three of us. Monty had slumped back on the bunk with his back resting against the bulkhead. I sat myself on a small built-in sofa. In their day these officers' cabins must have been immaculate. Now, like the rest of the ship, it was looking worn out and tawdry. Like Monty.

'Scotch,' said Monty. It wasn't a question and I didn't need asking. He struggled up and poured three generous measures draining the bottle that was on his bedside table. They might have locked him up but at least they'd left that for him. We each drank. It burned its way into my stomach and for a moment I sat there trying to gather my wits.

'Angus, you look like death. What have you been up to?'

I was dog tired, dangerously so. I got up, went into the tiny bathroom and splashed cold water onto my face. As I raised my head I caught sight of myself in the mirror.

Monty hadn't been exaggerating. And my arm ached like hell. I didn't want to even look at it. I went back in and told them what had happened: how we'd got Zoe off, how they'd murdered Ah Sun. I didn't mention what I'd found in the bosun's store.

'You were shot?' Watanabe asked. 'You're bleeding through your shirt. Here, let me see.' Second officers commonly serve as the ship's medical officer and are trained for that role. I let him look. He bathed it with water from the sink, first easing off the fabric from my shirt which had stuck to my arm, then washing the wound which had swollen up around both the entry and exit holes. There was no antiseptic in the cabin so he poured some of his whisky into it and made an improvised bandage from Monty's pillowcase. I winced as the alcohol burned down through the wound.

'So what's going on, Monty?' I asked, conscious of the urgency of our situation.

'We're in a fine old pickle I can tell you.' This much I already knew. 'These bastards! I never thought it would come to this.'

'Come to what, Monty?' He had failed to impress me so far and as of this moment I wasn't sure I could trust him. But I needed to hear his side of the story.

'I swear they're mad. They only want to take over the whole bloody world you know.'

'And how are they going to do that?'

It was as if he hadn't heard me. 'If I'd had any idea

what they were planning I wouldn't have gone near this lot with a barge pole, believe me, Angus.' He looked at me but I still wasn't sure whether he was being genuine or not.

'Tell me what they're planning, Monty. And make it quick.'

He gave me a sly look. 'You know plenty don't you. You're not just a P&I man are you, Angus. Otherwise you would never have come this far.' He held up his hand. 'Alright. I don't expect you to answer that.'

'Monty, for God's sake get to the point will you? We haven't got all night. How come you're sitting here sounding remorseful? Is this all a charade?'

'Christ no!'

'Tell me then.'

'Look. The last time I saw you I really did think this was all just about Dark Ocean and me, my ship, and the cargo. Believe me, they played down all this nonsense about reviving Japanese imperialism. There were long diatribes from Nakamura about how other right-wing nationalist groups were full of hot air, but not theirs; that the proceeds from any cargo we recovered would be split and their share would be used to fund their domestic activities - line their own pockets I assumed. But nothing about recreating a bloody co-prosperity sphere. That was never mentioned.'

He was obfuscating, to put it kindly. 'That's not the way it came across to me, Monty. Nakamura seemed deadly serious about their aims. And what about the Foundation of Oriental and Asian Studies? Isn't that just a front for another bunch of power-crazed psychos like Dark Ocean? I've encountered these types before. Believe me, they walk among us. Don't tell me you didn't know what the two groups were plotting between them.'

'Listen, to me they seemed just like you say, a bunch of power-crazed maniacs. I thought I could just use them as leverage to get what is rightfully mine. There's no way I could resource a salvage operation like this myself and the CMM weren't about to help were they.'

'So what changed your mind?'

'Alright, I won't deny I was in league with them. If they wanted to get control of a few owners, traders, charterers, then good for them. They promised me a slice of the action too. I saw a chance to put Sinclair Buchan on the map again, like it was in my father's day. Up there with the Swires and Jardines: a regional player.'

'But?'

'But, I didn't reckon on people getting hurt. I don't mean just Alastair Marshall and the girl they kidnapped. God knows that's bad enough, but the chemical weapon they've got for Christ's sake! I hadn't reckoned on that. It's here on board you know, this VX nerve agent.'

'I know it is, Monty. I've just been locked up with it in the bosun's store for hours while this old bucket pounded her way through the storm. For all I know the stuff could be leaking out as we speak. Do you know how it's contained? It was in crates with VX stamped all over them but I wasn't about to start ripping them open.'

'Apparently it's ready to be weaponised. And they've got the launchers stowed in the hold.'

'So what's their plan? Do they have targets in mind?'

Monty drained his whisky but said nothing, just stared down into his empty glass.

'Well?'

'Hong Kong,' he mumbled, then said it again louder in case we hadn't heard him the first time.

'They're going to launch VX missiles at Hong Kong,' I said, 'from this ship?'

'It's a threat but they mean it. They will do it if anyone tries to stop them from salvaging the *Lady Monteith's* cargo, or from any of their other aims.'

I was having difficulty processing this. Hong Kong's population, all seven million, was crammed into little more than four hundred square miles. It was close to being the most densely populated place on the planet. If what I'd heard about VX was true, they could wipe out hundreds of thousands, or more.

Monty carried on. 'If China, UK, the US ... if anyone stands in the way of their plan, they'll launch an attack. China's the main threat. They know China wants total control of the South China Sea. If China gets serious, militarily I mean, then their plans are jeopardised. But it's not just China. They'll have the whole world and its navies ranged against them. But what they're banking on is indifference, and procrastination. They don't want a military showdown with China or anyone else. They want to control the trade.

What was it Raleigh said?'

'For whosoever commands the sea commands the trade; whosoever commands the trade of the world commands the riches of the world, and consequently the world itself.'

'Yes. That's right.' He seemed put out that I'd pre-empted him. Alastair Marshall had quoted it so me not so long ago and it and it had stuck in my mind.

'How many launchers are there? And where are they? You say in the hold?'

'They'll deliver the stuff by UAV: drones. They've got a dozen of them stowed down there.' He looked utterly defeated, increasingly aware now of the part he'd played in all this and the peril he'd brought upon his own city.

'We've got to stop them, Monty. Any idea what size these drones are? And how the VX would be dispersed?'

'Japan has led the way in using unmanned aircraft to spray crops,' Watanabe interjected. 'For many decades we've used them to disperse pesticides on our rice fields. They say one in three bowls of rice consumed by Japanese households has been air-sprayed with agricultural chemicals using drones.'

'You're a mine of information, Watanabe-san, but the ones on board haven't been armed yet, have they?'

'Not yet,' said Monty. 'The VX is up in the bosun's store where you saw it. It's already stored in aluminium canisters. They just need fitting to the drones. They've got two technicians on board to handle it.'

'We need to disable the drones then.'

'If they caught me meddling they'd kill me in a flash, don't you see?'

'I'd have thought some things are worth taking a risk for, Monty.' I had to restore his confidence, and his sense of moral duty in case he had any. 'We're together in this. Remember Hong Kong's your town. It was mine too. And your own daughter is there. Are we going to let a catastrophe like this happen while we sit around drinking your Scotch?'

That hit home, but he was still unsure. 'You're right. Of course you are. But what to do?'

'Who's on board now? Besides the crew, I mean.'

'I don't know their names but there are eight of them: four from Dark Ocean, and four Europeans from FOAS who joined in Hong Kong.'

'Right,' I said without a lot of forethought. 'Here's what we're going to do.'

CHAPTER 30

The sea had calmed a little. Waves were no longer washing over the deck, although the ship was still rolling heavily in the swell left by the storm. I wasn't sure whether it had passed or whether we were in the eye and it would suddenly return, blowing from another direction with greater force. I looked out over the portside but could see no sign of the Marines or whoever it was that the IMTF was sending. I just hoped they were lurking out there ready to pick us up when we had to jump for it.

A steel door led into a small housing which gave access to the hold. Watanabe opened it. He was familiar with every inch of the ship and I was glad to have him with us. We had convinced ourselves that the helmsman and officer of the watch on the bridge would be too preoccupied with handling the vessel in the heavy weather to be looking down on the deck but we still moved with caution. A hold ladder was welded to the bulkhead. We descended into the darkness, encumbered by the heavy wrench I'd retrieved and the torch Monty had provided, pausing to listen for any sound other than the sea and the ship herself as she moved uneasily in the swell. We'd left Monty in hiding above us behind the access hatch with orders to alert us if he saw anyone approaching.

The *Toyama Maru* was not a cargo ship and the hold was small by comparison, perhaps thirty feet in length by twenty wide. And counting the rungs of the ladder I guessed it to be as deep as it was wide.

We reached the bottom and waited there listening. Then I switched on the torch and shone it around the hold space. At the forward end were twelve wooden crates lashed down to pad-eyes set into the deck. We moved forward and set about removing the lashings. Then I broke open the first crate and shone the torch down onto the drone. It crouched there like a giant, pregnant spider, its black rotor arms folded inwards, the white plastic tank strangely suggestive of a spider's egg sack. For a moment I pictured these things flying in convoy over the high-rise towers of Hong Kong's Central district, their lethal spray raining down on office workers and shoppers, schoolchildren and pensioners: a scene from some apocalyptic movie.

The eight rotor arms of each drone were made from thick carbon-fibre tubing at the end of which were the nozzles and propellers. I used the wrench to twist each propeller out of shape, then for good measure smashed it down heavily onto the electric motor, cracking its casing open. And to make quite sure, I used a marlinspike I'd lifted from the bosun's store to puncture the plastic of the drone's tank.

Meanwhile Watanabe was opening up the other crates. It was a laborious task and took the best part of an hour, but when finished we were both satisfied they were beyond repair.

When we emerged back on deck Monty was where we'd left him, well hidden from view.

'Did you do it?' he asked.

'All of them. They won't be flying anywhere, with or without the VX on board. No-one come out on deck?'

'All quiet.' The ship was almost hove to now with her head to the wind. I could make out lights away to the north east.

'If those lights are from Jiapeng Liedao then we've reached the coordinates for the wreck site,' I said.

'We could be right above her then,' said Monty wistfully.

'It's time we were gone, Monty. The Marines are waiting.'

'I'm not going. You go, Angus. I'm staying.'

'What? You've got to get off this thing, Monty. Why the hell would you want to stay?'

'I have to. Don't you see? You've destroyed the threat of delivering the VX by drone but they could still sail into Hong Kong and release it by other means.'

'Which would be suicidal for them too.'

'No. They have technicians who could still rig up some way of detonating the canisters remotely, or by a timing device. It would give them time to get away. It's a risk we can't afford.'

This was a change in Monty's attitude. Was it his determination to protect Susanna that had suddenly endowed him with courage? Was he seeking redemption for his greedy selfishness?

'Okay,' I said, 'but how are you going to stop them? Leave it to the military now, Monty. They may decide to disable the ship.'

'Sink her?'

'Exactly. Remember, the VX attack might only be a threat, but a threat is worthless unless you're prepared to carry it out. Those controlling the response on our side know they will have to remove the threat once and for all, however improbable its implementation might seem. See reason for God's sake.'

He didn't need further persuasion. Watanabe went off to get three life jackets from the passageway. We pulled them on and headed over to the vessel's portside. I was about to start the signalling sequence when Watanabe whispered hoarsely. 'Look!' He pointed back to the passageway from where he'd just come. Heading towards us was one of the heavies: the one who Ah Sun had immobilised earlier. He was no more than thirty feet away and lumbering along struggling to keep his balance, but with gun raised. He'd seen us and fired in our direction., the shot going wild. It was almost impossible to take a measured aim with the ship rolling like this.

I pulled the gun I'd taken from the other gorilla out from my waistband and fired off four or five rounds in quick succession. He leapt back into the cover of the passageway.

I handed the torch to Watanabe. 'Start signalling: SOS.'

More gunfire was coming from the passageway now, the aim more careful, and more accurate. Crouching, I ran back towards where the shooting was coming from. At the edge of the hatch I stopped, inserted a fresh clip and, still well covered by the coaming and with a better view of the passageway which was lit, started firing again. He was silhouetted – an easy target. Almost immediately I heard a cry and the firing ceased. Cautiously I emerged from the coaming to get a better view. He lay there, motionless. I went over to him. His eyes stared up into the night.

I ran back to where Monty and Watanabe were waiting. Watanabe was still flashing Monty's torch through the curtain of rain out over the dark waters. The noise of the gunfire would have alerted others on board, I was sure.

'We'll have to just jump for it,' I said.

But as I spoke Watanbe yelled: 'Look!' We were getting an answering signal.

The ship was rolling thirty degrees or more and jumping was going to be risky even in calm conditions. Besides the weather we had the ship's propeller to contend with. She was barely making headway, in effect hove to against the wind, but it would still be rotating. We would need to get well clear or risk being caught by it. And Monty was getting nervous again.

Our minds were made up when Watanabe noticed one of the accommodation doors opening. 'Two men coming!' he yelled. 'We must go.'

We climbed over the ship's rail and jumped.

CHAPTER 31

We'd waited until the *Toyama Maru* was listing over to port in the swell before we leapt, but when we hit the water a rolling wave slammed us back against the ship's side. Pushing off we struggled to swim away from her but again were knocked back onto the steel wall of the hull, further aft now towards the lethal threat of the ship's churning propeller.

Watanabe was young and fit but I worried about Monty who was struggling desperately in the maelstrom. Eventually, by kicking against the hull then swimming with one arm while linking to Monty's with the other, we dragged him clear and into open water. I watched the ship move away into the night as we were tossed around in her wake. We'd been just a few feet from the propeller.

The open water was almost a relief, though one minute we were deep in the trough of a wave with seething grey water towering above us, the next, lifted twenty feet or more to the crest. This roller-coaster ride went on for what seemed an eternity And Monty was virtually unconscious. What chance would our rescuers have of spotting us in these conditions? The lifejackets were equipped with whistles and lights. The lights had automatically activated when we entered the water, but this was a mixed blessing: they could attract the attention of those on the ship as well as our rescuers. As if to confirm my fears there was a sudden burst of gunfire from the *Toyama Maru*. With the lifejackets' lights flashing we were sitting ducks and it would only take a lucky volley to get one or more of us. But the distance between us and the ship was widening fast and there was too much motion both on the ship's deck and in the water for the firing to be accurate.

I knew we couldn't hold onto Monty indefinitely while struggling to save ourselves. Thank God Watanabe was with us, but we were both near the end of our endurance by the time the searchlight spotted us. We'd seen its beam sweeping across the sea for minutes. It would appear then vanish only to reappear as our rescuers scanned the turbulent waters. Whether it was the high-pitched whistles or the flashing lights of the lifejackets that saved us I don't know but suddenly hands were reaching down to grab us.

We were hauled aboard a long RIB-like boat manned, to my surprise, by four burly Japanese Marines. We lay there in turn gasping for breath and throwing up seawater. Watanabe was the first to react bursting into a torrent of Japanese which turned into a high-speed dialogue with the crew.

Meanwhile, Monty lay collapsed in the bottom of the boat as we sped away and at Watanabe's behest, one of the crew bent over to attend to him. Between us, besides being battered against the ship's hull, we'd swallowed several gallons of the South China Sea and in Monty's case the experience had left him so exhausted I worried whether they could bring him round. But as he was propped against the rubber side wall of the boat he began vomiting up the salty water and looking around him trying to make sense of what was happening.

'Where are we going?' I yelled to Watanabe above the roar of the engines.

'To their ship. Japanese Navy destroyer.'

I grabbed Monty's shoulder. 'You okay?'

'I'm okay,' he croaked managing a weak grin.

We'd escaped and we'd been rescued. I'd never felt so glad to leave a ship. I looked back at her dark silhouette barely visible now as she disappeared into the spray thrown up in our wake. Ahead of us dawn was dragging itself up, a thin grey band of light on the horizon only slightly paler than the sea below it and the leaden cloud above.

'Are they taking us to their mother ship?' Monty shouted making it sound like an alien abduction.

'Japanese Navy Special Boarding Unit,' explained Watanabe. Like your SBS, or US SEALS.'

We were silent after that, clinging on as the coxswain guided the craft expertly keeping the weather on the port bow so we crossed the peak of each wave at the right angle. As we picked up speed we were flying from crest to crest, the deep V-hull slicing through the waves.

It was half an hour or more before the lights of the naval vessel appeared ahead of us. We drew up deftly beneath one of the ship's access ports. A pilot ladder was lowered and, while Watanabe and myself clambered up and into the bowels of the ship, Monty was hoisted up on a stretcher.

We were met by two officers who escorted us to the sick bay. We showered and were then fussed over by a young medical officer who prescribed a mild sedative for Monty and cleaned and dressed my arm. The bullet had missed the humerus by a couple of inches. Tracksuits were dispensed and we were ushered up to the wardroom where the ship's commanding officer, Captain Harada, and two of his subordinate officers, introduced themselves in English. We were aboard a Hyūga-class destroyer as guests of the Japan Maritime Self-Defense Force.

As we talked there was a discreet knock on the wardroom door and a female officer entered. Bowing then stepping to one side, she made way for the new visitors: Claire Scott followed by Ishikawa from the PSIA.

When we'd finished with the pleasantries, which added a surreal quality to the occasion, we sat down round the wardroom table. Food arrived. To my relief there were burgers and chips, and Coke. Junk food would do just fine.

Claire spoke across the table. 'Angus, a sitrep would be helpful.'

I finished my Coke and leaned back feeling an immense weariness settle over me. 'Monty here tells me there are eight of them on board,' I said. 'Four from Dark Ocean - *Genyosha* - and four from the FOAS.

'The FOAS crowd were in Hong Kong for a meeting and to witness the salvage operation,' Monty supplemented.

'Monty discovered that they'd acquired twelve UAV crop sprayers. Two technicians were on board ready to fit the VX canisters to them. We destroyed the drones but the VX is still there. So are the technicians. That's about it.'

Claire turned to Ishikawa for his response.

'Thank you. We did not know of their plan to use UAVs. You have degraded their ability to launch an aerial attack. However, as I think you are saying, Angus-san, with the VX still on board they could still use the ship herself as the delivery weapon and our planning has been based on that assumption.' He looked across at Captain Harada as he spoke.

'Yes,' said Captain Harada, addressing Ishikawa, 'it is possible, if they do intend to attack Hong Kong.'

'Is what possible?' I asked.

Ishikawa replied: 'We have clearance to launch a strike on the *Toyama Maru* if we, the people sitting at this table, believe it is necessary. This authority comes as a result of direct talks between our Prime Minister and the President of the People's Republic of China. You will understand that their dialogue has great geopolitical significance. They are in complete accord on this matter.'

'So are you saying there is the prospect of rapprochement between the two countries provided this operation succeeds?'

'Exactly.'

Monty spoke. 'I can't believe the Chinese authorities have agreed to you waging a war in their waters.'

'As I have said, the Chinese are collaborating fully with us in this operation,' Ishikawa reiterated. 'They have no wish to see Japanese terrorists run riot in their territory. We are sharing all related intelligence with them.

'Now, all of you I think will agree that the correct course of action is to remove the threat posed by the VX nerve agent on board the *Toyama Maru*.'

I spoke to Ishikawa again. 'What would be the effect on the VX if you attack the ship? Would it still pose a threat?'

'We have discussed this scenario with The Japanese Defence Ministry's experts, and Ms Scott has discussed it with the people at Porton Down. If the ship is destroyed by the use of explosives and sunk, then there is no threat from the VX. The Americans disposed of their Okinawa nerve agent stockpiles at Johnston Atoll by incinerating them. I understand from Captain Harada that his weaponry is more than capable of achieving this result – of incinerating the ship and the VX simultaneously.'

'My ship is equipped with Type 90 SSM-1B guided missiles. Very suitable for this task,' added Captain Harada, his manner calm.

'What about the crew?' asked Watanabe.

Ishikawa sucked his teeth. 'Cannot be helped I'm afraid, Watanabe-san.'

There was silence as we all pondered the forthcoming fate of the ship's largely innocent crew.

'Can we warn them?' Watanabe asked quietly. 'They are seafarers, many of them are my friends. They had no knowledge of *Genyosha's* involvement when they signed on.'

'Too dangerous,' Ishikawa spoke emphatically. 'Lady, gentlemen, we have the authority to destroy the *Toyama Maru*. Captain, please prepare. I will give you final confirmation shortly.'

'*Hai!*' Captain Harada stood up and bowed. 'Straight away.' And with that he left.

Claire stood and walked over to the coffee machine. 'They've been discussing it all night. We were just waiting to get you off safely.'

'So it's a fait accompli,' I said.

'A consensus.'

'Yes, but she's sitting right on top of the wreck site – my wreck!' Monty exclaimed.

'Buchan-san,' said Ishikawa, 'it is my belief that once they see that their drones are destroyed and their radar shows a Japanese warship in their vicinity, they will make their move towards Hong Kong and away from the wreck site. Remember, they are fanatics. They will not surrender. It is not in accordance with their code of honour.'

'But we can't be sure they'll release the stuff can we?'

'It doesn't matter,' I said. 'Once they're in Hong Kong harbour the threat is sufficient in itself. It's a ticking bomb they can use to bargain with.'

At which point an officer burst into the room. After a hasty salute he spoke rapidly to Ishikawa who spoke to us in English.

'The *Toyama Maru* is underway,' Ishikawa said getting up from his chair. 'We must act now.'

***

We watched from the destroyer's Combat Information Centre. The *Toyama Maru* was eleven miles to our north and heading in that direction back towards Hong Kong as we'd predicted. We watched her on the radar screens for a minute or two. 'She is making eighteen knots,' said Captain Harada. 'Very fast for that vessel: flank speed I expect.'

We all knew what would happen next but that didn't detract from the spectacle. Captain Harada barked out his order which was repeated by another officer. There were a few seconds silence before the missiles shot from their vertical launching cells with a series of great whooshing sounds audible even from where we were gathered. A trail of flame and white smoke was left in their wake as they took off seeking their target, their trajectories no more than a hundred feet above the surface of the sea. The acceleration was almost inconceivable. By the time they reached the *Toyama Maru* they would be travelling at Mach 4 – over 3,000 miles an hour.

The missiles vanished over the horizon and barely a second later, struck their target. We saw the light first, a white flash that bleached the dark sky spreading out horizontally. Then, as smoke mushroomed up into the sky, the sound of the explosions reached us. There was no discernible blast wave at this distance and the whole event lasted no more than a minute from beginning to end. It was only after I watched it all in slow motion on the ship's video monitors later that I could separate the sequence of events and make out each distinct element of the strike.

There was total silence as we continued to stare out at the plume of smoke marking the *Toyama Maru's* last position.

Monty was the first to speak. 'Bloody hell!'

CHAPTER 32

Monty, Claire and I were flown to Hong Kong in one of the ship's H-60 helicopters later that night, exhausted and a little dazed.

'The salvage op next?' Monty asked as we alighted at the Shun Tak Heliport.

'We'll need assurance that the marine environment around the wreck site has not been contaminated,' Claire said. 'The Hong Kong government will want to do that anyway. But from what we heard from the Porton Down people, and based on the Americans' Johnston Atoll disposal programme, the fact the VX was incinerated by the explosion should ensure no contamination from that source. Inevitably though there will have been damage to the marine environment, temporary we hope.'

She was right. In the days that followed the Chinese and Japanese sent their own teams in to assist the local authorities. Four days later the Hong Kong government released a statement saying a privately-owned vessel had suffered a catastrophic explosion five miles south of Lamma

Island resulting in her total loss. The Hong Kong Marine Department declared an exclusion zone around the area with an accompanying Notice to Mariners. On the day following these statements they approved the commencement of salvage operations at the *Lady Monteith* site, twelve miles south from where the *Toyama Maru* had gone down.

We met in Sinclair Buchan's offices: Monty, Susanna, Claire and myself. I tried to read the mood between Susanna and her father. They'd had time to discuss the ramifications of what had happened including Monty's vanishing act. Superficially at least. Back on his home turf, Monty had returned to his former urbane self, while Susanna was looking concerned.

We were discussing the Sino-Japanese collaboration in the survey and analysis study around the exclusion zone.

'Don't forget,' said Claire. 'China and Japan have been working together to destroy World War Two chemical weapons for years now so there's plenty of precedent. Between them they know what they're doing.'

'But I have read that VX can persist for long periods in ocean waters,' Susanna countered.

'Yes, that's believed to be true, but the power of the explosion would have incinerated it. Anyway, the consensus is, having checked the numbering on the crate you memorised, Angus, that the VX was old stock dating back at least fifty years, which could well have degraded to the point of becoming harmless. And remember, they took two hundred seawater samples from the exclusion zone, which includes the *Lady Monteith* site, and they were all clear.'

'Ergo,' concluded Monty, 'the salvage can go ahead.'

And that is what happened.

Monty invited us both to dinner that night but Claire declined. She'd told me she had something important to discuss with me before she returned to Scotland so the two of us dined at her hotel.

'The CMM would like you to stay on and attend the salvage operation. Can you do that?' she asked sipping her Martini.

'Sure, it's what I'd figured.' We were having a pre-dinner drink in the Pacific Bar of the Conrad overlooking the harbour. Claire was wearing a simple black dress.

'You look sexy in that,' I said.

'My little black dress? Every girl should have one.'

I stretched back in my chair and looked out across the garish office blocks to the harbour. I was feeling relaxed.

'There's something else,' she said, serious now. 'Amber wants you to come on board, permanently. She says we can hardly cope, particularly now Alastair is no longer with us.'

'I don't know,' I said, taken off guard. 'I'm getting too old for all this action-man stuff.'

'No-one could have anticipated how this could have turned out. And you do tend to bring it on yourself don't you: wading in with all guns blazing.'

'I didn't have much choice, did I? I wasn't going to leave Zoe in the hands of those maniacs.'

'Of course, and you sure pulled it off this time. But

we're not talking about the 007 escapades. You could do so much on the investigation side, Angus. We don't have anyone with your talents, your feel for it. You're a maverick, we know that. Alastair was the same. We don't have a problem with that.'

'Give me time to think about it.'

'Good. I'll tell Amber you're seriously considering it. Now, there's something else.'

'Yes?'

'There's something I want you to do tomorrow, before I leave.'

'And what's that?'

'You've never been to the site have you? In the Mid-Levels.'

Knowing what was coming I reached for my Martini and emptied the glass. Then I signalled the barman for another round. 'No.'

'I want you to come with me. Will you?'

'I don't know why you think that might be a good idea, Claire.'

'Because you've never really confronted your demons have you? I know it's hard but I really believe you'd be better for it. It'll bring relief, closure.'

'I doubt that. Listen, I've been through all this a thousand times in my head. Going up there isn't going to change a thing. What would be the point? It would just open old wounds.'

'Wounds that have never healed, Angus. I've spoken

to our psychologists. They agree. They did a vetting report on you.'

'What? You've had your shrinks nosing into my personal history? That's a bloody liberty isn't it?'

'You shouldn't be surprised. It's normal procedure. Anyway, your strengths outweighed any reservations they may have had. But anyone who went through what you did, as a child, is bound to carry it around with them. We all have our personal baggage.'

'Exactly!' I said angrily. 'That's what it is: my personal baggage. We all have our demons.'

'All I'm asking is we go up there in the morning, walk along the road, look around and reflect. There's little sign of it now, just where the hillside was stabilised and replanted. Pause and reflect.'

'I'd remember things, Claire. Things that are best left buried.'

'I know you would but I'm saying, and our shrinks agree, that it's best unburied. I know how sensitive this is for you. I wouldn't dream of raising it if I didn't think it would help. I want to help you, Angus. I can't bear the thought of you carrying those nightmare memories locked away inside your head for the rest of your life.'

We argued on about it but eventually, in a way only Claire could, she brought me round and I began to see the logic of her argument. Then we ate, we drank, we made love. Everything was perfect.

And in the morning we took a taxi up there to that

corner of the Mid-Levels on the northern slopes of the Peak where many years ago my world was literally turned upside down.

Minor mud slips had already been noticed. The road was blocked by falling earth and mud from a construction site, and several cracks had appeared in a retaining wall. Days later a slip occurred over the whole width of the road above ours. The surveyors noticed subsidence affecting several buildings and residents were urged to leave as a precaution. The following day it was still raining and the situation got worse. More cracks kept appearing in retaining walls, and more mud was falling down the hill. The road above us was cordoned off and nearby apartment blocks were evacuated. A large landslide was coming but no-one thought it would affect the road below.

But that evening it did. In less than ten seconds the mudslide cleared a path straight down the hill destroying houses and retaining walls on its way. As it reached our road it knocked our apartment block completely off its foundations. In less than a minute, sixty-seven people were killed. The final toll was eighty-seven.

The rescue operation was sporadic, hampered by the torrential rain and broken transport links. More landslips occurred and emergency personnel were pulled back. Eventually, after two days and along with a few other survivors, I was rescued.

I'd read dozens of accounts of it over the years, particularly in my teenage years. But I'd never been back.

We paid off the taxi and walked along the road. It was raining. A mist hung over the hill wrapping itself round the upper floors of the tower blocks, most of which had been built since the accident and were twice as high as the one that had collapsed.

'It must have been a day like this,' I said. Claire linked her arm in mine as we walked. A Filipina maid walked past us pushing a buggy with a small child in it. A reluctant young boy dragged along behind her. He was carrying a school bag. The two children were Europeans. The maid was wearing a cheap waterproof, jeans and flip-flops.

We reached the point where the slope had been stabilised. Trees covered the site now. They had been planted in neat rows, their purpose obvious.

We stopped there. I looked back and saw the maid with her two charges entering a block of flats down the road. The boy looked back towards us. I waved at him. 'Ghosts,' I said.

She gripped my arm. 'No, Angus. Just people, like you and me.'

***

I went out to the airport with her that night. We sat having a drink in the VIP lounge to which she'd magically arranged access for me. She was quieter than usual, withdrawn. Finally she turned to me. 'I need you, Angus. I don't mean just professionally.' Her eyes were full. I held her hand, but before I could say what I wanted to say they were calling her flight and we left the lounge. I took her in my arms and we hugged tightly for a long time. Then she broke away, hitched her carry-on bag onto her shoulder and headed off. She didn't look back.

Claire and I would always be close but I didn't often express my true feelings to her. Had I ever? I just assumed she knew. We both lived separate lives and perhaps that's what kept our love for one another so alive, so urgent. Did she want our relationship to become permanent, for us to live together? I didn't think so. We were both resolutely in-dependent, but then she'd never said she needed me before. Whatever the answer, I resolved to talk to her about it.

***

But there was another matter that I had chosen not to raise with her. And that was the question of who had betrayed us?

Whoever had revealed the wreck coordinates to Dark Ocean had either done so by accident, under duress, or as a deliberate act. I was convinced it was the latter. My intuition told me so.

Of itself it might not have seemed so serious since, in the grand scheme of things, the salvaging of the golden Buddha from the wreck of the *Lady Monteith* was not criti-cal to the success of the Dark Ocean/FOAS cabal's overall plans. But that was not the point. The point was that whoever had betrayed us, if they hadn't been aboard the *Toyama Maru*, was still out there.

My worry was that we were dealing with a Hydra: that we had decapitated the so-called Revival in a previous case which had led to the loss of the *Astro Maria* and her crew, and had nearly cost us, Claire and myself, our lives; and that now the *Hydra* had grown more heads in the shape of Dark Ocean and FOAS. Had we decapitated them only to see yet more appear?

CHAPTER 33

The weather had settled and only a gentle swell disturbed the seas around the wreck site. And the sun had finally made a tentative appearance, struggling to shine through the dense cloud cover left over from the storm.

The salvage operation had been replanned and was now being run by a Japanese firm with a China Coast Guard vessel, much like the one that had chased me across Mirs Bay, attending as observers. Monty chose to remain on site throughout, taking up residence on the salvors' support vessel. Along with Susanna and Nya Wang, I hitched a lift out from Hong Kong every morning on the agent's launch. By the third day, using side-scan sonar and an array of ROVs, they had found the wreck of the *Lady Monteith*. Monty was beside himself. He went around hugging everyone he could get hold of. His voice breaking, he exclaimed, 'I've waited so long for this. Now it's here and I can't believe it.'

'They've still got to locate the cargo.'

'Yes, yes. They'll find it, don't you worry.'

'Remember too, Monty, your ship is a designated war

grave under the definition of the Military Remains Act.'

'Claire told me that had all been dealt with.'

'Yes, the MoD has declared it a controlled site. You can dive onto it, but the rule to divers is look don't touch.'

'Yes but that applies to the skeletons right? Not the cargo.'

'You're right, Monty,' I said. 'Just don't forget that over two hundred POWs drowned when your ship went down and they're still down there. They deserve some respect.'

'You're absolutely right, old boy. Don't think I've forgotten that.'

On the fifth day they found the Buddha. It had fallen away from the ship as she'd turned turtle. The crate that had protected it during its transit from the mountains of Yunnan had long since rotted away. And its appearance from the video footage taken by one of the ROVs, showed just a dark form encrusted with barnacles and other forms of marine life that had taken up residence. But the size was right. There was no doubting it was Nya Wang's precious statue.

On examining the footage, the team elected to use underwater air-lift parachute bags to raise it. Calculations were made on the assumption the Buddha was solid gold. Nya Wang had said it weighted nearly six tons and the salvors' calculations confirmed this. It was therefore decided that eight-ton capacity bags should be deployed. These were air-freighted in from Japan and arrived the following day.

I asked the Japanese salvage master about the operation. These men were at the top of their game. My previous encounters had mostly been with Dutch salvage teams but I recognised the same qualities in this man, chief amongst which was an immunity from stress given the extreme sea conditions they so often encountered in their work. No one in my business would disagree that it was the most dangerous sector of the maritime industry to be working in.

As Salvage Master, Captain Fukuda was responsible for planning the operation while protecting his men against the many perils they faced. Salvage teams were expert in matters of naval architecture as well as chalking up years of seagoing experience. Besides a cool temperament, there was a need for adaptability and inventiveness for things were rarely predictable in a salvage operation. For these reasons I had respect for Captain Fukuda.

'Force required to lift submerged object from bottom can depends on two things,' he explained. 'Weight of object minus buoyancy of displacement, we call this apparent weight. Then breakout forces due to embedment in bottom, in the mud. This can be nothing, or sometimes major part of load. We see. When Buddha breaks free of bottom, only apparent weight remains. Then must manage decrease of resistance to lifting force. Understand?'

Four divers went down to attach the lift bags to the Buddha which had settled deep into the silty sea floor. Underwater blowers were used to create a pit surrounding the statue. Finally on the seventh day the lift bags were attached and the controlled ascent of the Buddha began. We were watching an array of video monitors in the control room.

The breakout force Fukuda had mentioned was considerable. The divers had swum well clear. As the air-lift bags did their job the Buddha suddenly sprung free, released from the mud which swirled around it.

Now it rose from the mud cloud, eerily yet with a serenity, the bright orange air-lift bags buoying it upwards into clearer water. As it approached the surface the load was transferred to the crane of a flat-top barge waiting to take its precious cargo on board.

We watched as it broke the surface. On the video feed we had seen the four divers swimming around it serving as reference points and giving us an idea of its size. Now we went out on deck and only as it was swung up into the air a few feet from where we were watching, did we see the full scale of the thing. Although seated in the lotus position it measured over fifteen feet from top to bottom.

Beneath the marine growth, the statue was covered with what looked like plaster or stucco, which had been painted blue at some point long ago and inlaid with small pieces of coloured glass. But much of the plaster had crumbled away revealing the gold shining brightly beneath.

It took another hour to get it safely loaded into the right position on the deck of the barge and temporarily lashed to keep it from shifting or toppling back over the side.

Only now did the impact of what we were looking at strike us. And the mess of broken stucco, coloured glass, barnacles and weed that covered it made the thing all the more awesome.

Nya Wang was as close to excited as I'd seen him. 'This is a truly important moment,' he said. But he didn't seem quite able to comprehend that finally it was actually standing, or sitting, there before him. 'May I go to it?'

Captain Fukuda assigned one of his crew to accompany him onto the barge which was tied up alongside the salvage tug. We watched as he walked around it reverentially touching the patches of gold where the stucco had worn away. Then he stood silently before it for several minutes. When he returned he asked Fukuda if it could be covered.

'We have heavy-duty tarps, dunnage too. We will secure your Buddha for the voyage, do not worry, Nya Wang. It will be safe.'

Nya Wang turned to Susanna and Monty. 'Our Buddha will always be yours too. We will return it now to our monastery, but you must know it is shared.'

I looked at Monty wondering how he felt about it all. But it was Susanna who spoke. 'Nya Wang, my father and I both know this. We hope one day to visit you in Ganlanba, if that would be possible?'

'You are all welcome. Angus, you particularly are welcome. I thank you most warmly. Without you, we would not be standing here now.'

And Ah Sun, I thought, and Alastair, Ronnie and Zoe.

The following day the divers resumed their search of the wreck, this time entering the holds in case there was anything else of value. They found nothing. They stayed clear of number two hold which was where the POWs had been imprisoned. There was enough grisly evidence of their fate lying around the wreck in the form of skulls, bones and even a few skeletons still intact after all this time.

The tug and barge carrying Nya Wang's Buddha left the wreck site under escort of the China Coast Guard cutter bound for the southern port of Beihai where it would be transferred to a low-loader. Nya Wang would rendezvous with it there and accompany it on the long road journey westwards to Ganlanba.

Meanwhile, in Hong Kong he was being feted as a national hero, albeit a reluctant one. The destruction of the *Toyama Maru* had received huge local media attention; the recovery of the gold Buddha even more. Not only this but the collaboration between Japan's PSIA, China's PLA Navy Intelligence, the Japanese Navy and the China Coast Guard, was being heralded as a breakthrough in diplomatic relations. The South China Morning Post was calling it Buddha diplomacy.

At the invitation of Jardines, Monty, Susanna and I joined Nya Wang and his small entourage of monks, to fire the Noonday Gun on the waterfront at Causeway Bay. Jardines' uniformed guard rang a bell to signal the end of the forenoon watch. Then, looking awkward, Nya Wang pulled the lanyard and fired the gun. It provided a little light relief but he was impatient to get down to Beihai having now become preoccupied with the task of supervising the Buddha's return to his monastery. Four days after the tug and barge with their escort had sailed from Hong Kong they arrived in Beihai with their prized cargo.

'We owe you a great debt.'

'But you can repay it, Nya Wang.' I'd gone to the house in Kowloon Tong to wish him well before he caught his flight.

'Anything.'

'I'd like to take you up on your offer and visit your monastery.'

'You know you will always be welcome.'

'Not as an honoured guest but as a retreat.'

'Yes, a *vassa* we call it. You would meditate, practise a little Tai Chi perhaps?'

'No Kung Fu though. I'm too old for all that jumping around.'

'Yes. Our Kung Fu training is intense. It is for young men and those who have been studying for many years. We do not have a training programme for older men.'

'Tai Chi would suit me fine. But mostly I wish to experience your routines. Breathe your mountain air, a little Buddhist philosophy, and think about the future.'

'This we can certainly do,' he said. 'I personally will teach you. It will be an honour for me to do so.'

'First though I must return to Greece to see to my business, and to Zoe. I haven't thanked you for arranging her return.'

'Ah yes, the poor girl. When she came ashore from the sampan she was in a bad way, but a little better by the time she left Hong Kong. It will take time for her to recover.'

And so it was settled. On her return to Scotland, Claire had called to say the IMTF's file on the case had been closed. The CMM was closing its own file too. The cost of the salvage operation was being covered by the Japanese government and Monty Buchan had to accept that he wasn't going to get rich from the venture. But Monty was a changed man. He'd been lucky to come out of it with his life, never mind a windfall. Humility wasn't a trait I'd have associated him with but he'd accepted the outcome stoically. And he'd had the sense to step to one side by appointing Susanna as the firm's CEO.

I had dinner with her before I left. We talked about everything except the *Lady Monteith*. But we both knew the case was closed, as far as she was concerned at least. She had big plans for Sinclair Buchan's future: selling off some of the older bulkcarriers in the fleet, and a liner service between India, Southeast Asia and Japan.

'That's a well-trodden route,' I said.

'Show me a trade that isn't. I've been in talks with a Japanese carrier about a joint venture. I'm confident it will work. Just watch.'

'Well, good luck. By the way, Claire said not to worry about your P&I cover. All things being equal, CMM will be glad to renew with you next year.'

'Typical lawyer. Tell her that all things being equal, we'll be glad to accept.'

I booked my flights back to Athens. In Hong Kong I'd exorcised some of the ghosts from my past. I'd even grown to like the place. As the plane climbed heading northeast, I looked down from my window seat and realised we were passing over Mirs Bay. I could see Tung Ping Chau island. A couple of fishing boats were anchored there. It looked a peaceful spot.

But I wasn't thinking about an idyllic little island in Mirs Bay. I was thinking about who gave the wreck coordinates of the *Lady Monteith* wreck site to Nakamura and his gang.

CHAPTER 34

'Coffee, black,' Zoe announced, placing a mug on my desk. I worried about her. Her sense of fun was gone. I missed her insolence, her jibes, her self-confidence. Now she rarely smiled. I feared she was suffering from PTSD, just as I'd known Claire had suffered it after what had happened in Perama and on Alastair's island a year earlier. I'd broached the subject of therapy with Zoe but she'd rejected the idea out of hand. I'd talked to Claire about it and we'd agreed we should get Zoe over to Scotland. Claire had seen a psycho-therapist herself and she'd promised to get Zoe in to see the woman. It would also be an opportunity for her to meet the CMM people, and refocus on her career and her legal studies which had lapsed.

I blamed myself for what had happened to Zoe. I'd wake up in the night, my mind full of recriminations, and then the desire for revenge would creep into my mind. For me the case was far from closed, but there was more to it than just vengeance.

I watched her walk back across the reception area. She'd

lost weight for all the wrong reasons. She paused looking up at the wall. Then she turned and came back into my office.

'What happened to him?'

'Who?'

'Boris Kaliyagin.'

I hadn't heard that name for a while. She'd been looking up at the golden fleece that hung framed on the wall in the reception area. Boris Kaliyagin, an oligarch from Georgia, had sent it to me after he escaped, or was allowed to escape, following the showdown in Perama. From early times his people in the North Caucasus province of Svaneti had pegged out sheep's hides in the river beds. The water from the mountain streams was heavy with sediment which carried flecks of gold that clung to the fleece. It glistened beautifully and Zoe and I cherished this unusual gift. She'd worried that it would be stolen and had insisted that we had it insured.

Boris was an oligarch but he had a conscience, of sorts. He'd enriched himself by smuggling ethyl alcohol across the border into North Ossetia where it was turned into *cacha* vodka for the Russian black market, but he wanted to enrich his people too. Not just his native Svans but all Georgians. And that meant grabbing power, which I presumed was still work in progress. Despite his dubious business dealings, or perhaps because of them, he was now an elected Deputy in the Georgian parliament serving on various committees each of which gave him access to various influential foreign government officials, NGOs and quangos.

'Boris? I haven't heard anything recently, Zoe. Why?'

'I know you think there are still people out there,' she said. 'Remember, I found the list of passengers on the *Toyama Maru* when she came into Greek waters. When I was imprisoned on board in Hong Kong I heard things. You know as well as I do there are more than just the four FOAS people who came aboard there and were killed when they sunk the ship. Now you can't let it go can you. You worry about me but you come into the office every morning looking like, I don't know, not yourself. You haven't met any of our clients. No new cases. We can't go on like this, Angus, or the business will fail. Anyway, this FOAS. They're still there aren't they. Why doesn't your IMTF do something about them?'

'They say they are. It's a political matter they say.'

'What does that mean?'

'I don't know, Zoe. And I don't want you worrying about it.'

'Don't you think I want these people finished?' she suddenly shouted angrily. 'After what they did?'

'Of course.' I was beginning to realise that therapy for Zoe meant exacting revenge.

'I know you've always thought that there are people in your British government, your Foreign Office, your secret service, who are mixed up in these things. First they try and take over gold mines and countries that are broken. Now this, this co-prosperity thing. Don't you think there's a connection?'

'It's occurred to me,' I said. 'What, you think because Kaliyagin was involved the first time, with the Revival, that he might know something about FOAS?'

'Exactly!'

'It's worth a try. Can you track him down, Zoe? Start with Gelovani Trading. Remember that was the front company he used to charter Kyriakou's *Delfina*. Michael Kyriakou will help you.'

'Okay, she said. 'I'll find him.' And at last I saw a spark of her old resolve. I wasn't sure whether Kaliyagin could or would want to help but if it gave Zoe some sense of purpose, it could do no harm. She wanted justice but she wanted revenge too.

***

That night I called Claire.

'I told you, darling, the case is closed, at least as far as you and I are concerned. And how many times have I also told you that the IMTF operates on a need-to-know basis. They might well be pursuing this as we speak but they wouldn't feel it necessary to give you a running commentary, or me either for that matter.'

'Listen, Claire, someone leaked those coordinates to Dark Ocean and/or FOAS. The only people besides you and me who had them were Amber, Benedict Wood, Admiral Carvill and Tim Younger. One of them, willingly or under duress, disclosed them.'

'I think you know who the most likely candidate is don't you?'

'I know who you think it is: Younger, right?'

'Yes, of course.'

'Well, I'm not so sure.'

'Are you looking for a mole, Angus? A traitor within our own camp? You've been reading too many spy stories, my love. They got to Younger after you'd seen him. They must have followed you up to Pitlochry and you never knew it.'

'Thanks for that. By the way, did you ever learn who was behind FOAS? I mean who founded it?'

'Now you're asking me things you don't need to know.'

'But you're going to tell me anyway.'

'It's a man called Helmut Gertch. He's a Swiss national. We've no reason to believe he had anything to do with the Dark Ocean business. That was a rogue faction. Anyway, Gertch might have founded FOAS but he's retired now. And that is all you're getting out of me because that's all I know. They'd shoot me if they knew I was still talking to you about the case.'

I left it at that. I'd been stood down and I didn't want Claire getting flak for betraying confidences. I spent the next hour searching online for anything about Helmut Gertch. There was nothing. The man was a spectre.

CHAPTER 35

'He's on line two,' Zoe called through.

'Got it.' I picked up the phone. 'Boris?'

'Ah, I recognise that voice. How are you my friend and to what do I owe this honour?' Boris Kaliyagin's English was remarkably good. He was a dapper man, an elegant dresser who sported a neat goatee beard. The first time I'd met him he was wearing an expensive grey overcoat with a black fur collar, the coat draped casually over his shoulders. The encounter took place in the tawdry outskirts of Tbilisi. He was surrounded by a gang of his henchmen all wearing dark glasses and black leather jackets. The contrast was palpable and the effect menacing, as was intended.

'We were just looking at that fleece you sent, Boris. It hangs on the wall of the office here.'

'Yes, and I hope it brings you good fortune. Now tell me.'

I told him what was worrying me, namely the possibility of a connection between the so-called Revival, of which he had been a fully paid-up member, and FOAS.

'And why would you want to know this?'

'That I cannot say, Boris. But trust me, it's important.'

'I'm sure. And I am in your debt so I will tell you what I know which I'm afraid is very little. Only that the Revival had amongst its members powerful individuals from Whitehall and from your intelligence services, even your government. This much I think you knew, or suspected. I understand that some of those people later became associated with this Foundation for Oriental and Asian Studies you speak of.'

'Do you know any of these people by name?'

'I'm afraid not. They do not broadcast their identities you understand.'

'And what about Helmut Gertch? He set up FOAS, right?'

'I know little about this man except he lives in Lucerne, or nearby. I am not associated with FOAS you understand.'

'Can you find out?'

'Let me see, Comrade. But give me time. Tomorrow I will send you something.'

True to his word, Boris emailed a report on Helmut Gertch the following day revealing details that were nowhere to be found on the internet. I had my suspicions where it came from but I knew better than to ask.

Gertch, a Swiss citizen, had been born in 1940. He'd studied Economics at Universität Mannheim before earning his PhD in transport economics at Princeton. A career at the Asian Infrastructure Development Bank followed where he spent much of his time arranging and dispersing

Western-funded port and transport infrastructure loans to the emerging Asian tiger economies of the time. His star was rising until he became embroiled in a corruption scandal in Indonesia. Nothing was proven against him but it wasn't long before he parted company with the Bank, after which he returned to Switzerland and set up the Foundation for Oriental and Asian Studies.

As an interesting footnote, Boris's report stated that Gertch's father and two of his uncles had run a bank in Zurich after the war that had allegedly laundered vast sums of Nazi loot for various members of the ODESSA, the organisation set up to help SS and other Nazi ne'er-do-wells escape justice to establish themselves in South America.

Then came what I was looking for: a link, albeit tenuous, to Dark Ocean. Between March 1949 and September 1953, the Gertch family bank had received eight deposits totalling seven hundred and twenty-three million dollars from an undisclosed source in the US. According to Boris' intelligence sources, which I was sure originated from within Russia's FSB, these deposits came from the proceeds of Imperial Japan's Golden Lily loot syphoned off by the Americans after the war and allocated to assist a number of allied democracies in fighting off the Soviet communist threat during the Cold War.

Gertch Senior and his two brothers disbursed these funds from the bank's Zurich headquarters. Some of the money went to agents of the Soviet Ministry for State Security, later to become the KGB, and later still the FSB.

These were agents who had agreed to reveal details of Soviet military and espionage activities in return for generous pay-outs. Whether this operation was carried out willingly, or whether under threat by the Americans of revealing the Gertchs' ODESSA connections for which they would have almost certainly faced prosecution, was not made clear.

Today, Helmut Gertch himself was a director of several Swiss-registered companies which Boris had thoughtfully listed in an appendix and which I now gave to Zoe.

'Go through these and see what you can find out. I'm wondering if any of them own shares in shipowning, chartering or terminal and port operations, Zoe.' I gave her a contact in a Cologne-based firm I'd used in the past that provided risk-management services including money laundering investigation and due diligence reports. 'Use them if you need to. They're good.'

In his covering email Boris Kaliyagin had added a final note. 'I do not know why but I am told Helmut Gertch is not who he seems to be. Others are pulling the strings. Take care, Comrade.'

It didn't take Zoe long. Anchinvest, a company in which Gertch was listed as a director and shareholder, had acquired a controlling share in a prominent Croatian shipowning firm just three weeks earlier. Along with that acquisition came another, a significant share in a profitable Rijeka shipyard. Anchinvest also declared controlling interests in a Philippine port and terminal operator and an Indonesian fertilizer trader and charterer. Both these deals had been concluded within the last six months.

Anchinvest's other two directors both shared the name Gertch: still a family concern it seemed, and still active.

'Zoe,' I said, 'It's time I paid Herr Gertch a visit.'

'How do you know whether he will be there?'

'Only one way to find out. And remember, Zoe, this is between you and me. If the CMM, Claire, anyone wants to know where I am, I've gone to China to visit Nya Wang's monastery, okay?'

'Okay, Angus. I understand. And stay safe.'

***

Boris's report had also included Gertch's address near Meggen on the northern shores of Lake Lucerne. I decided to drive to give myself time to think how I was going to confront the man, and because I wanted to have my old Webley service revolver with me when I did so. Greek and Italian ferry terminals were less rigorous than airports when it came to checking luggage.

Taking the go-bag I kept packed in the office for such short-notice departures, I set off in my ageing Alfa Romeo, the route taking me from Piraeus to Patras from where I caught the overnight ferry to Ancona. From there it was a seven hour drive north on the E35 skirting round Milan, up to Como and, having bought my motorway vignette, over the border and north from there. I booked into a small hotel up a side street in the town of Lucerne. As on all my previous visits to Switzerland, it was raining.

After the long car journey, that evening I was glad to walk through the streets of the old town. The rain was light now and after a while I found a bistro in a back street away from the lakeside tourist traps. There I ate Rosti accompanied by fried eggs and spinach with a bottle of Chasselas. After I'd eaten I continued my evening stroll. I couldn't be sure that I wasn't being followed, either here in the town or on the journey up from Ancona. I'd lost all confidence in my evasion tactics.

And as I returned to the hotel I still had only the sketchiest idea of how to handle my meeting with Herr Gertch.

CHAPTER 36

The following morning the sun was shining through gaps in the storm clouds which loomed above the Alps. There was still a chill wind off the lake but the birds were singing perhaps sensing that the best was still to come. I wasn't so sure.

Helmut Gertch's estate was on the shores of the lake just a few miles southeast of the town. I had found some details of the place from the address Boris had given me. The estate had been on the market a few years back and the estate agent's description, helpfully, was still online; an uncharacteristic slip-up by the secretive Herr Gertch.

Meggen, it said, was a charming, idyllic lakeside community whose attractive setting and proximity to Lucerne made it one of the most sought after locations in Switzerland. Built in 1926, the estate comprised a seven-bedroom, 9,000 square foot house occupying a modest one and a half acres of well-kept grounds stretching down to the lakeside. All this enjoyed a secluded location which guaranteed a high degree of privacy. The pool, the gardens, the views across the lake and the house itself left nothing to be desired, said the blurb; except perhaps the character of the man who had purchased it.

I drove past the tall iron gates slowing down briefly. There was no lodge but there was a gatehouse, a security measure I guessed. I saw no guards around but figured there would be CCTV cameras. A mile or two up the road I turned the car round and headed back to town. There I ordered sandwiches from the hotel and asked the waitress to fill a thermos flask with black coffee. My next acquisitions were a super-telephoto lens and a heavy-duty tripod I bought in a photo equipment store I'd spotted the previous evening.

Then I hired a small motorboat. The weather had turned again and rain was slanting across the water driven by the wind coming down from the mountains. Waves flecked with white foam crests raced across the lake's grey surface. The man who rented me the boat had warned of the lake's fickle microclimate and had insisted on seeing my ICC licence, a certificate intended to provide evidence of competence to operate a pleasure craft when requested by officials in foreign countries, so if I capsized and drowned he could tell the police and his insurance company that he'd ticked all the boxes so it wasn't his fault.

Keeping well offshore I slowed the boat down as I passed Gertch's place. The jetty was occupied by a Riva motor launch of the classic design. It was poorly cared for with varnish peeling off the wooden deck and hull. I carried on down the lake for another ten minutes or so then crossed over to the southern shore. After a while I found what I was looking for: a dilapidated jetty serving an equally dilapidated chalet that, if not abandoned was certainly not occupied. I tied the boat up and climbed ashore. The property was surrounded by conifers providing the cover I was looking for. Having found a discreet vantage point, I attached the new lens to my camera, mounted it on the tripod and focused on Gertch's place diagonally opposite. The detail of the scene jumped to life through the powerful lens: the jetty, the boat, the garden and the house itself in front of which was a large terrace accessed through a number of French windows. I settled down to watch and wait.

The house had been built in the Swiss chalet style. According to the estate agent's description such architectural designs had originated in the Romantic era of the early nineteen hundreds when ideas from the stereotype English landscape garden had inspired residences across Germany and Switzerland. It had come to be appreciated by noble landowners impressed by the simple life of mountain folk though I could see no resemblance to either an English country garden or Heidi's grandfather's chalet. But it had been modified over the years and although the styles competed with one another, skilful landscaping around the house and its terraces had softened it and lent charm to its appearance.

It was a couple of hours before anything happened. I'd eaten the sandwiches, drunk the coffee and was beginning to feel the cold. A large car glided to a halt on the gravel drive alongside the house. The car was partially hidden by a low wall so I couldn't make out the number plate but I could see it was a right-hand drive, black and gunmetal grey Bentley Mulsanne. The car was spattered with road dirt suggesting a long journey. A man climbed out of the driver's seat, placed a black Fedora on his head and stretched. I began taking stills and video clips. He was wearing a black coat with an astrakhan collar. The boot opened and he removed a dark brown leather suitcase. The boot closed and the man walked towards the front of the house.

After another half hour one pair of French windows opened and two men stepped out, both were smoking cigars and holding tumblers of what looked like whisky. The man on the left was Astrakhan from the Bentley. He had a familiar air about him. But the man he was raising his glass to I recognised straightaway. It was Vice Admiral Randolph Carvill.

As I was about to jump to a number of conclusions, a woman pushing a wheelchair now entered the scene, carefully manoeuvring it down a ramp which was in position beneath another of the French windows, which I presumed led off from another room in the house. The wheelchair's occupant was huddled under a tartan rug and wore a woollen hat. The woman pushed the wheelchair up to where the other two were standing and turned it to face the lake. I could see now that the man in the wheelchair was leaning over to one side. He looked enfeebled as if he'd suffered a stroke. The woman disappeared into the house returning with a tumbler of whisky for him. The three men drank and stared out onto the lake. The woman stepped back inside.

By now it was after six and what sun there had been had disappeared behind the mountains. I watched and filmed as they talked, drank their whisky and smoked their cigars. Eventually the woman returned and the three of them went back into the house. Lights went on and curtains were drawn.

I guessed the man in the wheelchair was Gertch but what the hell was Carvill doing there? Was he the mole who'd leaked the coordinates? Or did he have some other role? Was he working undercover himself? Having met the man it seemed improbable. And who was Astrakhan with the right-hand drive Bentley? Four people, no sign of a security detail but I couldn't take that for granted.

I recalled what Claire had told me: espionage is all about waiting; another gem from her beginner's guide to tradecraft. I waited another couple of hours. It was raining harder now. Water dripped from the branches down my collar. For the hundredth time I stared through the camera's viewfinder across to the villa. Then, just as I was about to pack up, a crack of light appeared where the curtains weren't fully drawn. The French windows opened and Carvill stepped out onto the terrace followed by Astrakhan. I could tell from their body language that they were both well-oiled. Astrakhan had almost tripped coming down the step through the French windows. I packed up, transferring the camera's memory card to my pocket, and walked back to the boat. It was time to pay them a visit.

CHAPTER 37

The wind was still blowing hard from the south. Frayed clouds swept across the rising moon as I motored down the lake before crossing to the northern shore giving Gertch's villa a wide berth. I spotted a small shingle beach and ran the boat up onto it. Then I worked my way back on foot for half a mile or so until I reached the perimeter wall of the estate. I walked along it in both directions hoping to find a gate or some alternative way in. There was nothing. I could chance entering via the main gate or the point where the wall reached the lakeshore, but judged both to be too conspicuous.

The wall must have been a good distance from the house itself. When I'd been watching earlier from the opposite shore I'd seen no sign of dogs or guards but the wall was an obstacle. It was of natural, rough-hewn sandstone. There was no sign of glass shards or barbed wire on the top. I estimated it to be some ten feet high, too high to haul myself up without some upward drive. But a sprawling ivy plant was clinging to it at this point so I decided to try it. Leaving the bag with the camera in it at the foot of the wall but buttoning the Webley into my jacket pocket, I eyed the waist-high spot where the ivy was thickest and where I wanted my foot to land. I moved back, enough to get a good run at it. I ran, hit the wall with the ball of my foot in the spot I'd chosen and thrust my other leg up into the ivy to gain momentum. Swinging my arms and shoulders up I reached and grabbed the top edge of the wall. Then I hoisted myself onto the top and without waiting, dropped down onto the other side.

Instead of the soft yielding bushes I'd hoped for I landed hard onto a gravel path making contact with my injured arm. It had been aching before, now the pain shot through it like a red-hot knife. I grunted and lay still, slowly regaining my breath and looking around me.

The house was at least fifty yards away as I'd estimated. There was no sign of life in the grounds but lights were on in several rooms both upstairs and down. The Bentley was still there parked beside a black BMW.

I checked the Webley and waited five more minutes adjusting to the surroundings before approaching the house. There were several doors opening onto patios besides those which faced the lake. Now I worked my way round the building looking for a way of gaining access undetected. I moved around to the landward side where the cars were parked, then onto the far side but could find no easy way in without breaking a window and probably setting off an alarm. I was considering my options when they were decided for me. Someone came up from behind and smashed my head against the wall.

***

When I came round I was lying on my front. I opened an eye. Someone had thoughtfully provided a towel for my head to rest on. Then I realised it had been placed there to prevent blood from a gash on my forehead from spreading out across an expensive looking rug I'd been dumped on. I didn't move.

'What do you want to do with him?' said a guttural voice.

'Nothing. Leave him here with us. You may go now but stay in the house. Gudrun will feed you. You did well.' I recognised Carvill's voice. He was speaking to my assailant.

I stayed where I was. 'Get up, McKinnon,' he said. 'We see you've woken from your slumbers.'

I raised myself up and touched my forehead. It was sticky with blood.

'Gudrun, go and get some water and a rag so he can clean himself up will you.' Carvill seemed to be in charge.

Gudrun left the room. I looked around. It and the people in it were swimming. I felt sick. Gudrun returned with a bowl of warm water, cotton wool and bandages. She bent and began cleaning, first the blood from my face then the wound itself.

'For God's sake, woman,' Carvill remonstrated, 'stop

babying him. He can manage himself.'

She took no notice and continued cleaning me up. Finally she fixed a large gauze pad over the wound. I could see she was concerned. Her grey hair was tied back into a bun. She was dressed in a plain brown woollen dress. She had the appearance of a school mistress but I suspected she was a trained nurse, here to look after the ailing Herr Gertch.

When she'd finished she left the room. Carvill was seated in a wingchair pointing a pistol at me. My own Webley had been removed from my jacket pocket. He looked pleased with himself. Over by the French windows stood Astrakhan. This was the first good look I'd had of him.

The man in the wheelchair who I took to be Gertch was wearing pyjamas, a camel-coloured dressing-gown and slippers. What was left of his hair was grey as was his skin – a ghostly pallor. I thought back to Jim Brodie. It seemed a lifetime ago.

Carvill spoke again. 'Angus McKinnon. Rest assured, if you hadn't found me I would have found you. So you have saved me the trouble, though you have also caused me a great deal of it.'

I recalled with irony what Claire had told me in one of her tradecraft lessons: by appearing vulnerable you will find it easier to win the trust of the person you are interacting with. I didn't need to just appear vulnerable.

'Who are your friends?' I asked wearily and struggling to my feet. 'Herr Gertch?' I said turning to the man in the wheelchair.

'I am Gertch,' he said sounding as weary as I did.

'And him?' I nodded to Astrakhan who was still leaning on the wall beside the French windows.

Carvill spoke. 'He is a colleague from London.'

But then as I looked across at him I had it. 'You're a politician aren't you, from the Foreign Office?'

'Well done.' His voice was slurred from the drinking. 'Junior Minister actually, yes.'

We stared at each other. I shrugged. 'No harm in telling me what this is all about. I'm fascinated. What have you cooked up here?'

Again, it was Carvill who spoke. 'This is a serious organisation I am running and you have repeatedly interfered with and obstructed our plans. Do not expect me to start explaining what this is all about. You know what it's about.'

'You mean you've used your position as a senior military officer to satisfy your lust for power and control. In doing so you have betrayed your country, not to mention the values of the Royal Navy. You're a traitor, Carvill.'

He was on his feet too now. I was angering him and as with all such men with an irrational desire for power, he couldn't stop himself reacting. He would always need to have the last word and in that, I told myself, lay some hope.

'How dare you speak to me like that. What do you know of our ideals? Of the benefits our plans will bestow upon the world.'

Here we go, I thought. 'What? You want to turn the whole planet into one big co-prosperity sphere by controlling the world's shipping lanes and its trade? In your dreams you mean.'

'You know nothing.' He spat the words out, his anger rising.

'You just relish the idea of bringing down the established order. You relish aggressive nationalism as a means to hoard power. You're delusional, Carvill - ignorant of the realities around you. You belong in an asylum.'

'Now, now gentlemen.' It was the Junior Minister who spoke. I'd remembered who he was now, the Right Honourable Albert Acton, MP. I'd seen him on the news when he'd been on a trip to Thailand ostensibly drumming up business for British business.

Carvill ignored him. 'The end justifies the means. Those who obstruct us must be removed. And that includes you, McKinnon.' He said it with quiet menace, his anger back under control now.

I pressed on because I'd seen something and I needed to hold Carvill's attention. 'Not only that but you're a murderer too. You ordered the killing of Alastair Marshall and Ronnie Eastfield because they were onto you, and getting in your way. Now it's me.'

Now Carvill moved towards me raising the gun as he did so. But behind him, framed in the doorway, a slight figure had appeared standing in deep shadow like an apparition. The figure was holding something big and heavy. I stared as he raised his arms high. Just as Carvill turned to see what I was looking at, the newcomer moved forward and smashed a large china vase down onto Carvill's head. He staggered forward still holding the gun. I grabbed a fire iron from the grate and swung it at his gun hand as he crashed to the floor. The gun skittled across the parquet. I went for it but Acton got to it first. Still holding the fire iron I struck him on the arm. He screamed in pain as again the gun went flying. This time he backed off holding his arm. I picked up the gun.

The whole sequence resembled what had happened in the saloon of the *Toyama Maru* when Ah Sun had lost his life. It was over in less than thirty seconds. Carvill lay unconscious. Acton had sat down nursing his arm and looking affronted. Gertch sat slumped in his wheelchair looking confused. And standing by the door holding the remains of the vase and looking unperturbed was Takeo Ishikawa.

CHAPTER 38

'Christ, where did you spring from?'

'I believe you needed assistance.'

'Have you killed him?' I bent down and felt Carvill's pulse, something I was getting used to. His pulse and his breathing were regular. I left him where he lay.

'There's another guy. The one who whacked me when I was coming into the house.'

'We have looked after him too, Angus-san.'

Gudrun had entered the room and was fussing over Gertch. Ishikawa walked over to a drinks trolley in the corner of the room and poured us each a large Scotch. I checked Carvill's pistol. It was a 9mm Glock similar to the one I'd lost when they'd blown up Ronnie's flat. The clip was full and there was a round in the chamber. He hadn't been joking .

I slumped into a wingchair. 'Gudrun, I will need to question Herr Gertch as well as this man here.' I waved the gun at Acton.

'Herr Gertch needs his medication,' she said.

'Go and get it will you. I need him to pay attention to my questions. And that applies to you too.' I pointed the gun at Acton who was still looking affronted. 'Ishi-san, would you go with Gudrun? I don't want her trying anything.'

Unobtrusively I switched on the voice recorder that they hadn't found in an inner pocket of my jacket and focused my attention on Acton. 'Suppose you start the conversation. What's your role in this charade?'

'I'm an elected representative of the British people and a minister of state. I don't answer to you.'

'Think again, Acton,' I said. 'I also represent the British government. What distinguishes us is that I'm the one with the gun.'

But as it turned out Gertch was the key to the interrogation. 'I will tell you everything you want to know,' he interrupted. The old man was weary but he had a few things to get off his chest. Ishi, who had returned to the room with Gudrun, joined me with the questioning.

After twenty minutes or so Carvill began to come round. We watched him closely but needn't have bothered. Once Carvill heard what was being revealed he kept stumm.

I went easy with the whisky. This was going to take a while. But as I felt myself relaxing and for no apparent reason I started thinking of Monty Buchan. And I remembered something he'd said before I left his office that last time. 'Just mind yourself, Angus. Something I overheard on the *Toyama Maru*. It was one of the FOAS people and he'd had a lot to drink. We all had. He said there was a lot more behind the man who started FOAS than was apparent. I didn't think it was important but you might like to mention it to your masters."

I'd not thought it important at the time either, just a throwaway remark, except that Boris had said something very similar.

Then the man who wasn't who he seemed, slumped in his wheelchair but helped by the Cholinesterase inhibitors that Gudrun had fed him, began to talk.

I guess he felt safer now someone was there to protect him from these two Englishmen who had usurped him and, he insisted, had been the prime movers in executing a plan that had started as just an exercise in theoretical idealism. It sounded a weak argument but the way he told it, a credible one. He didn't try to conceal his own complicity in the scheme either. He looked spent, beaten. I sensed he was treating this as a confession.

The economist, Ikuo Takahashi, he said, had believed that Dark Ocean was the organisation that could turn the dream into reality, the theory into practice. Dark Ocean wasn't just another ultra-nationalist society harbouring dreams of a resurgent Japan. It was backed by a syndicate of Japanese industrialists ready to support them. But, Gertch maintained, what for him had started as an academic exercise to illustrate an alternative course for economic development in Asia and beyond, had become much more than that for Carvill and Acton. These two were already active members of FOAS and to them the co-prosperity idea became a strategic goal, one to be executed with ruthless determination.

At this point Acton interjected. 'You're lying, Gertch. You love the idea of the region powered by a resurgent Japan just as he and I do,' he said pointing to Carvill. 'And not just Asia. It took a Neocon American to point to Old Europe,' he said in reference to Donald Rumsfeld. 'He was right. Europe's destruction as a union is in good hands: its own. The rebuilding will be ours; the same in Asia too, you said so yourself.'

'Yes,' Gertch snapped back, 'by peaceful means. Not by spraying nerve gas over Hong Kong!'

'Such drastic acts are sometimes necessary.' They glared at each other in open hostility.

'I understand your family is in banking, Herr Gertch,' I said moving the questioning in another direction.'

'Yes. So?'

'I was told your father and your uncles laundered Nazi loot and used the proceeds to fund the ODESSA organisation, the flight of Nazis to South America and elsewhere.'

'I have no knowledge of this. It was long before my time.'

Ishi stepped forward, a gun in one hand and a whisky tumbler in the other. 'Then what happened to the bank, Mr Gertch, in the nineteen-fifties and beyond that? What kinds of business did your bank conduct then?'

With effort Gertch moved himself from his slumped position. Now he leaned forward. 'Every kind of business: investment business. Who are you anyway?'

'I represent the government of Japan, Mr Gertch. We have a keen interest in this matter, as you can imagine. Now, please tell me about the gold deposited into your family's bank during the early nineteen-fifties and thereafter. You must know about this.'

Gertch hesitated. He turned to Gudrun who passed him a glass of water. But he stayed silent.

Ishi pressed on. 'We have traced cargo manifests belonging to one of our shipping lines that is no longer in business. These manifests show the shipment of gold from Japan and the Philippines to the USA and to London. But the biggest consignment of gold was shipped to your bank, Mr Gertch, in Zurich. That consignment that you received was part of the Golden Lily fortune. Gold looted by my country during the war, looted from across China and Southeast Asia. It did not belong to Japan. And it did not belong to you.

'You will understand that this is a sensitive matter for my country. As a nation we have moved on from those dark days, but it is my job to discover the truth of what happened to the gold plundered by my country. Am I right in saying that much of that gold has been laundered and reassigned to fund *Genyosha's* efforts to take over all shipping, trade and port activities throughout the Asia-Pacific region?'

Gertch was shaken. Carvill and Acton both looked at him to see how he'd respond.

'Tell him, man,' Carvill said. 'Tell him what it was for.'

Gertch looked agitated. He turned to Gudrun again as

if seeking her support.

'Yes, you are right. If you have the manifests they are the proof. I did not know they still existed. The first gold was shipped to our bank in 1953. Twenty-five tons. It was worth twenty-eight million dollars then. Today's value is a billion and a half or more. The money came from the Americans. They shipped out most of that gold and it went to fighting the rising tide of Communism. It was disbursed to governments around the world wherever there was perceived to be a threat from the Soviet Union or Mao's China. The money kept coming, right into the nineteen-seventies it was still coming.'

'And how was your share disbursed?' I asked.

'It was supposed to be used for payments to Soviet defectors and double agents working within the KGB in return for intelligence on Soviet military plans. But in reality, only a small proportion, perhaps ten percent, was used for that purpose.'

'And then the Soviet Union collapsed. What about the rest, that which remained?'

'Much has been transferred to *Genyosha*, to Dark Ocean's accounts for their plans.'

'But not all?'

'No, not all.'

He hesitated. 'And the rest?' I said.

He looked at Acton and then at Carvill. 'Ask them. My two co-directors, these English gentlemen have done very nicely out of this project.'

'That's an outrageous lie!' Acton shouted. 'How dare you accuse me.'

'You fool, Albert,' said Carvill. 'Don't you think these people will gain access to our accounts? Once they start an audit trail from Helmut's bank we'll soon show up despite the elaborate veil, the concealment measures we took. Rest assured.'

Acton was silent. Again it was Gertch who spoke. 'I trusted these English but they were more interested in their own power and their own pockets. Now it is all over.'

Then, as we watched transfixed, he reached into the pocket of his dressing gown and pulled out a pistol. I could see it was a Luger – an old Swiss Army gun by the look of it, iconic yet menacing, recalling its use by the Nazis and later, the East German Volkspolizei. In retrospect, I knew in that moment what was coming, but I did nothing. The others in the room were watching him too. Only Gudrun moved but she was too late. Gertch raised the gun, placed the barrel in his mouth and fired.

Gudrun screamed and then, sobbing, moved to hold him as he slumped forward. The bullet had exited through the back of his skull spattering splinters of bone, blood and brain matter onto the wooden panelling behind him.

Ishi stepped forward taking the gun from Gertch's hand and gently pulling Gudrun away. He held her as the hysteria subsided. I walked over and took the Luger from him to check how many rounds were in the magazine but it was empty. There'd been just the one in the chamber.

'We need to get these two dealt with, Ishi-san,' I said. 'Do you have back-up?'

'There is a team standing by. The Swiss have been co-operative.'

'I see.' Actually I didn't. How he could have set all this up, or how he could have followed me here, wasn't clear to me, but I wasn't going to get into that discussion with him now.

Ishi made his calls and within ten minutes a squad of Swiss heavies turned up. They didn't identify themselves and they weren't wearing uniforms or insignia though clearly Ishi knew their commander. Three of the men set about securing the house and grounds while the others took charge of Carvill and Acton. I looked enquiringly at Ishi.

'Swiss Military Intelligence,' he said.

CHAPTER 39

I called Claire. This time we didn't bother with the coded language we usually used on our calls.

'Hang on, Angus, I'll go downstairs.' I presumed she'd been in bed but not asleep from the sound of her. She'd no idea where I was or what I was doing. I told her what had happened. She had the sense not to challenge my unilateral decision to take the case forward, or what I thought had been unilateral until Ishi had appeared.

'My God,' she said. 'Carvill was the one who leaned on Amber to pull you off the case. It all makes sense now. But how on earth did Carvill manage to hide his activities with FOAS and Gertch's bank from his masters in the MoD, never mind from us?'

'That's what I was wondering. Don't people like him go through a vetting process, like I did?'

'Of course they do. But he was non-exec within the IMTF so his activities weren't monitored that closely I guess.'

'Right now we need to know what to do with him and Acton. Swiss Military Intelligence are acting for Ishi and his

PSIA. But I don't want Carvill and Acton slipping through the net on some legal technicality over here.'

'Give me an hour, Angus. Hold them there and I'll get Amber to send the janitor team in.'

'Who are they?'

'The clean-up people. We'll fly them over.'

'What about Gertch. He's still in his wheelchair with his brains spread across the wall.'

'They'll handle him too, don't worry. Let me speak with Ishi-san would you?'

Just what mountains had to be moved with the Swiss authorities by her and Ishi in the middle of the night I didn't ask but true to her word, within the hour Claire called back to say the janitors were on their way in an RAF transport plane.

'How many?'

'Three guys. Can you meet them at Buochs airfield? It's a military base on the other side of the lake from you.'

'Sure. Do they have much equipment?'

'One case apiece. They're flying from Northolt. ETA Buochs 0630.'

'Okay, make sure I can get through airside onto the tarmac will you. I'll be driving a Bentley.'

'Fine, as long as you're not charging us for car hire, darling.'

'It's Acton's. I'll try not to break it.' I gave her the registration number.

'Angus, we want Carvill and Acton returned to London

with the janitors, okay?'

'They'll look forward to that.'

'Get the janitors to take care of them. They'll know how to handle it. And don't touch anything. Don't touch Gertch. Just leave it to them.'

'Okay.'

'Oh and Angus, best you come over too. You'll need to be debriefed. It could take a while.'

I agreed reluctantly and returned to the living room. The military intelligence people had handcuffed Carvill and Acton and placed them under guard. It was interesting to observe these two. Normally, you would typecast them as alpha males: confident men with an air of authority and expecting others to do their bidding. Now, both were subdued. Carvill sat staring out of the French windows watching as the moonlight cast a silvery light across the lake, lost in his own world. I was reminded of when we'd looked out at *Big Lizzie* as he called her: the Royal Navy's brand new aircraft carrier HMS *Queen Elizabeth*, as she'd headed out for her sea trials just a few weeks before. Pride of the fleet he'd declared. He was a skilled deceiver, I'd give him that.

Acton was different altogether. As might be expected from a politician, he maintained a façade of self-righteousness. From time to time he would turn to one of us and, bristling with indignation, deny all knowledge of his own wrongdoing without offering a shred of evidence in his defence.

'Just shut up, Acton. I've had enough of you,' Carvill

said in the end. But it didn't make any difference.

'We're returning these two to London,' I said to the unit's commander. 'You'll get confirmation from your own people soon.'

There wasn't much more Ishi or I could do. We'd covered Gertch's body with a sheet and left everything else as it was.

At five o'clock I left and went out to meet the janitors. A young military policeman greeted me at the gate of the airfield. He checked the car's number plate and asked for my ID. I told him my passport was in my hotel in Lucerne but he waved me through anyway. The plane they'd sent was one of the RAF's BAe146s. I watched it come in low through a pass in the mountains and land just as the sun came up. Customs and Immigration officers boarded first, followed by a Swiss Air Force officer and ten minutes later the janitors emerged each carrying a large aluminium suitcase. The men and their luggage only just fitted into the Bentley. One of them was Benedict Wood. The others were hard-looking men dressed in dark blue coveralls. Ben Wood looked out of place in his business suit. Back at the villa they exchanged muted greetings with their Swiss counterparts who then departed taking a still shocked Gudrun with them and leaving two officers to liaise with our janitors.

By six that night they were more or less done. Besides cleaning up the mess in the living room, they went through the whole house with a fine tooth comb. Computers, external hard-drives, hard-copy files of correspondence and documents going back years; nothing was overlooked. Everything was recorded, placed in plastic bags and receipts issued to the Swiss intelligence officers and copied to Ishi. Gertch's body was handed over to the Swiss after photos had been taken and DNA swabs collected from his body using an evidence collection kit they'd brought along. Ben Wood supervised the whole operation. Ishi and I stayed close to Carvill and Acton until it was time to leave. I said goodbye to Ishi and invited him to Scotland on behalf of the CMM.

'Very sorry, Angus, but I don't play golf.'

'Neither do I, Ishi, but we both like whisky. We could drive around visiting some distilleries. Maybe borrow Acton's Bentley.

'Then of course, I accept,' he said, laughing.

Then I asked him how he'd known where to find me.

'I knew you would not accept that this case was closed, Angus. And when you drove up here from Greece, you left a trail a mile wide in that old Alfa of yours. Buy a Japanese car: more reliable, less conspicuous. Oh, and we placed a tracker device under the car to make it easier. But good job done. No more trouble from these people now. It is finished.'

'I hope so, Ishi,' I said wondering why I hadn't thought to check under the car.

We piled into a black van provided by the Swiss to take us back to the waiting RAF plane.

'What about my bloody car?' said Acton as we walked past his Bentley.

CHAPTER 40

The plane jumped about, buffeted by the turbulence created from the erratic air currents which streamed down off the mountains. We laboured out of the valley before turning west and reaching more stable air at our cruising altitude.

I sat back and let my mind run over the events of the last few weeks since I'd left Mindanao. Was it finished as Ishi had said? What would happen to Carvill and Acton I wondered. They were both handcuffed to steel rings attached by a chain to the foot of their seats. Ben Wood sat beside Carvill and one of the other janitors guarded Acton. I was sitting a few rows back content with my own company.

After a while Ben got up, stretched and walked back to where I was sitting.

'Carvill's getting restless. There's a medic on board. I'll get something for him.'

He walked further back to another compartment in the rear of the aircraft returning after a few minutes with a man in civilian clothes. He held a stainless steel kidney tray with a syringe in it. I watched him bend over Carvill. Then he left and Ben took his seat again.

Exhausted, I slept for the rest of the flight.

I woke as we were descending towards RAF Northolt. From the window London looked grey and dismal. Before we disembarked an ambulance drew up beside the aircraft steps. Two men boarded with a stretcher and with some difficulty hauled Carvill from his seat and carried him off the plane. I walked up the aisle to where Ben Wood was standing.

'He passed away as I sat there beside him,' he said. 'Heart attack I guess.'

'Convenient.'

'What do you mean?'

I didn't reply. Two military police were next to board and escorted Acton off. He was still protesting about his treatment.

A car was waiting on the tarmac close to the plane, a black Jaguar with darkened windows. The rear passenger door opened as I walked towards it and Claire stepped out in the way Hollywood actresses do when arriving for a premiere.'

'Hello, Angus. Goodness, you look done in. What happened to your head?'

'I hit it off something. Where are we off to?' I asked getting into the back seat with her.

'Somewhere you can rest and we can deal with things.'

'Carvill died on the flight.'

'Yes, so I heard.'

'Heart attack Ben reckons.'

'I expect so. He never looked particularly healthy.'

'He was given an injection, Claire – a sedative apparently. Then he died.'

'What are you getting at?'

'It just seems a little too expedient.'

'Expedient? What, you think he was murdered?'

'I don't know.'

'They'll do a post mortem I'm sure.'

We drove west eventually reaching the Buckinghamshire countryside. Before Amersham, we turned into a private driveway stopping at a lodge where Claire showed her pass to a tough looking man with a military bearing and a moustache to match. The drive led through an avenue of lime trees at the end of which an ugly nineteenth century red brick pile appeared. We were shown into the house by another ex-military type and through to a lounge overlooking the river. Amber Dove got up from her armchair and greeted us.

'Angus, you poor man. You must be exhausted. What have you done to your head? Here, let me pour you tea.'

'What is this place?' I asked sitting down opposite her and helping myself to the chocolate biscuits.

'Oh, the MoD uses it for various purposes. For us it's handy, in this particular case, for holding some detailed conversations with the Minister.'

'Interrogation.' I'd heard about these places. Black site detention centres they were called. Whatever went on here would be deniable.

'It could go on for weeks if not months.'

'I trust he'll be charged.'

'Why on earth would we want to do that?'

'Because he was at the heart of an international criminal conspiracy committed to overthrowing the established democratic order that we all love and cherish so dearly and with the intent of committing mass murder along the way,' I said patiently.

Amber smiled. 'You do have a way with words, Angus. But he's more useful to us where he is. We can use him to our advantage. He knows we have sufficient evidence to have him convicted of all sorts of offences including treason. He'd be locked away for the rest of his days. This way he can help us root out any other nasty elements hiding away in the corridors of power. This case is far from over, but you've done more than your fair share, I have to say.'

'What will happen to those firms that were victims of hostile takeover by this cabal? There were some big names there.'

'Your friend Ishikawa-san will look after that side of things; in liaison with us of course. It's a matter of undoing the transactions, which will be complicated to put it mildly. Claire here will be helping too.'

'And Carvill?'

'What about him?'

'Was he murdered on the plane?' I asked, holding her eye. 'Was he injected with something lethal?'

'We really shouldn't be discussing these things, Angus.' She hesitated, then leaned over and refilled my cup. 'Our masters in the MoD were very anxious to avoid any scandal involving one of their senior officers, you understand.'

'You mean they ordered him to be bumped off.'

'Expedient demise they like to call it. For the sake of the nation's security. Potassium chloride given intravenously causes almost instant cardiac arrest. One gram does the trick but two to be absolutely certain. There, now you have it.'

'You speak as if this is common practice in your profession.'

'Heavens, no. Of course not, not these days anyway. It was different during the Cold War.'

'How can you cover it up? I mean someone needs to do a post mortem surely.'

'Of course, the great advantage is that because potassium levels shoot up hugely after death anyway, poisoning by potassium chloride is pretty much undiagnosable. He wouldn't have suffered,' she added sympathetically.

'Carvill was Acton's puppet master. That's the impression I got.'

'Spot on. Carvill was the puppet master all right. He was running Acton, Gertch and, in effect, Dark Ocean too.'

'And you - us, the IMTF?'

She fidgeted. 'And that's why we're so eager to talk to the Minister – at length. We need to get to the bottom of this once and for all. I'm not sure our Vice Admiral colleague would have cooperated. He'd have been a hard nut to crack.'

'But Acton will?'

'Oh, he'll talk alright.'

'And then? Another expedient demise?'

'We'll have to see, Angus. Don't you worry about that. But as long as there are people of the same persuasion as Messrs Carvill and Acton at the heart of our government and our intelligence services, this case will not be completely closed. There are failed states out there with natural resources waiting to be exploited. The seas are still, in many senses, lawless. And look at what's going on in the South China Sea now. What did you say in Tokyo? Two-hundred billion barrels of oil and up to seven-hundred and fifty trillion cubic feet of natural gas the Chinese estimate. Not to mention the five trillion dollars' worth of trade passing through every year. If ever there's trouble brewing somewhere it's there. But I rather think this case of yours may have calmed matters. They're still talking of Buddha diplomacy between China and Japan, which is a helpful start.'

'Yes.'

'Something else: would you say that you and Claire got along well in your respective roles?'

Was this a loaded question? I looked at Claire for a clue but got nothing in return.

'Yes, of course,' I said.

'Excellent,' said Amber. 'Strictly need-to-know, and I deem that you do, we feel so too. But as you will be aware, Claire has micromanaged this case, particularly towards its conclusion. She directed the rescue operation with support from Ishikawa and the Japanese Navy; she persuaded the Japanese and Chinese to work together thus becoming the architect of so-called Buddha diplomacy; she worked with Ben Wood and MI6 to ensure harmony between our two organisations despite old animosities, which is a breath of fresh air I assure you; and with commendable diplomacy, she brought the Americans on side too, just as they were beginning to feel alienated. So she has proved herself a worthy successor to our dear departed friend Alastair.

'That said, it was your own determination throughout that drove the case forward, and then just yesterday, your tenacity that uncovered Carvill and Acton. Very impressive indeed. So on behalf of the MoD, and from me personally, wholehearted congratulations to you both.'

At this point I'd have thought a bottle of champagne would have been more appropriate than a pot of English Breakfast tea. I looked at Claire who just smiled.

'Now, we'll get you cleaned up and rested, Angus,' said Amber Dove in her most matronly manner. 'Then they'll be an extensive debriefing. It could take a while, several days anyway.'

'That reminds me, Angus,' Claire interjected. 'Susanna Buchan's been trying to get hold of you. She's in Ganlanba. The Buddha has been reinstalled at the temple apparently. Nya Wang is expecting you to attend a formal ceremony to mark its return. She seems eager for you to visit too,' she added.

I thought of my father's little Buddha statue. I hadn't got to the bottom of that. Where had it come from and who had given it to him? Nya Wang had promised to look into its origins. Along with his notebooks, it was the strongest link I had to my family. Perhaps it was time to head for Ganlanba.

ABOUT THE AUTHOR

Nick Elliott began his career as a boarding agent attending ships in Edinburgh's port of Leith. He moved to Hong Kong in the Seventies and lived throughout the Far East for twenty years before relocating to Greece and eventually back to the UK.

Throughout, he has worked, lived and breathed shipping and more than a few of the events described in his books are inspired by his own experiences. He is a Fellow of the Institute of Chartered Shipbrokers.

Married with two daughters, he divides his time between Scotland and a Greek island.

Sea of Gold was his first novel. It was followed by Dark Ocean, Black Reef and in 2021, The Code, a prequel to the first three.

ACKNOWLEDGEMENTS

My thanks to Helen Bleck, my editor; to Peter Flannery and our Scottish Borders Scribblers, and to Sarah Eakin and members of the Edinburgh Society of Independent Authors, for again sharing their ideas, their views and their own travails; and to Mags Fenner for her proofreading.

My thanks also to Doctor Jane Stanford, Claude Carletide, David Gourlay, Rear Admiral (ret'd) Roger Lockwood and Christos Makrialeas for their input on matters within their respective fields of expertise.

I am also indebted to Sterling and Peggy Seagrave and their excellent book, Gold Warriors, for much of the information concerning Golden Lily and the recovery of gold bullion and other treasures after the end of World War II.

IF YOU ENJOYED THIS BOOK

If you enjoyed reading *Dark Ocean* I'd be very grateful if you would leave a short review on Amazon. Good reviews help other readers find and enjoy a book.

If you would like to get in touch, please contact me via my website: **www.nickelliott.org**

And thanks for buying the book.

Nick Elliott

SEA OF GOLD, DARK OCEAN, BLACK REEF AND THE CODE

Buy The Code here: https://amzn.to/3lGVtDq

What readers have said about The Code

"The Angus McKinnon thrillers are set within the maritime industry. Speaking as an ex seafarer, Nick Elliott's many years of industry experience shine through, bringing credibility to the scenes he sets and depth to the profiles of the main characters. A gripping read, I have enjoyed all of the Angus McKinnon series."

***

"Another cracking read from Nick Elliott. Once again, the story, a prequel, moves with breathless pace and, in common with his other books in this series, he guides us across an enormously wide geographic landscape - this time from Lebanon, Latvia, through the Balkans and ending up in the West Indies. It's also good to know now how Angus McKinnon became the maritime sleuth we know so well from the first three books. Very highly recommended."

***

"Just finished Nick Elliott's 4th book, The Code. A great prequel to his Angus McKinnon trilogy. His writing gets better and better."

Buy Sea of Gold here: http://amzn.to/1jkQUYT

What readers have said about Sea of Gold

"Nick Elliott ticks all the boxes in this fast-paced yarn, with a keen eye for descriptive detail and solidly drawn characters. The first-person narrative, complete with ironic internal asides, is the perfect vehicle for a thoughtful and witty style that draws us swiftly into the shoes of its protagonist, a credible and consistent character."

***

"A unique twist on the spy detective thriller featuring impeccably re-searched action that is set in a host of well invoked locations. I look forward with intrigue to Angus McKinnon's further adventures."

***

"This is a first rate, well-constructed first novel which benefits from the author's learned insight into the maritime business world and his familiarity with interesting parts of the world. In addition he introduc-es us to some interesting characters who fortunately survive the tricky circumstances in which they find themselves and who we look forward to meeting again in the sequel(s). I predict a successful future for Nick Elliott who will I feel sure continue to set his stories in fascinating parts of the world. I thoroughly enjoyed this book."

***

"In the tradition of Eric Ambler, this is a well written crime novel. What starts out as a case of insurance fraud turns into a battle of international intrigue."

***

"A fascinating and very well-written story in a world I knew nothing about, commercial shipping. If you are a mystery fan, enjoy reading about international intrigue, appreciate well-developed complex charac-ters and are curious about or fascinated by the high seas, this is for you. A powerful first book."

Buy Dark Ocean here: http://amzn.to/2vIPRyJ

What readers have said about Dark Ocean

"This really is an expertly researched, very well-written and fast-paced international thriller. The protagonist, Angus McKinnon, is a character with real dimension and credibility, which is something often lacking in this kind of fiction. You believe in him, and you believe in the streets, alleys and seaways he travels: every location is atmospherically and authentically created as your drawn deeper and deeper into a dark world where nothing is what is seems. Superb book."

"Felt like I was back in the Orient when I was reading this book. I could easily visualize every aspect of the author's descriptions of people and places. So many plot twists. Thoroughly enjoyed this book."

***

"Dark Ocean hit landmarks with which I am familiar (Kowloon and Hong Kong), and I loved all the interesting tidbits of shipping detail, description of ports, and customs of the locals, including the exchange of commerce with Japan. This book grabs your attention immediately then quickly widens to that of international intrigue that includes the collusion of a major cabal in what might be a hostile takeover--a far-reaching takeover. The threatening organization is deeply rooted and far ranging and has Angus flying to retrieve information from sources he thought well buried in his past--only to have to retrieve, relive, and sort. But as with any good thriller, a piece of the puzzle only leads to hints of acquiring the next piece."

***

"The book is a well-plotted, multi-layered suspense with slightly rogue alpha male management style being ever more deeply entangled in MI6 as they coordinate between agencies. There is so much (fictional?) information here reading as gospel that it becomes scary."

***

"Nick Elliott has done it again. Following Sea of Gold he has come up with an equally gripping, intelligent and well-paced thriller in Dark Ocean. Set in the shipping industry which he knows intimately and in countries which he knows like a native and in which you can feel the pulse of the street life, the plot leads you on in an unputdownable way. Once started you have to read on to the end. The characters, especially the female ones, are excellently crafted and true to life. Who knew that shipping could be so interesting?"

Buy Black Reef here: https://amzn.to/2zVBo4e

What readers have said about Black Reef

"I have now completed the Angus McKinnon trilogy and they get better and better. Like the previous two, Black Reef covers a tremendously wide geographical canvas written with Nick Elliott's intimate knowledge of those parts of the world together with the people who live there. So the book is fascinating on that count alone; add the breadth of the story, the excitement and suspense at almost every page and the quality of the writing and you have an action thriller amongst the very best.

This book stands alone from the previous two, but if you haven't read them yet - do!"

***

"Nick Elliott does it again, his work just gets better and better. If you have read Nick's first two books this is a must read. If you haven't read the others then you have three must read books to enjoy. Can't wait for the next one."

***

"I really enjoyed meeting Angus again and being drawn into this third thrilling case. What a great trilogy. I particularly enjoy the depth of knowledge Nick Elliott shows when it comes to the different locations Angus finds himself in, as well as the fascinating mysteries of the shipping world. What great reads!"

Or buy the trilogy box set here: https://amzn.to/2Ov8WhE

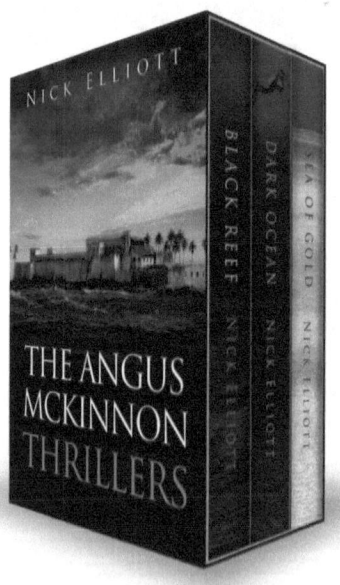